THE REPUBLIC OF EAST L.A.

OTHER BOOKS BY **Luis J. Rodriguez**

poetry

Poems Across the Pavement ❑ *The Concrete River* ❑ *Trochemoche*

nonfiction

Always Running: La Vida Loca, Gang Days in L.A. ❑ *Hearts & Hands: Creating Community in Violent Times*

children's literature

América Is Her Name ❑ *It Doesn't Have to Be This Way: A Barrio Story*

anthology

Power Lines: A Decade of Poetry from Chicago's Guild Complex
(Edited by Julia Parson-Nesbitt, Luis Rodriguez, & Michael Warr)

THE REPUBLIC

OF EAST L.A. *stories*

Luis J. Rodriguez

rayo *An Imprint of HarperCollinsPublishers*

FIRST EDITION

book design by shubhani sarkar

Movie-still on title-page spread and chapter-opener pages
is from *La Jetée* (1962); reprinted with the permission of
chris marker.

PRINTED ON ACID-FREE PAPER

Library of Congress Cataloging-in-Publication Data

Rodriguez, Luis J.
The Republic of East L.A.: stories / by Luis J. Rodriguez.
p. cm.
ISBN 0-06-621263-4
1. East Los Angeles (Calif.)—Fiction.
2. Hispanic Americans— Fiction.   I. Title.

PS3568.O34879 R46 2002
813'.54—dc21
2001048887

02 03 04 05 06 BVG/QW 10 9 8 7 6 5 4 3 2 1

V ersions of these stories have been previously published in the following publications:

THE REPUBLIC OF EAST LOS ANGELES: The title is from a quote attributed to barrio evangelist Jo Jo Sanchez in a *Los Angeles Times* article published in the early 1980s.

"SOMETIMES YOU DANCE WITH A WATERMELON": An earlier version of this story won a 1983 Second Place Fiction Award in the University of California, Irvine, Department of Spanish and Portuguese Chicano Literary Contest. It appeared in the *Los Angeles Weekly* in 1979 as a nonfiction piece by Tracy Johnston and Luis Rodriguez. It also appeared as fiction in *The Southern California Anthology* magazine, 1982; *The Best Chicano Writing—1986* (Bilingual Review Press); and *Mirrors Beneath the Earth: Short Fiction by Chicano Writers,* edited by Ray Gonzalez (1992 Curbstone Press).

The EPIGRAPH is from *Cantares Mexicanos: Songs of the Aztecs,* translated by John Bierhorst (Stanford, Calif.: Stanford University Press, 1985).

ACKNOWLEDGMENTS

Tlazokamati, muchas gracias, thanks—to all who have made this particular literary journey possible: Camila Barros, her mother Felicitas, and their quintessential East L.A. family; the Los Angeles Latino Writers Association of the early 1980s and its publication *ChismeArte;* the *Los Angeles Weekly,* which allowed me some space in the late 1970s and early 1980s to write; Eastern Group Publications, where I had my first full-time newspaper job; the publications *Q-Vo, Catholic Agitator, People's Tribune, Obras, Quinto Sol,* and *Milestone* (of East Los Angeles College) that published some of my early work; the *San Bernardino Sun,* where I first worked as a daily newspaper reporter; KPFK Pacifica Radio and the now-defunct California Public Radio where I did my first radio pieces; my compadre Anthony Prince, and goddaughters Janelle and Micaela; Leo Oso, Francisco Chavez, Juliana Mojica, Jorja Wade, Pablo Mendoza, Manazar Gamboa, Reynalda Palacios, Susana Gil, Maria Elena Tostado, and other friends and family (sorry, I can't name them all) who helped fuel some of these stories with their stories. Also a heartfelt thanks to Dan Spinella and my agent Susan Bergholz for help in editing the drafts. And to René Alegría and Rayo Books for believing in the stories and furthering their vision.

Much gratitude also to the Lila Wallace–Reader's Digest Fund for honoring me with a Writer's Award, the Illinois Arts Council for a few writers' fellowships over the years, the North Carolina Writers Network for a ten-week residency, and the Lannan Foundation for providing me space and time to write in Marfa, Texas.

CONTENTS

Canio nican in antocnihua tontotlanechuico in tlpc. y ticcauhtehuazque yectli yan cuicAtly ticauhtehuazque yhua in xochitl a ohuaya.

Only here on earth, O friends, do we come to do
   our borrowing.
   We go away and leave these good songs. We go away
   and leave these flowers.

THE REPUBLIC OF EAST L.A.

MY RIDE,
MY REVOLUTION

The long sleek limousine lays into the curved street as kids of all sizes, of many coughs and giggles, skirmish around it, climb its blinding chrome and white armor, smearing dirt and fingerprints on its tinted windows. The unshaven men gather around to put words together about this wonder on the roadway, to excavate a new vocabulary for this intrusion that seems to smirk at their poverty, to lay like a diamond on a garbage-strewn lot. But still, it's kind of their hostage. Here in a run-down section of East Los where limos don't belong—although here it is, laughing at fate, at "everything in its place," at a segmented society of "who has" and "who hasn't," and practically telling the world, "see . . . here I am, in the barrio—how about that!"

I'm awake, sitting at the edge of my bed with my hands on my head, startled by the wedges of daylight through torn curtains, by the voices and inflections, their wild abandon, and by the men's search for living poignancy from the polished enormity in their midst.

We're all neighbors of small cottages near Prospect Park in

Boyle Heights. The cottages face each other and onto a dry courtyard as *vecindades* are wont to do wherever old Los Angeles still rises out of gray ground, which I know something about because I read, because I spend many hours in libraries, because I care to know most everything about most nothing. One of the cottages, I swear, has twenty people in it: children, grandparents, wives, husbands, uncles, aunts, and probably a stranger who nobody knows, but they make him breakfast anyway.

I'm the limo driver. It's hard to believe that me, a longhaired, chiseled-faced, brown-red man can be the chauffeur of a luxury vehicle that we mostly only see in movies or magazines. But this is just the latest gig in a lengthy row of short-term and sometimes bizarre jobs I've had in my twenty-nine years—mostly because I won't do any work that demands commitment or an emotional investment. Like I won't clean the windows of downtown high-rises or dig ditches—which only the undocumented would do anyway—or kill rats in sewage tunnels, or sit in an office cell, surrounded by half walls, bulletin boards, and phones.

Man, I hate phones.

I've been an extra in obscure movies, though I have to say I'm like an extra extra—you'd never spot me in a crowd of nobodies. I've played acoustic guitar at the Metro station downtown when it first opened—and before the cops started pushing the musicians out. And I've sat for people's apartments with their flea-bitten cats—one time I had to bomb a place with Raid to clear out the annoying blood-sucking vermin that practically ate me alive. Those cats were probably the most grateful co-workers I ever had.

What I like are jobs where I can think, listen to music, maybe read a book, and check out every mole and pimple of the city.

Like a limo driver.

I've just started. Only the other day, I first brought the limo home. It's not your basic paint-peeling Chevy or rusty pickup like the rest of the junk heaps around here. It is an extra seventy-one inches of curved metal-and-glass epiphany—creamy white, tinted windows, and dark gray leather interior. And apparently it's a big hit. I don't normally score big points with my cottage neighbors as it is.

My name is Cruz Blancarte. I'm Mexican, but I'm Indian. That's what everyone around here always brings to my attention—like they're not. Only I happen to look like I come out of the reservation. That's because I'm what you call a Purépecha. It's good to be clear about these things, especially for those who don't have an inkling about these matters. Some people call us Tarascans. We're known for taking on the Aztecs—the Mexikas—back before the *conquista*. We even made the Spaniards wish they'd never crossed our paths. We're a tough people from the hardiest parts of Michoacán. Many Purépechas still speak their original tongues and don't have anything to do with the mestizos—who are mostly Indians who've forgotten they're Indians. But the Purépechas are getting close to their last stand as poverty and neglect piles up against them. They're now too hungry, too drunk, and too despised most of the time to do anything substantial about it.

The thing is I don't wear my hair long because I'm Indian. I wear it long because I'm in a rap-and-rock band. The group is called La Cruz Negra—the Black Cross. It's a play on my name but also on darkness, Christ, and not being Christ. Somebody may consider us a rockero band—you know the Spanish-language rock groups that have streamed out of Mexico and other Latin countries. But except for our name, we only throw in Spanish words here and there. We sing mostly unintelligible English. But nobody cares. It's yells and hiccups. It's gravelly throats, guitar feedback, and ass-kicking drums. It's heart jumper cables—this is what we are.

There are four of us—four like most garage bands, like Metallica, like Rage Against the Machine, like Limp Bizkit. There's Lilo, Dante, Patrick, and myself. The other guys in the band don't know how to play that good—I'm the only one who's actually studied some music: guitar, a little piano, and bass. But they're the shits, man. They rock.

My mom, Ruby, is a Chicana activist from back in the day— you know, the sixties and seventies: the Chicano Moratorium, *el movimiento,* Aztlán Libre. Ruby taught me many things, including being proud of what I am, which is why I know so much about my heritage. Ruby never married after having me, though. She's a community organizer—holds a master's in social work, too— helping families around the Flats neighborhood with a not-for-profit agency.

Ruby's had boyfriends, sure, but she's put almost everything behind me—behind my eccentricities, my dumb ideas, my music. I know she doesn't like some of the decisions I've made—and that at times I'm wasting my time with frivolous pursuits—but she never discourages me. I love Ruby.

I think she's raised me okay. Single moms aren't bad. Sometimes they make miracles happen with little to work with. But love is love, man. I'm not into drugs, for example. I don't drink much—it messes me up so that I can't think, can't create, can't do anything worth a shit. I pride myself in having my wits about me, so I stay away from anything that deadens the senses. I also don't get into trouble with the law, except sometimes for the noise we make when we play in my cottage room.

As you can imagine, I'm not like most people. I spend most of my life trying to be different. In the neighborhood, whenever the cliques break off into their own worlds, I stand aside, listening to my own rhythms. I don't want to be one of the cholos, the gang-bangers. They have their own problems, I'm sure, their own identity issues. I can't relate to them. Like I *want* to live. I don't care about the dance crews too much. I don't want to end up a working stiff, stuck in some sweatshop, waiting to retire, only to sit in the backyard with beer in hand, bored to death. I don't want to be like those *ranchera*-loving *mejicanos* in bars drowning in their losses. I don't enjoy wearing a suit either—like the salesmen on First Street that try to sell covered-over worn-out furniture for more than they're worth. Or the fast-talking swindlers at the used car lots on Atlantic Boulevard. Like I said, I hate working in a bank or a store.

But I also don't want to float in the world. I consider myself a philosopher—and I don't mean like they say that everyone is. Sure, we all got opinions. We all have our beliefs and ideas that we stake our lives on. But, to repeat, I love to read—Buddha, the Bible, Marx, Jung, Black Elk, Stephen King. I mean if you're going to put everything behind anything, you might as well know as much as you can about everything. I have a spiritual curiosity that isn't just to fill in the voids. It's also not about hooking onto any one belief—it's the satisfaction one gets from learning about the vibrant universe of arts, words, images, and ideas that human beings have created over time.

I have Ruby to thank for this. In her heart stirs a revolutionary. And I'm not talking about a malcontent or a party pooper. For Ruby, a true revolutionary believes in the best in people, in their courage and brains.

"You want change—you have to study," Ruby would always say. "And you have to impact the people and world around you."

Not just theory. Not just practice. Truth is both. Although at first I thought Ruby was half off her *mecedora.*

Eventually, I came around. This isn't hard if—like Jesus or Zapata—you care about those at the bottom. It isn't hard if you don't fit in. If you feel and taste the daily injustices and hypocrisies—and it makes you gag. If it seems that the churches, the schools, the politicians, and corporations are all in collusion against you. That's the way I see it—it's good to be about something *they* hate.

So I play bass for the La Cruz Negra—thumping out a bloody rage and calling for a worldwide uprising. *Claro que* hell yes!

For now, I also have to drive this shiny slick white limo.

There's a certain advantage in being a limo driver. It's being able to see the world through a lens that few ever get a chance to do. Not just the "lives of the rich and famous." But about *our* lives, the rest of us—the fool-hearted talented whose glories never leave a garage; the hip-hop rebels and the dream-starved street women; the urban vaqueros in their tightly woven molded hats and ornate leather boots and the assembly-line kings and queens waiting for the week's shift to end so they can reign on a dance floor.

I'm talking about all those who get convinced that watching TV, shopping on weekends, or drinking tequila and singing tear-drenched ballads at the *compadres'* house is all that matters.

In my limo, I see the world beneath the world, the undercarriage of the glass-and-marble city—every pothole and manhole along our greased byways, every piece of dust and mold on brick, slate, or stucco edifices.

The limo service allows me on rare occasions to take the "beast" home when I've been out all night. My boss trusts me, if you can believe that—but he should. Despite my weirdness at times, I won't ever burn anyone. That's not my nature—that's not the way Ruby raised me.

So I bring the limo to the block—and pay for the extra car washes because of the kids—and I'm special here. A local hero. But, you know what? This won't last long. Because life goes on. The streets don't stop being crummy. The cottages are still sullen matchboxes.

The fact is no limo is going to make things better in the long run. Even for the factory-slaving men who have been standing around this royal carriage discerning the mysteries of life. Even for the little bit of magic that I pull from the only bona fide symbol of power and wealth ever to grace our little spot of God's funky, rooster-infested, weed-filled backyard. Nope. No limo's going to change that.

The airport is always holy hell. Especially for limo drivers. You have to pull up to tiny spots that a long limo won't fit into. There's always a cop telling you to keep moving. There're the long waits for your pickup to show. There's the chance you have to take running into the baggage area with a crudely made sign with your pickup's name so they can spot you—and the skycap you have to bribe so he can watch your ride.

Then there are the people who just hate anyone in a limo. I can see why—you get the impression that people in limos think they're better than anyone else is because they see the world through dark glass. I try not to let this get to me—it's a job, one that I like for now.

I can tell you stories about these streets, about the partially lit office buildings outlined by night, and the angular houses on tired lawns. I can tell you about the nagging billboards—smoke this, eat that, buy this, look at that—flashing by like unwanted memories. I can tell you about the limo and the people who've graced its meticulously polished interior. I can tell you about the worlds that some of them spit on—and the world of spit where most of them have landed. How a silent laughter seems to em-anate from the asphalt as I pass.

I can tell you about the Taiwanese businessmen that I take to fancy hotels in Alhambra—down Valley Boulevard's Asia Heights with that beautiful oriental lettering on all the stores. The hotels look like any other—with the best service and smiling patrons—only these have gambling, booze, and women in a back room that's set aside just for these businessmen.

Or I can tell you about the California state senator with a hand in some young woman's blouse—not his wife—who I chauf-feured to a gala political ball on Santa Monica Boulevard.

Or about the Beverly Hills High School—*90210*—prom dates who leave fluids of all colors and shapes on the floor and seats . . . well, you get the picture.

The limo is my doorway to a world of glitz, power, and cor-ruption inside the canopied palaces of Los Angeles that I would never have otherwise known.

But soon all this gets old. Where I'm from, people get scared, desperate, mean, stupid, and downright ugly. East L.A. has its share of murderers, rapists, abusers, drunks, and psychos. What I realize, though, is that it's practically the same all over Los Angeles—only some of *those* people get their names on the marquees, the bank accounts, and the stock options.

After a while, the sheen on that white limo doesn't seem so bright. The leather seats don't look so sharp. After a while—like most things—the excitement wears thin. The celebrities, the bankers, the high school jocks, the white-hair society ladies, the airport call girls—they all start looking and sounding alike.

One day, I come to the airport to get some famous author. I read a lot of books, but I never read any of his. A best-seller, they say. But I had heard his name. Thaddeus Rosewood Turner. A Southerner, if you ask me. And he is—one of those Texas noir writers who ruminates about real murders, real places, with a real Texas accent.

There's something about some outsiders' view of L.A., though—they already hate the place before they even get here. Turner is no exception.

"Son, can you please pull up the air some—I'm dryin' up like a junebug in winter," Mr. Turner says while maneuvering his hefty body into the leather seats. "Man, this town ain't got no feel to it. I don't know how anybody can rightly stand it."

Famous or not, Mr. Turner turns out to be a real pain in the ass. First off, he has these weird gray eyes, like clouds in a darkening sky, an orange tan, and a pointy chin with globs of flesh pushed around it. His hands are pink hairy tarantulas with diamond-laden gold rings.

Unfortunately, we limo drivers belong to the pickup for the time a publisher or company pays for our service. So I am literally at Mr. Turner's beck and call. Most of the time, people are nice and don't demand too much. Most of them are just happy to be inside a limo, seeing the world through dark glass (maybe, for a moment, believing they're better than anybody else). But Mr. Turner has been in many limos. This doesn't stop him from whining about everything and everybody.

"Now this fruit bowl looks like a withered hat come out of a rain," he starts about the basket of fruit the limo service likes to have in the backseat. "Get me some real fruit, son—apples and peaches—not these California shits. These bananers, kiawas, and goddamned grapes."

So we make stops at fruit markets, tie stores, cigar stores, porno shops (I know, but what the hey), between the fancy-ass hotel Mr. Turner complains about, and the barbershop. All within a few turns of the Westside. All the famous people I pick up never ever go deep into downtown L.A.—or near East L.A. for that matter. It's all Westside with them—Beverly Hills, Santa Monica, Hollywood. They think *that's* L.A. They got no idea about L.A.!

And sometimes they pay attention to me, sometimes they don't.

Mr. Turner did.

"Hey, are you one of them injuns?" he asks, staring at my thick long hair and my sharp dark features. "You look just like an injun . . . has anyone ever tol' you that?"

"Once or twice."

"I got some injun in me, too," Turner replies smartly. "Cherokee. Got it on my mother's side, God rest her soul."

Many Southerners claim this, I find out, and usually it's Cherokee.

I also find out that it's no good telling them I'm Mexican. When I do, all of a sudden I'm no stoic heroic Indian (that some of their ancestors killed, robbed, and left to starve in funky reservations in the first place). But I tell Turner anyway.

"God dang, Meskins—they're everywhere," Mr. Turner obliges. "Now they're drivin' limos—hell horse, I've seen everythin' now."

The limo service sends me to this colossal hotel on Wilshire Boulevard—a castlelike structure that you have to pull in almost a mile from the street to get to the front steps. I have a CD of Pavement in the limo's CD player—I mean, this beast is loaded with all the electronic conveniences. I wait for my pickup, bopping my head along to wailing guitars.

When I see her, I can't believe my eyes. She's one of those dream honeys—pretty with tight silk pants, see-through blouse, and a lacy black bra underneath. She has dark shiny hair to her shoulders and a made-up face that accentuates her cheeks and lips. Rouge and gloss galore. I get out to open the back door.

"Hey, hon, I'm set, how about you?" she says.

I don't know what she means, but I say, "Like always."

"You know, I don't feel like getting anywhere just now—how about we just drive around for a while?"

"Whatever you want," I say, a little nervous. "'I'm yours' for the night."

"Whoa there, tiger, let's just cruise, and we'll see about *that* night."

"I . . . I didn't mean nothing by it, ma'am. I just mean the service is at your disposal for as long as it's paid for."

"Yeah, I know what you . . . just drive will you."

She's bad-tempered beneath her bubble of beauty. That's okay. It's my job to be as nice as I can, regardless. At least she's a looker.

We end up in Hollywood, which for those who haven't been

here is really nothing to write home about. I think of Hollywood as having unexpected ordinariness. I suppose it's had its glory days—they try to recapture this even now with new specialty bars, sparkling theater marquees, and tourist buses. But Hollywood to me is more about lost middle-class teens hooked on smack; about bikers sitting around their hogs at tattoo shops with their pierced girlfriends; or Saturday-night cruising with hydraulic-hopping lowriders and sporadic gunfire. It's more about the lonely white-shirted men entering X-rated bookstores and peepshows.

There's the Salvadoran and Armenian street gangs, the homeless on crack, and the hourly rate motels where once in a while some prostitute is found murdered in a bathtub. Most people with stars in their eyes don't make it to the movie lots or the good-paying modeling studios. You've heard this before, I know, but it's true. I'm not sure many of them even want to make it, really. They get stuck on motel row, on the next dope high, on the street life with its yelling, violence, and fast sex—and that's it. They're gone.

Beneath the bright lights and glamour of movies there's this Hollywood—one is connected to the other.

So Miss I'm-Gorgeous-And-You're-A-Stupid-Limo-Driver starts talking again.

"This sure is a long way from Nebraska."

I think she's making a reference to Dorothy and Kansas and Oz.

She grabs a bottle of Chivas Regal from the bar in front of her. She turns on the TV set, mutes the sound, and with tiny mani-cured fingers takes out a thin brown cigarette from a silver case. *She's all that,* I think.

"You got a light, hon?" she asks. I push in the lighter on the dashboard and wait for it to pop out. She starts pouring a drink into a glass. One thing about these limos is that they're smooth. So we're gliding down Hollywood Boulevard. Gliding through dreamland and bright lights, and somehow from behind the windshield of this vehicle, Hollywood starts looking like it's sup- posed to—carefree, inviting, and safe.

"I got lots of plans, hon," she says as I hand her the lighter. "I'm going to make my money—you better believe that! And I'm going to put it away. I ain't going down like some of those whores and bastard pimps who don't got nothing to show for their fuckin' efforts."

She keeps drinking. She keeps talking. I keep driving. And pretty soon my vision of loveliness is drunker than shit.

"I was just visiting with this really rich guy—you know, where you picked me up."

I nod while getting glimpses of her in the rearview mir- ror. After a while, another face comes through from below the makeup—a lived-in face, a street-sculpted face, a slash-and-burn kind of face.

"I party with the best of them, hon, and they pay me real good, too. And you know what—I'm worth every cent."

I understand now what she is—one of those high-priced es- corts. I calm down. Nervousness gone, I guess, because I know she's not going to give up anything for me. So I listen—the biggest part of my job is to drive, listen, and hope nobody goes off on my ass.

"Only his money can't make his shit smell sweet," she says, dropping ashes on the floor rug. "Trying to tell me what to do. I make *him* look good! I'm not his slave or piece of ass. But he starts in on me, yelling, pushing me around. Hello!"

I turn into a side street, make a couple of left-hand turns, and glide down the Boulevard again.

"Sometimes, though, I wish I were in Nebraska—you ever been there, hon?"

"No, ma'am, only to Arizona . . . Mexico."

"Oh, Mex-i-co. I just love Mex-i-co. Cancoon. Alcapoolco. Porto Valarda. I love margaridas—you don't got any margaridas, do you?"

"No, just what's there in the bar."

"Yeasss, Chivas—the best!" she exclaims, wiping the hair that has fallen across her face. "I'm from Nebraska. Small town called Brewster. Real small. Knew everybody. Everybody knows you. I was homecoming queen, if you can believe that! That's why I'm no street *'ho*—I'm high class, all the way. I always was, always will be."

I can see she's a sad lonely person, despite her job. Somewhere she's made some wrong turns, met some wrong people, and now she can't see her way out of this except in a dream of money— what everybody tends to do. Money, though, is an illusion with green faces. I think this is so money has personality—like the way our deities end up with traits like the rest of us. People create money and then they let money create them. Money is a facade but it has a force greater than nature. Sure, we've all gone to the woods, to the most mellow of beaches, or a serene desert, and praised the Creator for the handiwork. But as soon as money becomes an issue, *olvidate!*

My lovely friend here is like many of the people I drive around in this glimmering city. They are so removed from whatever fire they were born with that all their dreams become mud. She's no different—wounded and truly beautiful.

"Brewster's got some pretty fields—ripe green and yellow corn ones. I loved those stalks, straight up into the sky, like a sea more alive to me than any ocean," she says softly. "Tall stalks with leafy arms to hold you. We lived in town; we didn't do any farming or anything. But I just loved to go out into those fields. Just wading through the stalks. And there're bugs, but I don't worry about bugs. Something about the corn, the smell, the late afternoons with the sun hanging low in the sky and then later as the lightnin' bugs flash here and there like Christmas lights. I don't know—I guess I miss it about now. I miss not seeing my sisters, my ma and pa, those green fields, and that sun. I guess I miss not being who I was. But I tell you one thing—I'm doing better now. Got me more money than I would ever have with a lifetime in Brewster. Got money to put away, invest; get me a nice big mansion in Hancock Park. Yeah, better than Brewster, I tell you. . . . But there are days, hon, days like around midsummer with that orange light over the horizon, small birds crying out, and them crows fluttering like black hands across that sky—umm, umm, sometimes there are days."

Driving around most of the night, I finally drop off my Homecoming Queen from Brewster, Nebraska, at a secured apartment complex of low buildings in Hollow-wood. I open the door for her. She hands me a twenty-dollar bill, which is mighty nice of her—or anybody for that matter. She also gently places a card in my hand. The card is glossy black with words in embossed gold lettering: "She-La's Premier Escort Service." There's a beeper number below the letters.

"Just in case you get lonely, hon," she says.

I smile and thank her. When she's not looking, I crush the card in my hand and put it in my coat pocket to toss later.

"Hey," She-la asks as she walks away, "has anyone ever said you look like an Indian?"

When I'm not with the limo, I'm with the band.

As usual, we crowd into my cottage room. Lilo tears into the lead guitar, slashing the strings with callused fingers; Dante pours the sticks down on top of his drums like ceaseless rain; and Patrick shouts incoherent hate into the mike. I'm bopping my head, pulling on the bass strings like I'm pulling weeds out of a cactus garden—something I've done in my spotted work record, by the way.

> *Lies, betrayals, this system smells—*
> *My brain is crammed with rusted nails,*
> *Time to blow it all down—got to fight it—*
> *Tear it all down—*
> *Can't be cruel to the Brown—*

These are the words that Patrick mouths into a handheld mike while the rest of us envelop him with backbeats, feedback, and screeching guitars. As for the song . . . well, let's just say I drive a limo better than we write lyrics, okay? But we're learning, as Ruby points out. We're La Cruz Negra—there's mean intention there. Besides, the few people who come to hear us at the downtown bar where we sometimes practice don't seem to give a shit. Raw is better. Raw is power.

Raw means we're never gonna get a record deal.

I know this. Right now, it's just about being there—losing oneself in the venomous three-chord assaults, in the blood-boiling guitars, heart-stopping bass, and the drums with mayhem on their mind. It's being in that unnameable space between voice and microphone, flesh and metal alloy; between what screams I pull from my bass-plucking hands and the suicide eyes of the people listening to us.

Patrick's girl Luz, the bleached-hair metal chick, likes it. She sits lazily on a beanbag with a thin halter top and worn jeans as we hammer the walls with deafening noise. It's a good ten minutes before I realize there's knocking at the door.

"Hold it . . . hold it—someone's here."

I step over the amp in the middle of the room to unlatch the bolt. Ruby comes in, grimacing, as she usually does when she visits. She's bearing a bucket of Pollo Loco chicken for us to munch on.

"Darn, *m'ijos,* you could peel paint with that noise," she offers.

"Hey, Ruby, how does it sound today?" Lilo asks.

"Better, really—a lot better. I could almost hear a melody."

"Damn, we messin' up bad then," I add.

As it turns out, most people in the cottages can't stand our playing. But even after the initial death threats and cursing, they eventually get used to hearing us. Like the way we've all gotten used to the incessant roar of traffic on the San Bernardino Freeway. We just can't play at night or during the weekdays when the night workers rest—people like me, actually. But on Saturdays, we're allowed to jam during the day with a slight downturn of the volume so as not to tax our neighbors' immense generosity (by rights, they should have lynched us).

I walk out into the noontime sun with a piece of chicken in my hand. Our neighbors are out on this warm summer day. The kids are playing everywhere; one ten-year-old girl is pushing around a toddler in a dirt-encrusted wobbly carriage in the courtyard.

Across the way, a cholo and his robust girlfriend relax on two lawn chairs in front of their doorway, brews in hand, next to a three-week-old baby in a bassinet. The six undocumented guys who share a room at the far end are working on a Dodge sedan that sits on top of cinder blocks in the alley behind the cottages.

My prized limo is parked on the street, now watched over by almost everyone whenever I leave it there in case some fool thinks about ripping it off.

And then there's Bernarda.

On that bright and immaculate day, Bernarda is standing at her doorway with a bikini top and tight black shorts around her ample hips.

"So when are you going to take me for a ride, Cruz? You promised."

"Oh, hi, Bernarda . . . how are you doing today?"

"Don't change the subject. You told me the first time you brought that thing that we'd go cruising—well?"

"It's not that easy. I could get in trouble if something happens to the limo when I'm not on the job."

"So why did you bring it down here—to tease?"

This exchange between Bernarda and me is of recent vintage. Before the limo, Bernarda had nothing but bad things to say about La Cruz Negra and me. But the limo has become like a bargaining chip—I believe it's why people now tolerate our playing once a week.

So let me tell you a little bit about Girlfriend. Bernarda lives alone in that cottage of hers. She also works at night in a downtown dancing joint where men—mostly Spanish-speaking—pay for tickets that allow them to dance and drink with the women for a set amount of time. Supposedly no hanky-panky accompanies those ticket purchases, but you hear stories about guys paying a little extra to get a little extra.

I'm not sure where Bernarda stands on this issue. I consider it degrading to work in a place like that, but I don't blame the women. It's kind of something they fall into—and sometimes they're unable to get out.

Bernarda is unusually tall—for a Mexican. She's five feet eight inches, without heels. A real giant. I'm only five six. She's also dark-skinned with thick curly short hair and an oval face. For all her supposed dancing and partying, she's got a complexion like silk and a to-die-for figure.

"Well, Cruz, I'm not letting you off the hook. You owe me a night out in that thing."

Bernarda is in a long flamingo pink skirt and a tight white silk blouse. She's looking as nice as she ever does when she goes to her dancing jobs. Only this time she's going out with me. Finally, after months of prodding, I decide to take her and that beast out for a spin.

Things slow down in winter—even in L.A., where you better believe it gets cold. It may not be Minneapolis or Buffalo, but I hear that as many homeless people die of hypothermia in the streets here as they do in Chicago. I don't have stats, it's just what I hear.

Bernarda has a friend—real nice, sweet almost—who works at the same dance establishment. Her name is Suyapa, and she's Honduran. They're quite a pair—Bernarda and Suyapa—especially before they leave for work, wearing the slickest dresses, tallest high heels, and hair curled and brushed back with the most delicate of strokes.

"Cruzito, we better get going so we can get Suyapa before it gets dark," Bernarda says while putting on a leather coat and taking one last peek at herself through a mirror hanging on her bathroom door.

Yes, her Honduran friend is joining us this evening. You didn't think I'd get an actual one-on-one date with Bernarda, did you? I know the score. She's in for the ride, nothing more. That's okay. Ruby taught me to be realistic—even with dreams.

I got on my finest beige jacket and slacks with my favorite white-striped blue shirt—the few decent clothes I own. Needless to say, when you're in a rock band you don't need fancy duds. And I didn't think it was right to put on my black suit and white shirt that I wear for working. Even if it's not an official date, I'm going to hang loose and have me one hell of a good time.

There's a fast-breaking wind coming through the trees, hitting the city at intense speeds and at strange angles. Dark clouds menace the sky. I hope there's no rain with those winds. The problem is that in winter, drastic weather changes can occur in any given hour.

Suyapa lives in Echo Park. From our block, we turn west on Chavez Avenue and go straight—past small homes, taco joints, darkened bars, and dollar stores toward downtown's lit skyline as the sun begins to set. We pass the twin towers of the county jail, Union Station, and Olvera Street's open stalls of Mexican and old California trinkets and wares with Japanese and Anglo tourists crowded into the alleylike thoroughfare. Then over across Chinatown with its banners, pagodas, and restaurants, and onto Sunset Boulevard and the E.P. barrio.

When we hit Alvarado Street, we turn north, then left on another street. After a few blocks, we hang a right where I promptly double park in front of a set of small family homes.

Suyapa emerges from a beige duplex in a dark red satin dress that swerves around her every curve. Man, these are some beautiful womens, I think. But my plan is to be a gentleman—a real caballero—and try to enjoy myself without imposing any base desires. I really want Bernarda to think the best of me—although in the back of my mind is the issue of a possible future one-on-one date with her.

You should see the people that surround the limo, which I had buffed to a perfect luster. Most of the residents on Suyapa's block are Central American. A limo for one of their own—now there's something to recall for days to come. I feel a tinge of manly pride, I must say, to open the doors and let in songs of nature like Bernarda and Suyapa into my castle on wheels.

Men in front of tireless car frames smile at me, then chatter among themselves. Others, including a pregnant woman, circle the limo as if they're evaluating its worth. Then the kids start to run up, and I decide it's time to leave.

"So Cruzito, where do we start?" Bernarda asks from the backseats that face each other as we transition onto Sunset Boulevard and Suyapa waves from the opened sunroof to anybody on the street. I drive toward the much more famous and ritzier sections of Sunset Boulevard on the Westside.

"Wherever your little hearts desire," I say. "See me as your personal chauffeur."

The evening starts out nice: The girls snicker, enjoy the imbibements, tell jokes, make fun of my hair. We go from club to club—not so much to spend time in them, it seems, but to see the people's faces as the statuesque Bernarda and sumptuous Suyapa get in and out of the vehicle.

I only drink sporadically—since this is not my thing. But the girls are going buck wild with the booze. As the night wears on,

Bernarda eventually pulls herself in next to me while Suyapa crashes in the backseat. I put on an old AC-DC cassette tape, *Highway to Hell*—and Bernarda just about back flips.

"No, no, no, *querido*—we're not going to listen to that monstrosity," Bernarda insists. "Don't you got nothing nice and soulful?"

"No, I'm sorry, I don't," I say, crossed. "But you can put on whatever you want from the radio."

Then Bernarda dares to ask me the big limo no-no question— she has enough nerve to ask if she can drive the beast.

"No, I can't do that," I explain. "I'm the only one qualified to drive. Besides, I'm not drinking that much."

"Oh, Cruzito," Bernarda purrs. "We don't have to go into traffic. A parking lot is okay. How about at the beach? Then we can get out and sit on the sand for a while."

I'm weak. I know, I know. I figure it won't harm anything if Bernarda drives the limo around a parking lot. So we cruise on over to Malibu Beach on Pacific Coast Highway. It's three A.M. The ocean view is nice and tranquil—nary a soul lingers. I pull over into a lot next to a beach condo. Suyapa is snoring big time. It seems the lot is large enough for Bernarda to get a feel for driving this thing.

Meanwhile, I'm fantasizing about kissing her full wet lips later on a blanket near the waves.

Bernarda runs over to the driver's side. I jump over to the passenger's. I know she knows how to drive because she's got a Nova or something. She sits there for a while—taking in the extraordinary number of lights on the dashboard and the sensation of the steering wheel under her fingers.

"You ready?" I ask. "Now put it in drive and go up a ways, then stop, make a turn, and come back. Got it?"

Easy enough. But that's when you know that Tatadios has other plans. That's when you know that there's a reason you shouldn't give in to purring stoned women against your better judgment. It's times like these when the word "*pendejo*" has salient significance. I think Bernarda has everything in place—wheels straight, lights on, hand brake off, gears on drive. That's what I think anyway.

She punches the accelerator—which is bad enough—but she had inadvertently put the stick shift in reverse. The Limo thrusts backward and rams into a row of squat bushes and into the condo behind us; an explosion of glass and wood soon follows as we smash through the plate glass wall that separates the living room from the bushes. We shatter antique china cabinets, ceramic-topped coffee tables, and Tiffany lamps before Bernarda gets the presence of mind to brake.

Yes, two couples are relaxing on a sofa watching TV as we fly past them. Yes, Bernarda screams and Suyapa sleeps through it all. And yes, of course, a windy rain begins to fall as we wait for the police and tow truck to arrive while our reluctant hosts yell the most exquisite obscenities into our ears.

I suppose I don't have to tell you about the deep-ass trouble I get from this. I don't have to tell you that I lose my job (although the limo's insured for stunts like these). And that I'll never have another date with Bernarda again.

The last words Bernarda screeches from the driver's side are: "Why did you let me do that?"

B ack on the Eastside, sans limo, my stock among my neighbors greatly diminished, I practice on my bass with the power off. The smell of menudo and freshly toasted tortillas wafts through the open window. It's Sunday morning. The cottages stir beneath the brown haze. The twenty or so people next door start making their morning racket—cupboards slamming, balls bouncing, a Spanish-language evangelist shouting *aleluya*s on TV. I contemplate my next move, my next job adventure, the next possible gig for La Cruz Negra. I contemplate last weekend's events—and I know I'm gonna miss that limo for what time it lasted. I also think about the shame I brought to Purépechas everywhere. But I realize I have to get over it—and soon. The big three-O is around the corner for me. Where am I going in life? Who am I going to be? I think about this for about two minutes before I decide to ask my neighbors for a bowl of menudo—maybe as a charity case. As bad as I feel, I also know there's always another thing past the last thing. Maybe, someday, I'll get really serious about that revolution.

Rudy woke up beneath the shade of a full-leafed tree in Evergreen Cemetery, the afternoon sun teasing his eyes open, the dew tickling his ears and face. He took in the smells of freshly shorn grass and the exhaust of nearby cars, while his heart beat heavily in his chest, his breathing short and shallow, the humid air his only blanket.

During the day, the cemetery was Rudy's favorite place to lay his head, surrounded by weathered gravesites. Fresh flowers graced a few of the headstones, but most were neglected testaments to relatively uneventful lives. Rudy was at home here. He would often sit with his back up against one of the tilted headstones; in moments, he'd be facedown on the grass, passed out.

Today, as usual, Rudy rose unsteadily, not bothering to wipe the moisture and dirt from his stained and worn clothes. Briefly, he looked around to clear his head, trying to focus his vision. He searched through the brown corduroy coat that he wore regardless of the heat. In an inside pocket, he found an empty pint of White Port. Disgusted, he threw the bottle down, as if it had the Devil's face—and Rudy's name—on it. After a long pause, he started to walk.

Maneuvering along the asphalt road, Rudy exited through the cemetery's ornate gates. He took his time, stopping every once in a while to catch a breath. He headed toward his regular hangout, the corner of First and Soto Streets. It was a short stroll from the cemetery to that corner, but it seemed longer because he felt so many eyes following his every step—eyes from the other side of apartment windows, peering through wrought-iron fences, or from children staring out of the clamor that filled the school-yards.

Rudy reached his spot at the Major Liquor Store. Across the street, a newspaper stand sported Spanish-language magazines and cheap adult comic books from Mexico. Catty-corner to the newsstand, the Guadalajara Auto Sales graced the otherwise non-descript block.

People congregated on that corner: shopping, talking, peddling from food carts. Rudy sat down on the sunny side of the intersection against a bill-strewn wall that included a poster of La Virgin de Guadalupe near one of the singer Madonna with pointy breasts. Next to him, a young Mexicano sold bootleg cassettes of Mexican recording artists—Ana Gabriel, Los Tigres del Norte, and Vicente Fernandez in an elaborately decorated sombrero on his CD. A few of the tapes were from U.S. artists like Mariah Carey, Destiny's Child, and N'Sync; their music could be heard blaring from a huge boom box on the ground.

Rudy felt comfortable on this spot, even though most of the people pretended he didn't exist. He knew they saw him. What they saw wasn't just a strange broken man in a strange broken body. He was the specter of their deepest aches, a reminder of what happens when you leave so much of the old for the new. How once compact communities and families could turn up on the other side and completely fracture—about what it was they sacrificed to find "the good life" in America.

Rudy scrounged for food in trashcans and gutters. When he wasn't doing that, he just lay on that corner, looking at his feet, at the legs of pedestrians, and the tires of cars streaming by. He occasionally looked up at the people who strolled past him at that hour. These images floated through his mind—but he was never sure whether or not they were dreams or just memories. Rudy lay there and talked: to his feet, to the tires, to the wandering eyes trying to avoid his bent form, a sorry shadow on the sidewalk.

Rudy lay there until he sobered up a little. He wanted some distance from the drink before he started up again in the evening. He liked the sensation of his mind losing its balance, its clarity, to a kind of drowning, a dying without dying. Then a voice inside his head would demand that he get something to drink, fast.

As the sun's setting dimmed the corner, as the number of pedestrians thinned out, and as fewer cars passed by, Rudy rose from his spot and wandered toward the benches at the small park farther down First Street, across from the old CYO building. Others were already clustered there, and Rudy began his ritual drinking, always finding someone willing to share a bottle and lend an ear.

"Hey, dog, you got any change?" Rudy slurred at a young man with a portable CD player plugged into his ears and a backpack over his shoulder. The dude gave Rudy a fuck-you expression and kept walking. Rudy then spotted someone he could tell was recently arrived from Mexico.

"*¿Qué pues, compa?*" he declared. "*¿No tienes cambio? Para ayudar un paisa, ¿no?*"

He had all the lingoes down.

But every once in a while, he'd bug someone who didn't give a damn what Rudy wanted or his condition.

"Get out of my face, fuckhead!" yelled one hefty vato dressed in cholo-style short pants, cut off at the calves and neatly ironed, with elaborate skin art blooming from well-hewn muscles beneath an athletic T-shirt.

You'd think Rudy would back off, like many of the other winitos. But he followed the vato a ways; the dude stopped and then without saying a word slugged Rudy on the side of his head, dropping him like a swatted fly. Rudy tried to get up, but three other vatos emerged out of nowhere, kicking and pouncing on Rudy for a good minute or so. Others stood around ignoring the fracas.

Just about every other day, somebody would beat on Rudy. It didn't take much—something he said or how he said it or how he looked . . . he never knew why. More than once, he found himself waking up in the cemetery, one eye half closed, blood on his coat and his hands, sometimes on the grass nearby. Some nights he'd end up in the drunk tank at the Hollenbeck Police Station, vomiting, hallucinating, and screaming—the walls breathing a foul stench around him. But when he was released, it all started again.

To Rudy, this all made sense. All of this: his lonely walks, the drinking, the beatings, the drunk tank. Maybe others couldn't understand, but to him this way of life made all the sense in the world—Rudy seemed born for it.

The Godinez family lived near Roosevelt High School in Boyle Heights. Rudy Godinez knew only one house growing up there, on Fickett near Fourth. The family was made up of hard-working people. His father, a balding, well-trimmed man who took most things with a dedicated seriousness, managed a car wash. His mother, a polite, cheerful woman who seemed to always have cookies in the oven, sewed clothes for neighbors, teachers, and anyone who might have heard about her particularly fine work. At Roosevelt, Rudy was a decent student; he spent most of his spare time on the football and wrestling teams. He was fluid and graceful with a strong athletic build and sharp facial features. He could be called handsome, but he somehow lacked poise and confidence. Part of him moved well, especially when in the gym or field. But in the hallways, Rudy appeared naïve and awkward. Most of the schoolgirls, who were fairly street savvy, avoided him.

But Rudy had a strong competitive nature. He particularly liked the explosive rivalry with East L.A.'s Garfield High School. The football games were so heavily attended that they were played to overflow at East L.A. College Stadium. It was East L.A.'s most talked about school rivalry, lasting for generations, and once in a while, erupting in violence.

Rudy's school life was ordinary enough. He played guitar in the school band. He got average grades. He seemed to make out fine in a high school that had more students than any other in the country, confined by the sprawling city around them.

There was almost nothing spectacular about Rudy. He never joined a gang, despite the block-by-block street groupings in Boyle Heights. He hardly ever got in trouble and most people liked Rudy, which some might say was spectacular enough.

But nobody ever asked Rudy how he felt. For most of his life, he seemed to be emotionally empty, a blank. When asked about a future, he always responded with, "I don't know what I want to do." And he meant it. Sure, he did what he had to do to get by. But he didn't think much about what the grades, the games, and music were for. He seemed to be on a long, dull trip without a destination. He drifted through his adolescent years, never figuring out where he would end up.

"Why don't you go to East L.A. College?" Rudy's mother suggested one morning while serving him her famous chilaquiles— pieces of tortillas fried with eggs, tomatoes, onions, cilantro, sausage, and three kinds of cheese.

"I don't know, *'amá.* I'm not into studying anymore," Rudy replied.

"*M'ijo,* but you've always been good at your studies," his mother insisted. "And what about the sports? You can do that at college, too."

"I know, but I think I might take a break from school for a while, you know, work full time," he reasoned. "I'll go to college someday, I just need to do something else first. The thing is I've been going to school my whole life. I'm kinda' sick of it now."

Rudy's mother glared at him as if his good sense had walked out the door. But she didn't press the issue. She had always trusted Rudy, who never really gave her as hard a time as other sons in the neighborhood had their mothers. She thought about Señora Florez's three gangster sons—one who was killed, and the other two serving time for murder.

"*Pues tu sabrás,*" she answered, and returned to work in the kitchen.

Rudy's mother, whose name was Clarita, did recall how when her boy was small, he seemed withdrawn—reminding her of her father, Santos, an insensate man of immense size and immense silence. Santos never seemed to respond to anything around him.

He only moved to his own impulses, leaving his wife a cold, lonely, and withered woman. This bothered Clarita for years—how her father treated her mother with a lack of emotion, of connection. Santos never beat her mother, but he would give her a devastating look that caused her to wilt like a water-starved flower. Clarita recalled how as a little girl she hid away in her room, beneath blankets, surrounded by dirt-caked dolls, distressed that Santos would come in and destroy her with such a look.

One day, Rudy walked into the living room and announced to his father and mother that he was renting a place with his friend Augie.

"Augie just got a job at a mechanic's shop on First Street," Rudy explained. "I think I can add more hours at the taco stand. We'll live nearby; there are some rooms for rent on Boyle Avenue."

"I don't know, Rudy," his father interjected. "Maybe you should stay here until you can save up money to move out. What'll happen if you don't have enough to make rent?"

"Listen, '*apá*, it'll work out," Rudy insisted. "It may get rough at times, but with what Augie makes, if I'm a little short, we'll be fine. I think this will help until I figure out what I really want to do."

As usual, Rudy's parents, despite their doubts, had to believe their son would make it. So they didn't say anything when Rudy backed up a U-Haul van onto the driveway the next day, and he and Augie began to empty his bedroom of all its furniture, records, posters, clothes, guitar and amplifier, and trophies. Rudy was always responsible. He was their only child. He would be okay.

For the first few days, Clarita wandered through the house,

shaken at times, missing her son's music and conversation. Rudy, for his part, didn't make it any easier. He didn't call for a few weeks. But then his first visit back was fairly pleasant; he sounded relaxed, content in fact.

"*Cuídate, m'ijo,*" his mother said when Rudy told her he had to go.

Then the visits and calls came even less frequently, usually just to say hello or to ask after messages and mail.

One day, Rudy's father decided to swing by the taco stand and see how his son was doing.

"Mr. Godinez, how you been?" asked Mr. Perez, the manager of the place on Whittier Boulevard.

"*Muy bien,* thank you," Rudy's dad responded, smiling. "I wonder if Rudy is around just now."

"Well, no, in fact," answered Mr. Perez, a concerned expression on his face. "I guess you don't know, but your son doesn't work here anymore. I mean, he just stopped coming. We called and called him, but there was only an answering machine. He never came back, never returned the calls. I had to let him go."

Mr. Godinez's jaw dropped. A look of confusion fell across his face.

He got back into his car, drove home, and then took the address to his son's building from a bulletin board in the kitchen. He had to find Rudy. The room was in a large five-story brick structure near where Interstates 5 and 10 met. Mr. Godinez pushed through the main door, which led to stairs with darkened carpets, burned in a few spots. Children played on these stairs. Some adults sat on them or in lounge chairs in front of their apartments. With all the drive-bys in the neighborhood, people hung around the hallways of the buildings rather than outside.

Mr. Godinez found the apartment number on a door of the third floor. He knocked, waited. Then knocked again. He thought he heard rustling inside the apartment. But nobody came to the door.

"Rodolfo," Mr. Godinez called out, using Rudy's formal name, which he only did when he was worried.

Still, there was no response. The stirring inside subsided. Mr. Godinez knocked a few more times. But no one answered.

When Rudy stopped calling his parents, going to work, or returning phone calls, it appeared odd to those who had known him. Rudy may not have been an outgoing person, but he was respectful and usually thoughtful that way. The family and their friends talked about how Rudy didn't seem to care anymore about them or a job. Others tried not to say too much. They heard that Rudy was partying with Augie all the time, something he rarely did while attending high school. Drinking. Meeting people. Talking with women in the dance clubs around town.

At times, even Augie got tired of waiting for Rudy to extricate himself from the booze and noise.

"You ready to go, Rudy?" Augie would ask, wanting to head home.

Rudy would ignore him as he drank, like he was on a completely different planet.

"Come on, man, time to squint," Augie'd say.

But Rudy would only look up at Augie, shake his head, and keep on drinking.

"Okay, man, suit yourself."

It wasn't that Augie didn't like to party. He partied all the time. He'd put on his best duds, dance to almost every jam, and go out of his way to meet women. Only drinking to him was a tactic for a good time. Not so for Rudy.

The last time Rudy refused to go with him after a night of hanging out, Augie left Rudy at Tito's Tavern on Olympic Boulevard. When he didn't hear from Rudy for several days, Augie became concerned. He came home from the auto shop and knew that Rudy had been home. But nothing else—no note, no messages, no account of where Rudy may have been. Then one evening, Augie opened the door, entered the apartment, and nearly passed out. The place was a mess, as if a tornado had touched down and razed it. A lampshade lay on the floor. CDs and cassettes were scattered about, as well as pizza boxes and empty liquor bottles. In the middle of the living room was a guitar with food and spew on it. Augie moved toward the bathroom and there on the floor, curled up with a towel, was Rudy, vomit on the toilet and around his head.

"That's it, man, I ain't taking this no more!" Augie exclaimed. Rudy didn't move as Augie stepped over him to flush the toilet.

"Noche tras noche," he continued to yell. "The same thing. I'm tired of it, Rudy. You've had it, man. I'm getting rid of your ass."

Rudy didn't stir or say a word.

By the early afternoon of the next day, Rudy seemed to have sobered up enough to talk to Augie when he came home from work.

"Hey, Augie, I'll get it together. Don't worry, man. It's only a temporary thing, you know what I mean . . . I'm sorry, man," Rudy explained, slurring most of the apology.

"Temporary my ass," Augie replied. "I tried to help you, Rudy. I always thought you had it together. I thought you would be a big help here. The first time you overdid it, I just took it as good times. But it's been a few months, and this is all you do. You haven't paid me your share of the rent. You ain't cleaned nothing. I know you're not working either, 'cause your father called to ask me why you had left the taco stand. I can't keep doing this. I don't have the heart to tell your dad and mom about how fucked up you've become. They've always been good people."

"You don't have to tell nobody nothing," Rudy said. "It's all taken care of, don't worry so much. I got another job in mind. I already went to this place, a warehouse. It's a sure thing."

"Bullshit, vato!" Augie responded, then paused for a second. "Okay, I'm not going to throw you out into the street, but I'm telling you now, you stop this fucking around, start working and paying rent, or you're out of here."

For a while, it looked as if things were going to be all right. Augie came home from the shop one evening and saw that Rudy had picked up around the place. And he was out. It could mean he was looking for work. But, soon enough, it became clear when Rudy was not in the apartment he was at the corner liquor store, drinking and talking with local winos in an alley.

Rudy ended up returning to his old home with a few of his things. Most of the rest, except for his precious guitar, were sold or just gone, unaccounted for. His mother and father, bewildered, took him back in. Rudy's once handsome and bright face was drawn down, and his hair long and unkempt. His complexion was dry. By then they had heard from Augie about Rudy's state.

"We'll get you some help, okay?" Clarita said to Rudy as soon as he was settled into his old room. Rudy didn't say a word.

"*Contéstame, m'ijo,*" she demanded, but he only went to the TV and turned it on. What did I do? his mother thought as she turned away, hot tears streaming down her face.

A t night, the bottles seemed to have a life of their own. Rudy would even kick at the forty-ounce beer bottles or the cheap ports scattered about his room to make sure they weren't squirming about. During the day, he felt he could probably let the drinking go—that he would not cave in to it. But when night fell, the booze cast a spell, pulling him in. The nerve endings all over his body seemed to reach out for alcohol. Before taking even one drink, his mind responded as if he were already lost in the booze. He would get woozy just thinking about the first drink. He felt as if he had this overwhelming energy, and he needed to expend it. He moved around the room. He fidgeted. He talked to himself. He pushed his back against a wall. Then he grabbed a bottle and drank, letting the alcohol rush through his system, inundating all of him, the energy, the emptiness, the shame. It was his only comfort during those days. Days of not knowing. Days of not feeling. Days of not caring if he woke up or not. The only thing that mattered was the harsh warmth that greased his throat, its sting, and then the closing of the world around him till he resembled the shadows, the crevices on wood-paneled floors, the water-stained cracks in the ceiling. Finally, a steely voice somewhere in his mind, or maybe from the TV, which he kept on even if he rarely looked at it, would tell him that it was okay. No need to worry anymore. Everything would be just fine.

R udy landed an occasional job, but he'd lose it for one reason or another. He started to hang around unemployment agencies, day-labor joints, or in front of warehouses he had heard were hiring. The days he didn't have any work, Rudy stayed home, sat in his room, glanced at the TV or listened to the stereo, and never really talked to anyone.

One day, Rudy arrived home from working his first evening shift at an assembly line in Vernon. He had a grin on his face, which was unusual for Rudy.

"*¿Qué pasó contigo?*" Clarita asked. "You look like you swallowed the fish."

"You won't believe this, '*amá,* but I met somebody," Rudy said.

"Somebody? You mean a girl—you met a girl! *M'ijo,* this is great news."

"I know, but I don't want to blow it. You understand, *¿qué no?* I want this to work out."

Rudy began to clean up after himself. One day, he left the house early to get a haircut, a new shirt and pair of pants. He even got to work a half hour before the swing shift started. Her name was Fabiola. She had blemish-free skin, not too dark, not too light, and strands of dyed blond hair among her black ones.

Fabiola worked with a group of women, most of them older than her, all Spanish-speaking Mexican or Salvadoran. Rudy was on another part of the line with the men, doing basically the same task, assembling kitchen appliances. During his first supper break, Rudy spotted Fabiola with the women and just stared at her. For the first few days, it seemed as if Fabiola didn't notice Rudy's gaze. But one fine day, she looked up and smiled.

Rudy almost fell back in his chair. Fabiola smiled again and coyly looked the other way. After that incident, it was step by tiny step, day by day, stage by stage. One evening in the back room, Rudy situated himself behind Fabiola. After a few nervous missteps, he eventually reached out and tapped her on the shoulder. She turned around slowly.

"I'd like to get to know you better," he said; he could feel his heart beating through his chest. Fabiola smiled.

Everybody talked about what a great couple Rudy and Fabiola made. A collective sigh of relief seemed to accompany their small, but pleasant, wedding, with a cozy reception in the backyard of the Godinez house on Fickett.

The Godinezes had thought their son would never get over his binges. But since getting together with that beautiful and smart Fabiola, the binges were rare.

Rudy seemed back to his old nonintrusive, reliable self. The young couple found a small place to rent in a renovated garage behind a house on Gleason, just below First Street. They bought a few pieces of furniture, including a used kitchen table, chairs, and a sofa. Rudy kept the assembly job longer than any job he had ever held. Fabiola also continued to work there.

Something inside Rudy clambered to rise out of him, something alive and astonishing—he hardly ever felt this way. For Rudy it was a long time since he wanted something so bad, some life, some woman, a purposeful place in a world that seemed without purpose or meaning or surprises. The last time it was around his guitar. The wood shiny and strings tight—he stared at it for hours when he first got it. He felt the same way with his new home, his job, and Fabiola—he wanted to spend hours just taking this all in.

After a few months, the news spread around the neighborhood and among Rudy's family and friends: Fabiola was pregnant. Rudy seemed transformed. Perhaps a child would keep his drinking at bay completely. Perhaps the worst was over.

They named the baby Santitos, after Rudy's grandfather, Santos Cortez. Although the first Santos had been dead for a few years, Rudy thought of him fondly. As a small boy he would go down the street to visit Santos and his grandmother, Luisa.

Rudy remembered the elder Santos as a mountain of a man—large chest, hefty waist, and strong meaty fingers. He was testy and usually unshaven. His neighbors avoided him. They particularly complained about Santos's mystifying deep-dark stare that seemed to penetrate the features of flesh to the bones of soul—as if he could reach inside and present anyone their particular shames and secrets. Santos had worked in the railroad yards just south of East L.A. He worked, but other than that he didn't seem to care about anything else.

But to Rudy, abuelo had been a kind and funny old dude. After a work-related accident forced Santos onto disability, he usually just sat on the porch, drinking something out of a paper bag. When Rudy arrived home from school, however, Santos came to life, thinking up card and board games, like *lotería*, which he used to play in his old village in Guerrero, Mexico. Rudy saw a magical old wizard in Santos. He saw quick eyes, a sharp tongue, and a mischievous smile. While others turned away from this man, Rudy found a friend.

Rudy didn't know that Santos was a big-time drinker—his grandfather's alcohol breath mixed in with the old railyard grease smell on his worn overalls. His parents never talked to him about this. This deepened the nightmare of Rudy's condition for them. So, even with the marriage and the new baby, they were still anxious about Rudy.

"Maybe we should tell Rudy about his grandfather's drinking," Clarita said to her husband one day at the dinner table.

"No, it wouldn't help anything," Mr. Godinez insisted. "Rudy needs to deal with this on his own. It's his problem, not your father's."

"I hope you're right," Clarita said. "It's just odd how Rudy suddenly became so much like my father. I never thought this was possible. And even after I tried so hard to keep liquor out of this house while Rudy was growing up. But you saw how he got for a while, like my dad all over again."

"That's just nonsense," Mr. Godinez countered. "Rudy knows he has the power to change. If he thinks it's something he has inherited, that maybe this drinking can't be helped, he may go back to drinking. It's not the alcohol; it's his mind that justifies needing it. I don't want him to believe he doesn't have control over this."

"Well, you understand these things better than I do," Clarita conceded. "But look at how close my father and Rudy seem in character, as if Santos had possessed the boy."

"Don't be ridiculous, that's just *brujería* talk," said Mr. Godinez. "There are no ghosts involved here. The only possession going on is Rudy holding on to a bottle. He already has enough excuses to drink. Maybe with the baby, he will grow out of it. But, for sure, we don't need to give him any more excuses."

Clarita felt her husband was probably right, except that as far as she knew Rudy never gave an excuse for his drinking. He just drank, hard and heavy, and it had looked as if he couldn't stop. Somehow, she sensed that choice was not a big factor here, but she wasn't sure how to express this. Nonetheless, considering how well Rudy seemed to be doing, she decided not to bring up the disturbing similarities between Rudy and her father again.

It was chaos at the Hollenbeck Police Station: so much yelling, people scrambling about, tense officers in uniform, hands near their guns. Had there been a murder? Around the main entrance area, a couple of Spanish-speaking parents waited news of their son. Mr. Godinez concluded this couldn't be an everyday scene. It was probably dull most of the time. Like in a war. Probably, the majority of the time was boring. Waiting. Killing time. Then a battle breaks out. And everybody runs around, blood spills, adrenaline flows, and there is excitement everywhere.

A police officer behind a desk loomed over Mr. Godinez. "What can I do for you, sir?" the officer demanded with a thinly disguised disdain.

"I'm trying to get news of my son, Rodolfo Godinez. He's supposed to be in here."

"What's he in here for?" the officer inquired.

"I believe for drunkenness."

The officer didn't change his expression. Mr. Godinez figured this condition was probably all too common around here. Besides, such situations have to be considered tame compared with the more dramatic cases the police had to deal with.

"Yeah, we've got him here," the officer finally said after a long delay while he looked at logs and other paperwork. "He is still being processed. It'll take another couple of hours until his fingerprints clear before we can give you his status."

It was already four in the morning. But Mr. Godinez waited. As he had done several times in the past.

Rudy had begun drinking heavy again after he and Fabiola had a big fight. Rudy wanted to pick up his music again and play in bars. Fabiola wouldn't have it. Then, out of nowhere, Rudy went off. He even grabbed his guitar and smashed it to pieces against the furniture. The guitar had meant everything to him. Fabiola was frightened for the first time since she had been with Rudy. She wondered what in the world was going on with him.

It was scary for Fabiola, the suddenness of destruction, the way someone so right could go so wrong. Rudy went from being considerate and caring to someone who only saw himself, only his wants, like a baby, not a grown person—an unfeeling, insensitive being. Seemingly overnight, it became all about Rudy, only about his concerns, his rapidly shrinking universe, or nothing.

Unfortunately, Rudy's disposition worsened. He came home intoxicated, out of control, filthy. Fabiola, afraid and confused, would whisk little Santos away to a neighbor's house or to her in-laws. This drove Rudy to frenzied states; he would scream, throw things around, then leave. Soon Fabiola and the baby moved to the Godinez's. Then, she got another job so that Rudy wouldn't harass her at work.

"Rudy is such a different person when he's drinking," Fabiola cried to Clarita one night while the family watched TV in the living room. Santitos, on her lap, gazed up at her without a whimper. "I don't know him anymore when he's like that. I fell in love with a thoughtful, hard-working man; he was a man who spoke well, who had so much patience. My God, what am I going to do?"

Just then a hard knocking against the door pulled everyone's eyes away from the TV screen.

"Fabiola . . . open up, it's Rudy!" a deep, tired voice yelled from outside.

"No, don't," Fabiola said as Mr. Godinez went to the door.

"I have to, he's still my son," Mr. Godinez replied.

As the door opened, Rudy calmed down, almost sheepish, as he faced his father's stern face. Rudy's cheeks had premature lines, his eyes were sunken into his skull, his clothes were smelly and rumpled.

"Why, son? Why do you do this to your wife and baby?"

"It's none of your business, Dad," Rudy responded, looking down at the ground. "I just want to talk to Fabiola. I need to talk to her, Dad. Tell her to come out."

"No, Rudy, I won't," Mr. Godinez said. "She's scared to death of you. You can't go on this way—you have to get it together. . . ."

"Get it together—get what together, Dad?" Rudy suddenly looked up, angry. "You don't like who I am. I'm not any good to you no more. To Mom. Come on, Dad! Tell me what you really think."

"Son, I think you'd better leave."

"No, I'm not going—I came to see Fabiola, and damn it, I'm going to see her."

"Rudy, for the last time, go. Come back when you're ready to take responsibility for your family."

These words seemed to cut at Rudy. His face hardened. His bloodshot eyes, like those of hounds, fumed with fury. Then out of nowhere, he struck his father, who fell backward into the living room. Fabiola jumped up from the sofa, causing the baby in her arms to wail. Clarita rushed to her husband on the ground, got on her knees and held his head up. Then she looked over at Rudy, her face flushed with rage, her mouth quivering. Rudy stood there for a while, passing across his mind once more the words and the anger and the striking of his father. Then, without saying anything, he turned around and ran, rushing to nowhere, passing through thickening layers of night that seemed to wrap its dusky fingers around his shoulders and pull him deeper—where there was no mercy, no judgment, only dark.

The face of the dirty and disheveled figure who exited the Major Liquor Store was bloody and unshaven. Although a young man, he looked as worn as old shoe leather. He talked to himself and to someone nobody else could see. He said "abuelo." He said "Santitos," which local people knew was his son's name. He appeared to be talking with the air, as if the wind carried the voices of his grandfather or his son.

In the crook of his right arm he cradled a bag with an unopened wine bottle. Clumsily, the bottle fell to the ground. Rudy flew into a rage. The bottle didn't break, but he kicked it into the street, where a truck came by and crushed it. Rudy swore, turned around, and walked away.

As he crossed the street, the driver of a Nissan sedan, going slightly too fast against the light, put on the brakes and screeched across the crosswalk, striking Rudy's hip and thigh. He crumpled to the ground. People stopped and looked toward the sound of the collision, the thud of metal and flesh. They rushed over to the accident scene. Disoriented and hurt, Rudy pulled himself up from the asphalt, refusing the hands that were stretched his way. Slowly, he hobbled to the sidewalk and sat down on the curb.

In the sedan, the middle-aged, slightly balding man behind the wheel stared for a moment at the slumped figure on the curb but did not get out of his car. Others turned toward him. Someone asked, "*¿Está bien, señor?*" But he gave no response. A few of the bystanders walked away. One shook his head. Mr. Godinez then turned and looked straight ahead. As the light changed to green, he sped across the intersection, into the smoke and din of the traffic ahead.

LAS CHICAS CHUECAS

She just vanished.

That's the way Noemi described it, after her sister Luna's boyfriend threw her out of the car as he drove down the Pomona Freeway. Noemi was in the backseat. Luna and Eddie were in the middle of a heated argument, as usual, which is why Noemi, who was eight years old at the time, ignored their squabbling. While Luna and Eddie cursed and yelled, Noemi became fixed on the traffic on the opposite side of the freeway, a fantasy in her head, like the many she's always had, where she fought off armies of skeletons and goblins with swift thrusts of sword and powerful kicks.

Noemi paused for a few seconds when her high school counselor asked for details about the eight-year-old incident. Without emotion, Noemi remarked: "She just vanished."

Ms. Matsuda listened to the sixteen-year-old who was now only a year older than Luna was when she was killed that terrible day. Noemi was one of the "troubled girls" that Ms. Matsuda was hired to help at Garfield High School. But unlike the noisy girls she counseled, many of them involved with a gang, Noemi was quiet, unaffiliated, but also completely bored with school, friends, and counselors; she seemed to be in another world. Yet, of all the troubled teens, Noemi was the easiest to talk to. Ms. Matsuda found her easy to like.

"Tell me more about what happened," Ms. Matsuda pressed.

Noemi noticed a row of fallen scholarly books on a metal wall shelf and next to it, a single white certificate with Ms. Matsuda's name written in calligraphy. Noemi thought it looked gaudy, uncharacteristic of the Japanese-American counselor's straightforward manner. The girl turned toward a light-drenched section of floor, gathered her thoughts, and slowly began to relate back that day with Luna—for the first time since Ms. Matsuda had been dealing with the girl.

"They were arguing, miss, really heavy. I was in the backseat, minding my own business, humming a song in my head to drown out the yelling. I started thinking I was in some other place, a hero kind of thing, fighting monsters . . . I don't even know what they were arguing about. Ever since Luna started seeing Eddie Varela, they were always in some kind of *pleito*. Eddie was a real *pendejo*. Luna was fifteen, but she already had lots of boyfriends. Eddie was older, maybe eighteen. Anyways, one minute they were calling each other all kinds of *babosadas*, then Eddie just reaches over, opens the door, and pushes Luna out. It happened so fast. Luna was still looking at Eddie when she flies out. I just froze. Eddie kept driving, faster, going crazy. 'You stupid, you stupid,' he kept saying. He seemed to forget I was in the car. He drove for a little while, then took an off ramp, stopped the car, and started running. He left me there. I didn't know what to do. I couldn't scream or nothing. After a while, some people came to the car. Then police and an ambulance. They got Eddie when he was trying to leave for Mexico."

Noemi stopped. Ms. Matsuda wasn't sure what to ask next.

"*Ay que Luna,* she was pretty, and so sure of herself," Noemi continued. "And she was sure about whatever she felt was important—like being heard, like doing what she wanted, but also blaming nobody if things didn't work out. I was close to Luna. She taught me things. There was three of us girls, you know—Luna, then me, then Olivia. We call her Liver. You know her—she's a freshman, Olivia Estrada."

"Yes, I'm well aware of your sister, Olivia," Ms. Matsuda responded. Olivia was probably the loudest gang-connected, mean-spirited girl the counselor had to deal with at Garfield. Not hard to figure out, just hard to help.

"We didn't have a father you know—I mean, we had a father, it's not like La Virgen or anything. But we never had nothing to do with them."

"Them?" Ms. Matsuda inquired.

"Yeah, Luna had another dad, who is still around, working up north. Our dad—Liver's and mine—is a tecato from the barrio. You know my mom was a hype, right?"

"Yes, I knew that—she no longer uses, I understand."

"That's right, she began to stop using after Luna passed away. She's had relapses, but for the most part, she's been clean. I'm glad, too."

"I also understand you were taken away from your mother once," Ms. Matsuda said.

"Sure, for a while they split us up. But after Moms got her act together, she helped bring Liver and me back. Only by then—we were separated about three years—I didn't know Liver that good. She was so different, so angry . . . I don't know, she didn't like me—or nobody."

"Tell me more about your family, about Luna."

"Well, Luna was Luna, you know. The moon. The loon. A lunatic. She was in the streets all the time. I remember her as cool, real smart, and always watching out for me. When my moms and Dad were shooting up, Luna took us places, Liver and me: to the park, to the L.A. River, to the parties she went to. She was twice my age, but she was more of a mother, you know. My moms was out of it. I love Moms. She wasn't mean or nothing, just not all there. I didn't know *chiva* was bad. I thought it was medicine, you know. She calmed down with *chiva*. She'd put her head back and her eyelids fluttered, then her head would fall forward, like it was on its own. I know better now. My dad, I never talk to him. Moms got rid of him so she could stay clean. Once I saw him in an alley off Fetterly Avenue with some other dude, shooting up. He didn't see me, so I took off the other way. I never walked that way again. I just don't got no reason to deal with him."

"Moms? Why do you say 'moms'?" Ms. Matsuda inquired.

"I don't know—we just do. I think Liver called her that when she was a little girl and we all started saying it."

"You've had quite a life, Noemi," Ms. Matsuda said, her voice tinged with sadness.

"Oh, I don't know," Noemi said. "It's Liver, I mean Olivia. She's the one you really have to worry about."

Can someone love a name? *Graciela*. It sounded so nice, so sweet on the tongue. A name to be sung, to be tasted. A name with large brown eyes.

Olivia loved the name and the girl. Graciela—slender and slithery, with a body seemingly shaped by the most skillful hands and skin that was creamy and smooth. Graciela was older than

Olivia was—eighteen years old, out of school, and working. But the first time Olivia saw her at the hamburger stand on the Boulevard with the other girls from Las Chicas Chuecas, she fell into a trance. Although Olivia was fourteen and built big, with heavy breasts and fleshy thighs, it was as if an invisible thread from Graciela's forehead or navel pulled at her, keeping her at the right distance, where the tension was the strongest, where she was the most inflamed with desire.

Graciela looked over at Olivia, who felt so ugly at times that she wanted to choke somebody. But Graciela smiled. "Hey, what's your name, chula?" Olivia was gone. Spoken to by a poem with legs. Every detail in the world sharpened. The name imprinted like a song in her brain. *Graciela, Graciela.* Olivia didn't want to say she was called Liver. So, for the first time since she was a little girl, she answered, "Olivia—my name's Olivia."

"Good," Graciela smiled. "Let's hang out, all right? *O-li-via,*" pronouncing the name the way Olivia had said it, as if she were learning it for the first time. And on Graciela's tongue, saying her name the way she did, it felt like being baptized all over again. *Olivia. Graciela.* Names were no longer just names after that.

an, are you going or what, Noemi?"

"*Simón,* I just had to get my coat."

Olivia sat shotgun in the 1950 Chevrolet Deluxe that belonged to Graciela's lowrider brother, Mario. They were going out in style. It was a mix party, and Graciela, ever the creative one, thought it would be cool for Las Chuecas to ride up in the bomba.

Five girls piled into the short—Graciela drove, Liver sat next to her. In the backseat was La Crazy, Cuca, and Seria. As Noemi approached the car she saw the dilemma.

"Man, you guys give Mexicans a bad name," Noemi said. "How am I going to fit in here?"

"*No seas chillona*. Sit on my lap," Liver commanded. "We're *carnalas*, nobody is going to say nothing."

Liver's large frame took up most of the passenger side. Noemi was tiny compared to her younger sister, so she shoehorned her way in, with her back against the passenger door. For an instant, she thought of Luna being thrown out of the car from that side.

"I know now why I don't like hanging with you locas," said Noemi.

"You'll like it, don't worry," Graciela responded. "After this, you'll want to be one of us."

"I'm already chueca enough in here," Noemi replied, causing the other girls to laugh. Noemi played on the word that meant crooked or bent. The way the girls used the word, "chueca" stood for bent lives, bent minds—not the narrow, straight existence that girls were expected to have. Not these girls—abused by drunken fathers, humiliated by scornful mothers, beaten by raging brothers. They were pushed into all kinds of shape by forces stronger than their innocence could withstand. They also felt harder than most girls, survivors, who took the worst beatings, sexual assaults, putdowns, and were still able to stand up without tears and declare, "you ain't changed me."

Their hearts were bent, but not broken.

La Crazy, with L-C-C tattooed on her chin and three dots in a triangle, signifying La Vida Loca, below her left eye, began to pass out photos of her boyfriend, known as Chemo. He was serving time in the youth authority prison in Ventura. One photo had Chemo in his living room with a shaved head, standing in a cholo stance, penguin style with super-large ironed pants, his hands forming his barrio's initials, *LV,* for Lil' Valley. La Crazy had used a safety pin to mark around the photo, in cholo writing, the words *"La Crazy y Chemo juntos siempre."* Beneath this was a stylized *ele ce ce,* representing Las Chicas Chuecas, their barrio girl group. They went with guys from different neighborhoods, even with those vatos who were known enemies. It was a dangerous thing for them to do, considering how many other barrio girls would give them dirty looks, but they were bent lives, with bent minds. And they were fierce fighters, with Liver clearly the best fighter of the group.

The party was in Highland Park on Avenue 47. The Avenues, an old and large barrio gang, controlled these streets. Although most of Las Chuecas were from unincorporated East L.A. neighborhoods, they were never afraid to crash a party in another 'hood. Noemi, however, felt uneasy. She knew they were far from home, far from any help, far from anybody who would give a damn if anything happened to them.

Graciela pulled the Deluxe into a tight spot near the party house. She reached under the dashboard to pull on a "kill switch" that disconnected the power to the starter to make it harder for car thieves. The last thing she wanted was Mario on her back for leaving the car unprotected. The girls piled out from both sides. Noemi looked around. The neighborhood was quiet except for dogs barking and the mix beats coming from the party. She saw people standing around the driveway and on the front porch. *Please, God, don't let there be any trouble,* she thought. Noemi then looked over at Olivia, who had reached behind Graciela's back with an arm and held her for a second before letting go and taking on the feared Liver persona they knew well.

"*¡Aquí paramos—Las Chicas Chuecas—y qué!*" she yelled out while walking tough toward the house in front of the other girls.

Graciela shook her head, and with a certain practiced elegance, took her time behind Liver, pushing down her short leather skirt around her hips. Noemi looked at her and thought, *I'm not into women, but I can see why Liver likes her.*

When the girls walked in, people moved out of the way. Some congregated in corners of the room and around sofas and seats. A few of the other girls at the party gave out their I-don't-give-a-fuck look at Las Chuecas. But a few guys noticed Graciela and the others, and they began to brighten up, with smiles, compliments, and goofy gestures that guys tend to do when new girls are around.

Several people were already dancing; a few girls looked over their shoulders and bounced their behinds. Graciela jumped in right away, dancing with nobody in particular. Liver stopped her forward motion, looked at Graciela, whose enticing movements gathered steam with each beat, pulling in both male and female in a tight ring around her.

Liver liked to see Graciela dance, but she hated anybody else having the privilege. Liver turned around, walked to where the brews were and tried to act like none of this mattered. But Noemi, always the cautious one and the one with the keenest perceptions, knew that Liver was building up to some bloody scene. She knew her sister. She knew her rage. And this scared Noemi more than anything else did.

The night wore on. As usual weed and heroin powder got passed around. Whiskey, tequila, and beer bottles accumulated on top of chairs, mantels, and stairways. Graciela had by then

drunk several glasses of liquor. She began to dance with a fever—
her hands caressed her breasts, her waist, her hips. Liver was outside drinking with La Crazy, Cuca, and Seria. At one point she
looked over and through a window saw Graciela begin to lift her
skirt up her thighs. Several guys were smiling broadly and yelling
encouragement.

"Shit!" Liver said, pushing past the girls to enter the house.

Noemi was upstairs when she heard familiar voices in tones
higher than the rest of the party. She rushed down to see Liver
grab Graciela by the arm.

"What's wrong with you, girl," Graciela slurred, her eyes partly
closed.

"We're outta here—now!" Liver shouted.

"Fuck no! I'm dancing, *esa*," Graciela responded.

"You're losing it again," Liver said.

By then people began to shout back, "Let her dance" and
"Lighten up, man."

But Liver wasn't having it.

"*Mira chica*, you're a pip-squeak compared to me," Graciela
said. "I don't care if you can beat the shit of anybody here, I came
to dance, and I'm dancing."

Liver turned around and smacked Graciela hard on her
cheek; Graciela fell back, hitting the floor, and slid several feet.
Noemi ran over to Graciela who was moaning and bleeding, her
back up against a wall. Some girls began to jump on Liver, who
then turned around and squarely hit another girl, breaking her
nose. By then La Crazy and the other chuecas jumped in with
bottles in their hands.

"*Órale*... the *r-rucas* are going at it," yelled one plastered
partygoer.

Noemi helped Graciela up and took her to the bathroom. She was groggy, and blood flowed from her mouth. Graciela reached inside her mouth and pulled out a bloody tooth. Tears poured down her face. Noemi gently wiped away the blood with a towel dipped in hot water from the faucet.

"I love your sister," Graciela tried to speak. "But I'm four years older than her—she ain't got no right telling me what to do."

"I know—Liver loves you, too," Noemi assured her. "But you know her temper. You know how crazy she gets. For your sake, I think you need to get away from her for a while."

Graciela looked lost, her spirit dissipated. Even though she was the oldest and most sophisticated of the girls, at that moment she seemed like a child. Noemi figured that deep down Graciela was still trying to grow up.

When Noemi and Graciela emerged from the bathroom, the place was in complete chaos. Liver had a girl on the floor, pounding her face in, while the other chuecas pulled and scratched at others. After several minutes of this, some older guys came in, *veteranos* from The Avenues, and began to pull everybody apart.

"Fuck this—take it outside," said one of the guys, who pulled out a .38 magnum handgun.

Liver jumped up, staring at the dudes. They didn't step back, but they didn't move forward either. Liver didn't say anything. She just walked over to the door of the house, looking everybody over once; before leaving she kicked over a table topped with beer bottles onto the floor.

Noemi pushed Graciela out as well. The other chuecas began to exit, their backs to the door, one at a time. Nobody else did anything, except for those helping up several injured girls. The guy with the gun kept it in his hand as he watched the girls leave.

Cuca got into the driver's seat, while Graciela, Liver, and the other girls climbed into the crowded backseat. Noemi sat shotgun, alone.

"How do you start this thing?" Cuca asked, worried that people from the party might decide to pursue them and damage the car before they could leave.

"There's a switch below the steering column—you can't miss it. Just pull it toward you," Graciela managed to say, spitting drops of blood onto the seat in front of her.

Cuca pulled on the switch and turned the ignition, starting the engine right up. As they drove off, nobody said a word. In a minute, Liver held Graciela's face in her hands. Graciela began to cry, and Liver kissed her gently on her cheek and around her mouth. Noemi looked outside again, as she had done before, fantasizing of a duel she was having with a slew of humpbacked reptile men. She cut off heads, severed arms, pierced hearts.

"*¡Ajúa!*" yelled La Crazy. "*Las Chicas Chuecas rifamos.*"

T he front of James A. Garfield High School consisted of a beige three-story building pushed back from the street by a swath of grass. A multicolored mosaic graced a side structure. A rendition of the Mexika-Aztec sun stone glared from the top of another. A high chain-link fence surrounded the school like a prison. Volunteer parents in specially marked T-shirts monitored the hallways with walkie-talkies. Sheriff's deputies parked a patrol unit at the end of the block.

Every day, Noemi entered the four metal front doors on Sixth Street along with other students. The first thing she noticed was the school's mascot, the bulldog, prominently displayed on a wall. This was the only "official art" allowed after the administration cracked down on the barrio graffiti that had covered many of the walls and restrooms for years.

During the day, Noemi moved quickly from room to room after short class periods, which hardly accomplished anything. Some of her classes were in the makeshift bungalows in the back of the school. The bungalows were built to address severe overcrowding at Garfield—with more than five thousand students this was one of the largest high schools in the country.

And these were the school's better days.

In the 1970s, Garfield had the distinction of being so academically weak as to lose its accreditation. It was a school in which significant numbers—for a time, up to two-thirds—of the student body had dropped out or were kicked out. Gangs roamed sections of the school grounds like armies along national borders.

Then from the early 1980s on, Garfield amassed a measure of respectability. The 1988 film *Stand and Deliver* dramatized the work of math teacher Jaime Escalante who—with the help of teachers, parents, administration, and students—turned the school into a showcase of how a largely written-off public entity could become viable again. Garfield now boosted Yale- and Harvard-bound students.

Still, too many students were left out. The community that surrounded Garfield consisted of largely poor, stuccoed-over single-family homes or two-story apartment structures. Garfield also pulled students from the low-income Maravilla barrios, including its housing projects, and the hills of La Gerahty Loma and City Terrace. Two blocks south of the school lay Whittier Boulevard—once the cruising mecca for barrios everywhere until the sheriff's department forced its closing in 1979 with the arrest of 538 people and several beatings.

Instead of an oasis in a desert, Garfield was like a crowded interchange at rush hour. Inside the school, teachers, parents, and administrators admonished students who lingered in the hallways to get to their classrooms. Their policy was "zero tolerance." While adults sometimes yelled at the youth, the students weren't supposed to yell back.

As a freshman, Noemi recalled a provocative cartoon that caused quite an uproar. It showed several students stuck on the high fence. One of them proclaimed, "they sure make it hard for us to get in here."

That same year, President Clinton and his wife, Hillary, came to visit Garfield—the first time any U.S. president had ever done so. Noemi remembered how, for days prior, the Secret Service practically lived at the school. They checked out restrooms, classrooms, and every nook and cranny of the campus.

A tarp was placed on the fence so nobody could see from the street. The walkie-talkies used by the administration were taken away, replaced by Secret Service personnel with their own listening devices. As the president spoke, the school principal told everyone how impressed she was at the unusually quiet and still students. But Noemi knew why—all the students had clear views of snipers that had been trained on them from the rooftops and top floors of nearby buildings.

In a separate room in the crowded administration office, Ms. Matsuda sat behind a scratched metal desk. She looked over a sheet of paper in front of her that displayed a poem written in bubble lettering. A good poem, Ms. Matsuda thought, a revealing poem. Noemi had come into her office to show her the poem she had found beneath Olivia's mattress. It was called "Dreamer." At first, Ms. Matsuda couldn't believe that Olivia had had anything to do with it.

> There are girls that are poems
> Like a smile is a poem
> Girls who laugh their song
> Thru their eyes
> There are girls who see a world
> But touch beneath it
> And there are girls who are too much hurt
> Too much reality for dreams
> In your eyes, I've seen the dreamer
> Who sees a puddle of muddy water
> And gazes at rainbows.
> So all anyone can do, has done
> Is birth the dreamer past
> The doors of your fears
> Knowing the woman in you will lead
> Thru your eyes
> For your dreams.
>
> TO GRACIELA, "DREAMER"

"Wow, I'm impressed," Ms. Matsuda said. Over the weeks, she had gotten closer to Noemi, although Olivia remained unresponsive to her.

"I wouldn't do this normally—show you Olivia's poem without her permission—but I don't think she would ever show this to anybody," Noemi said. "She's good, no?"

"Yes, and she's expressing some strong feelings," Ms. Matsuda said. "I can't get these feelings by talking with her. But this says a lot about how much she is hiding behind her toughness. I won't tell her that you showed me this poem, but I do thank you. It's only going to help Olivia. Somehow, we have to tap into this side of her. You know, they are thinking of throwing her out of the school. She is doing badly in her classes. She hardly shows up, and then when she does, she throws fits and walks out on teachers. It can't go on much longer."

"I know, I wish I could do more to help," Noemi said. "But Liver doesn't listen to me. Like I said, we live together now, but we aren't like bosom buddies. She has her world and I have mine. But, still, I wouldn't want anything bad to happen to her."

"I understand. I'll see you tomorrow about the same time," Ms. Matsuda said. "And Noemi, again, thanks."

"No problem," Noemi responded as she got up and left.

Ms. Matsuda read the poem for a second time. She felt she had something to talk with Olivia about, something that may get her to open up. If not, Olivia was bound to do something terrible, something that might not be remedied.

Noemi, Olivia, and their mother lived on Ditman Avenue, a few houses from Hubbard Street. This area consisted of older stock wood-frame houses and duplexes, some with pots of flowers on windowsills and scattered gardens in backyards. Brick walls with wrought-iron gates surrounded some of the homes. Dogs barked constantly and the occasional rooster crowed the day into existence.

One of the neighborhood's claims to fame was how residents in 1985 captured, by beating into submission, one of the most prolific killers in the country—"The Night Stalker," Richard Muñoz Ramirez. Wanted in the murders of at least thirteen people, Ramirez had until then eluded police from northern and southern California.

That night, the neighbors had themselves one *chingón* of a block party.

The area was also the epicenter of the 1970 East L.A. riot. This began when armed sheriff's deputies attacked a crowd of around thirty thousand protesting the Vietnam War at Salazar Park (when it was called Laguna Park)—ending in the deaths of several people, including Chicano journalist Ruben Salazar, hundreds of arrests, and parts of Whittier Boulevard burned to the ground.

It was some distance from Garfield to Noemi's home. Many times, Noemi walked throughout the Eastside, taking her time, frequently passing her home. She particularly liked to visit El Mercado on First and Lorena to hear mariachis, eat tacos, and locate some hard-to-find Mexican music and clothing. Other times, she'd stop at La Curandera Doña María's Botánica ("daily *limpias* and spiritual readings, guaranteed!") on Chavez Avenue near Eastern to eye the elaborate and colorful *velas,* herbs, and spiritual items. Noemi also liked to observe the street peddlers as they sold mangoes on a stick, elotes con chile, churros, and raspadas on street corners, in parking lots, and parks.

Other sights graced Noemi's eyes: Mariachi Plaza on First and Boyle, where musicians congregated before hitting the bars and restaurants; the Buddhist temple on Fourth Street; La Luz del Mundo—House of God and Gate of Heaven, a gold-laden and Greek-column structure that loomed like an apparition from another century on First Street; and the various cemeteries, including the Chinese Cemetery on First and Eastern where Chinese funeral rites were often held, complete with incense and gongs.

One of Noemi's uncles worked at El Pedorrero (which translates to "the farter") Muffler Shop and Radiator Service on Whittier Boulevard and Record Avenue. There was a colorful welded-up art car parked in front. Noemi would stop by to say hello.

On these walks, Noemi imagined many battles and quests, armed with elaborate weapons in shiny attire, where worlds opened up to other worlds. She had on armor of the finest gold, lined with diamonds and emeralds. On her head was a helmet with images of serpents and wild birds. She was a fearless warrior meeting every challenge with boldness—be they other warriors, creatures, aliens, or devil-spirits from another dimension. In her thoughts, Noemi was nobody to mess with.

Once at home, Noemi rarely ventured outside (except when Olivia coerced her into hanging out with Las Chuecas). Noemi liked being there, with her mother, who slept late and watched a lot of TV, while Noemi did most of the housework—something Olivia would never do. Noemi didn't mind. She felt if she stayed home, became useful, her mother would not go out and party. She'd stay clean. She'd be a mother again.

One day, a particularly warm and calm day, Noemi arrived home from school as usual. As she entered the house, she felt something was off. The door was unlocked. Her mother, who usually sat on a sofa in front of the TV around that time, wasn't there.

"Moms," Noemi yelled out. Nobody answered.

Noemi picked up a couple of dirty plates and an ashtray full of cigarette butts from the coffee table. She entered the small kitchen and placed the dishes on the counter. She then opened the trashcan to pour in the cigarette butts when she spotted a scorched bottle cap. She picked it up and stared at the darkened middle. She placed it near her nose and the smell of sulfur entered her system. Noemi didn't want to believe it, but she knew. Heroin had been cooked. The girl dropped the bottle cap into the trash. She rushed into the bathroom, where she noticed a couple of cotton balls on the floor. She turned to the sink, where she saw the evidence—a hypodermic needle, her mother's *ere,* her "rig."

"No, Moms, no," Noemi exclaimed to herself, as she sank down on the closed toilet cover, the syringe in her hand, the blood not yet dry. Just then Noemi looked up and her mother stood in the doorway—her hair in disarray, her small body lost in a large nightgown, a euphoric gaze on her face while her fingers nervously moved at her side as she leaned against the doorframe.

"Moms, how could you?" was all Noemi said before she jolted out the bathroom, pushing her mother out of the way and almost dropping her.

Noemi was too messed up to do anything. She had drunk too much, smoked some weed, dropped a few pills. Now she was unable to stand up. This was something Noemi was not used to, and she felt scared. She managed to get to a bed in a side room and lay down. Earlier in the day, she was angry, confused. She didn't even go to see Ms. Matsuda; she didn't know how or if she could talk about it.

Her mother's using normally wouldn't hit her this hard, but she was having so much trouble with Olivia that everything seemed to come down on her at once. So when Seria and Cuca invited her to this party near the Ramona Gardens Housing Projects, she decided to go, even though Olivia wouldn't be there. Noemi normally did not go out unless Liver was with her.

Seria and Cuca were already out in the car making it with some vatos. Noemi was in and out of consciousness as she lay on the bed. Utterances, colors, faces, hands—they entered without any perceivable pattern into the room; everything was a haze, everything awash in dream tints and textures. Suddenly, two guys appeared above her. She wasn't sure if she was sleeping or what. She felt her body being moved, some of her clothing taken off, her legs pushed apart, but she seemed unable to say anything, to do anything. She couldn't scream or kick. Then she felt the weight of a body on hers. A mouth hammered out grunts. *Am I asleep? Is this a dream? Where am I? Where's Liver? Oh, Liver, where are you, man? Liver, Liver! Oh, Luna, querida Luna! Where is everybody?*

Part of her knew what was happening. Another part didn't care. Another part wanted to scream. Another part just wanted to fall asleep, forever and ever. To be in that world of swashbuckling adventures and daring battles where Noemi defeated all enemies, all challenges, with great flair and ferocity—oh, what a sight to behold, this fearsome hero, unafraid and triumphant.

"There's a *pinche tren* over here, homes," some guy said excitedly from the doorway to somebody behind him. *Was he really talking? Where is the hero, the sword? I'll take them all on. I'm La Noemi, with a horse and lance. I can take on anybody. Come on then!*

"Get off her!" somebody yelled.

Luna, Luna, is that you?

There was a commotion around her. Heads turned. More yelling.

"Get out of here, *puta!*"

"Fuck you."

"Hey, *pinche cabrones,* let her go!"

"It's none of your business—get out!"

Then, the thrusting and grabbing stopped. By then Noemi was in another place, another time, fighting off a dragon. She was dressed like an Azteca princess, like a knight from the Middle Ages, dodging flames and slicing through dragon flesh.

She never knew how she got home. But for weeks afterward she wouldn't say anything to anybody. Seria and Cuca knew what had happened, but they didn't say anything either. But Noemi knew that she had been raped—she didn't know who it was. And she especially didn't want to tell Liver.

After that night, Noemi also stayed away from Ms. Matsuda. She received calls at home from the counselor. Notes in her classroom. But Noemi didn't show up at school for days. Then she just stopped going entirely after Olivia was thrown out for fighting with a girl over an empty seat in the cafeteria. Noemi wanted to get out of everything. She wanted to stop the world from turning, but couldn't. It was easier for her to stop turning with the world.

O livia looked over at Noemi, who was sitting in front of the TV set with a remote in her hand. She noticed that Noemi wasn't really watching anything. Just changing the channels.

"What's up with you, *mujer?*" Olivia asked.

Noemi didn't respond.

"I'm talking to you, *boba.*"

Noemi kept staring at the TV, ignoring her sister, but trembling inside.

"Fuck you then—fuck you and Moms, that *pinche* tecata. I'm

tired of this house. This fuckin' place—all this bullshit melodrama. Both of you can go to hell!" Olivia yelled.

Noemi looked up, finally. Then without warning, she blurted out, "I'm pregnant."

Olivia looked hard at Noemi, like she was going to kick her or something, but then she softened, walked deliberately toward her sister, and in a less harsh tone asked, "You're pregnant? By who? Who's the asshole that did this to you?"

"I don't know."

"*Cómo que* you don't know? You have to know, *esa.*"

"It was at that party that I said I went to, you know, with Seria and Cuca.'

"They knew about this?"

"Yeah, but don't get mad at them. I swore I'd cut their throats if they said anything."

"Now I have to cut their throats for not saying anything."

"Listen, Liver, I don't know what to do. I can't tell Moms or nobody. I can't go nowhere. I guess I'll just have to have the baby."

"Tell Moms," Olivia offered, resignation in her voice. "She's fucked up, but maybe she can help."

"No, or she'll do what she did to Luna."

"What are you talking about?"

"You don't remember, you were maybe four years old, but I do. When Luna got pregnant."

"I didn't know Luna got pregnant."

"I know—nobody said nothing about it," Noemi explained. "Luna was thirteen. I don't know who did it to her—there was a rumor about some guy who lived down the street, some mexicano, you know, *sin papeles.* Anyways, Moms was pissed. For days, she yelled up and down the house. I never saw Moms like that—talking about killing somebody, about calling La Migra—all kinds of things. Luna yelled back, about how Moms can't tell her what to do, that she was older now—but she wasn't, you know. And I remember how Luna cried. Alone in the room. I heard her when she thought I was asleep. She was afraid, so I was afraid. I didn't know much about anything then, if you can imagine. I was only six. But one night—a night that feels more like a dream, even now as I think about it—I woke up to muffled screams. I got out of bed. When I looked into the kitchen, I saw Luna laid out across the kitchen table, her legs spread open, and blood everywhere. There was a towel in Luna's mouth. I could smell throw up. I should have left, but I wanted to see. I don't know why, I just did. I looked over and there was a syringe near Luna's arm. Moms had shot her up. And then I saw Moms—she went over to Luna's thing, you know, her *panocha,* and pulled out the dead baby. I saw this—I've tried to forget, but now I can't. It's all come back to me—especially now . . . especially that I'm like this."

"Man, Noemi, you've seen all this and I haven't, and I'm the one that's pissed off all the time," Olivia offered, acknowledging this for the first time. "But you're the one, you're really the one that has been through the shits, man. I always thought you were a *lambichi*—you know, uncool, weird. You never say much. You always dress like you don't care what people think about you. I wanted to look up to you, but I only felt bad for you. I get mad, and all you do is walk away. It gets me madder, let me tell you, but now I know. You just held all this in—all this shit you've seen. I'm sorry Noemi. Really, for once in my life, I'm sorry."

"What should I do, Liver?"

"I don't know, *'mana.* Let me think about this for a while. Maybe Graciela will have an idea. Let's call."

"I don't know about that—I really don't want anybody to know just yet."

The girls sat on the couch together, a large silence between them. Then Olivia reached over and placed her hand over Noemi's hand—the first time Noemi could ever recall.

M s. Matsuda entered the main office, saying hello to teachers and office staff before entering her cubicle. One of the teachers, Ms. Guzman, came up to Ms. Matsuda before she could sit down and asked, "Have you heard about Noemi?"

"Oh my God," Ms. Matsuda said with a hand to her mouth, expecting the worst. "Tell me she's all right."

"She's all right, but she is in the hospital," Ms. Guzman said. "We got the news this morning. She'll be fine—apparently it's a miscarriage."

"Miscarriage—oh, poor Noemi. I didn't know she was pregnant—what hospital is she in?"

Ms. Matsuda decided to visit Noemi at County Hospital. The girl didn't have much to say to Ms. Matsuda when she talked with her on the phone. After work, she canceled some sessions with students and drove over to the hospital on the western edge of East L.A.

When Ms. Matsuda entered Noemi's room, Olivia was there sitting near her bed, watching the TV set anchored to the ceiling. Olivia grinned, but didn't say anything.

"Well, hello girls. It's so good to see you—I missed you both."

"*¿Qué hubo?*" Olivia responded. "I wish I could say the same, but I can't."

"That's okay," Ms. Matsuda said, used to Olivia's smart mouth. "How about you, Noemi? How are you feeling?"

"I'm feeling better—they said I lost a lot of blood, and my insides are all screwed up, but mostly I'm okay."

"I guess we have a lot of catching up to do," Ms. Matsuda said, handing her a get-well card as she stood by the side of Noemi's bed.

"I don't know where to start—but I got pregnant. I didn't know what to do. I wanted to just die. I didn't tell you, miss, but my moms is using again. This really messed me up. I ran off but then came back and confronted her. She just mumbled. I screamed at her for the first time, and my moms jumped up. She finally spoke up. She said she was tired. She was hurtin'. I told her I didn't believe her no more. I didn't trust anything she said about loving us and quitting because she cared for Liver and me—it was all a big lie. Anyways, I got fucked up at a party . . . I don't want to get into details, miss, but I was raped."

"No, Noemi, this is terrible. . . ." Ms. Matsuda responded.

"I know—but then I wasn't able to tell nobody, not even Liver—and especially not my moms. I wanted to kill myself. I'm sorry, miss. I know this is wrong, but I really felt like it. I finally told Liver about the baby, and she stood by me. But we went to see Graciela, and this didn't turn out so good. Liver and Graciela got into a big ass fight—arguing over some bullshit. I don't know. I got scared. I started thinking somebody was going to get hurt, so I left. I just started walking. Graciela lives near Mission Road, close to the L.A. River. So I walked over the Sixth Street bridge. On the other side there's an entrance to the riverbed. I walked through this tunnel. There was so much garbage and glass in there; everything stunk. I made it to the river—all concrete with graffiti everywhere. There was no water, like it is lots of times. A homeless guy was sleeping in the middle of the damn thing, surrounded by a market cart full of cans and junk. I decided to walk—I didn't know where. Just to walk."

Ms. Matsuda pulled up a chair and sat down. "Please, make yourself at home," Olivia remarked. Ms. Matsuda ignored her.

"I kept walking, miss. I was crying. I walked as far as I could," Noemi resumed. "I kept thinking about Luna, my moms, Liver, and what happened that night of the rape. I started going into my hero thing. I started to win big fights. Slashing and punching and kicking ass . . . vampires, villains, whatever. Anyways, the problem was I didn't know how far I had walked or where I was. Soon the concrete became more like weeds and rocks. I fell over a few of them. It started to get dark. Pretty soon, I got even more scared. I felt some terrible pains inside of me. I picked up my skirt and looked down and saw blood trickling down my leg. The pain was awful. I looked up and I saw a lady putting up some clothes on a line on the other side of a fence. I told her in Spanish that I needed help. She's the one who called the ambulance. I realized, miss, I didn't want to die. I felt like Luna was watching over me. I kept hearing her voice, 'Don't worry. Everything will be fine.' I believed her because I have always believed her. Everybody lies, but not Luna. I know she's watching over me."

By then Ms. Matsuda brought her hand to Noemi's face and caressed it.

"I'm glad you're alive," Ms. Matsuda said. "You have so much to live for—you have so much to give to this world. Don't let anybody tell you otherwise."

Ms. Matsuda paused briefly, contemplating whether she should say what she wanted to say.

"Listen, I'll share something—with the both of you," Ms. Matsuda said. "I've never had the kind of life you two have had, but I was lonely too, long ago. I also wanted to commit suicide. My parents were real strict. They wanted nothing but the best for me,

I know that, and I love them for it. But there was so much pressure to get good grades, to be polite, to not have boyfriends or do anything that would waste my time. I was suffocating. Like as if I was not even important. I may not know what you know, Noemi, but I do know what it feels to want to destroy everything for nothing."

Ms. Matsuda then took Noemi's hand. Noemi could hardly say anything, but she felt good that Ms. Matsuda was there.

Olivia looked over at the two of them, rolled her eyes and said, "Oh, brother."

Noemi turned to Ms. Matsuda and asked, "Miss, is it true you wanted to die?"

"Yes, well—just because people have money and material things doesn't mean they don't feel empty inside," Ms. Matsuda explained. "Again, I can't compare my life to yours. But the pressure to succeed, to be better than anyone, no matter what, can be hard to deal with. The fact is, nobody is immune from feeling alone or desperate."

"I guess if I knew you would understand what I was going through, I wouldn't have shined you on," Noemi said. "So thanks, miss. I appreciate you coming here and talking to me."

"Does that mean you'll come back to school, Noemi?" Ms. Matsuda asked.

"Sure, I guess—yeah, I'll be back."

"And, Olivia, if you want the help," Ms. Matsuda said, turning to Liver. "I can get you into another school that can work with you. But you have to want to do this. You have to want something better for yourself—starting with a change in that attitude. I'll help, but you have to put in 110 percent. Understand, dear?"

"*Simón,* I understand," Olivia said.

Just then a nurse poked her head into the room and declared, "Visit's over, people."

After Olivia and Ms. Matsuda left, Noemi closed her eyes to rest. She felt good about the visit and Liver's apparent turn for the better. But Noemi still had a lot on her mind—she had to deal with her mother, although she realized that instead of putting her down, she should be there for her.

There was also her health to worry about after the miscarriage—the doctors weren't sure she could have babies again without severe complications. She thought about school and the classes she had to make up. And she thought about Las Chicas Chuecas—Noemi knew she was the only one among them who could get them real help. She reflected on this for a while and then made a decision: *I'm going to be a counselor like Ms. Matsuda— I could really get into this.*

As Noemi's mind drifted into sleep, she saw herself dueling against giant mutant knights, cutting their bodies in half or handing them back their arms.

She was a striking and valiant figure.

FINGER DANCE

The last time I searched my father's eyes for signs of love, all I saw was a vapid, dull mist, as if his eyes were marbles of glass or plastic—brown and lifeless. My father had long ago stopped acknowledging me with any emotion except anger. He had long ago stopped the hearts beating between us.

Ten years before, my father, whom we called Chi Cho, an affectionate term for Narciso, had plunged into a dark abyss, a long night; his once sharp and quick-witted mind shut out the world around him, enclosed in *un sitio de secretos*. As it was, his face had long held mysteries, a temple of stories, sins, and secrets that he never disclosed. I never knew his past, his visions, his intimate concerns. Chi Cho was more rumor than man. For years, he would sit with a beer bottle in hand, in front of the TV set or on the porch, without saying a word. Sometimes he'd turn to me when I came across him sitting there, his face taking on the expression of a question mark.

At first, I didn't notice when his mind began to tune out. It was like riding the Greyhound bus from Los Angeles to El Paso: You see mostly desert, the same landscape and outposts, but if you pay attention, a few signs and changing scenery along the way indicate you're almost there. Then before you know it, El Paso appears on the horizon.

Something like this happened whenever I dealt with Chi Cho: My father did strange things all the time. But over the last decade, his actions became increasingly odd, even for him.

First, he started to walk around the old house in rags. This didn't appear out of the ordinary in the beginning; he was always funny about his clothes. Chi Cho had a thin sinewy body—the metabolic kind, because he ate like a bull. But clothes betrayed him: they sort of dangled on him, on those shoulders shaped like wire hangers.

But then he would leave the house in those rags without telling anyone and take long walks. A hastily formed search party would bring him back. A couple of times, the police escorted him home. Chi Cho would act as if nothing had happened.

The most telling thing about his condition was his bedroom. Our old house was a two-bedroom stucco-over-wood-frame structure along a row of older, funkier, crowded homes on Sunol Drive. Growing up, my mother and my sister, Monique, slept in the living room. My brother, Teto, and I (I'm called Tutti, short for Arturo) were in the side bedroom, while Chi Cho had a room to himself in the back.

You might think this strange, but my mother, Mona, never seemed to mind. I think she liked it that way. She was the kind of mom who made it known that she sacrificed herself to be here— to be mother and wife, to walk the hallways, to take up space in the world. Although she was nondescript, usually dressed plainly in solid gray or brown dresses, her hair in a bun, she also had authority. Yet, she was resentful of what she had to do for husband

and family—nobody appreciated her, she'd say. But a part of her reveled in it as well.

My father's room faced out onto the backyard, where Mona's macraméd pots with lush tropical plants outside the windows blocked the view of the chicken coop and the partially falling-down garage. A lone rooster meandered around the yard, with the smaller hens pecking about the grassless plot for food. Patas, or "Feet" because of the long white fur that covered each paw, was our seemingly one-hundred-year-old brown-black mutt who lazily laid near a badly constructed wooden doghouse, which Teto and I had built when we were much younger. Even when Teto became a professional house builder, we never rebuilt Patas's home—but I think the dog liked it this way.

Then when we least expected it, after a decade of Dad's *loquera,* we got the news: My father had stomach cancer.

Chi Cho's mental decline was slow in coming, but when the cancer appeared it ate him from the inside out with devastating speed. The doctors said it was too far gone to stop. Chi Cho had weeks to live. The family took the news badly, but I felt relief; he already appeared to me to be dead, a body in motion, with nothing really ticking in there.

Chi Cho, confined mostly to his room, stayed busy. Next to his bed on an old secondhand dresser lay a number of writing tablets where he wrote with those long-fingered vein-covered hands—numbers over and over again. He put down different numbers, the same numbers, in different order, in no order. In one corner of the room, he had a pile of junk mail, most of it unopened and neatly stacked.

Chi Cho also developed the nasty habit of killing flies and other bugs unfortunate enough to land on the white curtains that Mona had so delicately placed over the windows. And, if that weren't enough, Chi Cho had positioned rubber band over rubber band at the end of a bedpost so that in a matter of months an immense rubber ball had sprouted there.

Whenever I called the house, Chi Cho always reminded me to give him my latest phone number, although he had already written it down some twenty times in his peeling brown phone book.

Mona was naturally concerned. If I mentioned his deterioration, she'd burst into tears on the phone. Yet, despite his growing eccentricities, she never once thought to abandon him. Mona continued to follow Chi Cho around, picking up after him, and seeing that he didn't get hurt or forget where he was going. Although they had long stopped being intimate, she was connected to him like a canary to a song.

Now, don't misunderstand. Mona was not dependent on Chi Cho. She ruled the house, really. But when he lost much of his sanity, he revealed a child there, and she responded—more mother than wife, more as little girl to boy doll.

If not for Mona, Chi Cho would have become one of those bedraggled men around Los Angeles, with shopping carts full of soda cans, filthy clothes, newspapers, and bottles. I'm sure of it. On the days he disappeared on his walks, Mona would jump into the family car, a well-kept 1960s Fairlane, to find him. Inevitably, she'd see Chi Cho standing on a corner talking to himself or sitting on a park bench, legs crossed, staring blankly at an invisible TV screen in the bushes, holding an invisible beer can in his hand.

"*¡Dios mio!*" Mona cried on the phone one morning after bringing Chi Cho home from one of his wanderings. "*¿Por qué me ha quitado a mi Chi Cho?*" Why had God taken away her Chi Cho?

"You're going to need a Chi Cho compass, Mama," I commented.

"How can you make jokes, *malvado?*"

"Mama, put Dad on the phone for me."

After a long wait and seconds of line static, Chi Cho came on the line.

"Tutti—*¿cómo estás?*"

"*Muy bien,* Dad—listen, what's going on over there?"

"Oh, wait a minute, Tutti, before I forget . . . give me your phone number."

T here were three children who remembered a different father, another Chi Cho, a man who was feared, respected, and to be honest, just plain ornery.

My dad was an artist. He worked with metal and welding rods to create the wrought-iron gates and window bars that now went up and down First Street in our neighborhood.

Chi Cho: *el soldadero del barrio.*

Before he began his street pieces, Chi Cho had worked in the factories of Vernon and Maywood. But when these mills and shops closed down in the mid-1980s, he established his own business in his garage—the same garage that now looked like it would topple with a swift wind or a long fart.

Chi Cho was resourceful, if nothing else. While many of his friends, after the plants closed, took to heavy-duty drinking, or to working in demeaning jobs, or worse still, to committing suicide, my dad began to design in metal.

Sometimes Chi Cho took Teto and me to Tijuana to gather design ideas and pick up the iron and the tools that would later transform, as if by magic, the run-down shacks of our barrio.

My father's most famous piece—his masterwork—was a wrought-iron Aztec sun stone at the entrance of a driveway in El Monte. I went with him a couple of times when he showed off the intricate work to friends; this piece was the essence of what his hands, mind, and eyes could conjure. His voice thick, almost with weeping, filled me with pride as he explained every elaborate detail, each welding pass, each twist and turn of the iron segments.

The image looked like a massive dial. Circular rings made up most of its structure, each one representing ritual or destiny time. There were many symbols, including those for wind, fire, death, water, and movement. There were also the stylized images of a rabbit, a monkey, a dog, a deer, a flint blade, an ocelot, a snake, a lizard, a flower, a vulture, an eagle, a crocodile, a house, and a reed. The sun's great face was powerfully rendered in the middle with two fire serpents on the outer bands transporting the sun through the sky.

"Here is the way of our heritage," Chi Cho explained to me once. "We put *toda el alma* into each piece. That's the Mexican way . . . *toda el alma.*"

In times like these, I looked up to Chi Cho. He appeared heroic, intense, perhaps unknowingly firing up the furnaces of creativity in my own mind.

That's why it was difficult to watch him become what he was becoming—his mind mutating, his memory scrambling, the electrons askew . . . no longer able to accomplish a simple weld or walk around the block.

One day I got a phone call.

"*¡M'ijo!*" Mona screamed into the phone. "Your father is gone again. *¡Que caray! Nunca faltan de líos con este hombre.*"

She reached out to me for consolation more than anything else. I knew she would soon grab the car keys, get the car going, and crisscross alleys and streets in search of him. I knew she would find him. This was a burden she would never be relieved of. Though there were times my sister, brother, and I tried to persuade her to do otherwise.

"Look, Mama, leave the old dude," Teto would tell her; he was the most adamant about this. "You can get a trailer to live in. We'll help you."

But, as always, Mona refused. Sometimes she expressed interest in the offer, but in the end, she was too much a part of Chi Cho to let him go.

Every once in a while, we brought the grandkids over to the old house. Between the three of us, we gave our parents nine grandchildren. I had three, Teto four, and my younger sister, Monique, gave birth to two. They were all fairly young, ages two to twelve—brats in any Buick.

When we all gathered at home, Mona would try to keep Chi Cho in his room, although he was harmless, really. Mostly he walked around, conversed with the walls, then hunkered down in the bedroom. But, surprisingly, he acknowledged everyone—all the grandchildren.

"*¿Cómo están mis niños?*" he would say. "Carolina, Antonia, Barbara, Soledad, Roberto, Titi, 'Jandro, Bebe *y* Israel—*vengan, vengan pa' ca.*"

We couldn't figure out how he managed this.

He recalled every face and the names attached to them. He always invited the children to come inside the house so he could talk to them, although by then Mona would intervene and tell the kids to stay in the backyard. In a second or two, my father would turn and go. The children looked toward Mona, searching for some sign from her that would tell them what to do next.

Chi Cho was okay with his grandchildren's names. He had problems with the big things, the damn things that really mattered.

Once when I was a kid, about six years old, I waited excruciating hours by the window, way past dusk, for Chi Cho to arrive in his battered green Fairlane, which he had owned forever, park, and slow walk the cement steps to our door.

"*¡Papi, papi . . . ya llegó!*" I yelled, forcing eight-year-old Teto to look up from the TV set, waking my three-year-old sister from slumber, and agitating the crap out of my mother.

Chi Cho pushed in the door and I rushed up to him so I could be held by his strong arms, surrounded by the smells of sulfur and iron. While in his arms, I sampled the stubble on his face with my hand.

In those days, Chi Cho worked at a small foundry about fifty miles from our home. Chi Cho left early in the morning, before I woke up, and he often came in late at night, after I had curled up beneath a moth-eaten blanket and had fallen asleep.

To make ends meet—since a welding job for a Mexican was not always a well compensated one—Mona took care of us kids during the day and did seamstress work for a garment plant owner at night. But she was always at home. It was Mona who kept us in shape, made sure we got dressed, picked us up from school, chased us down the street, and saw that we washed before dinner.

Mona was everything for us, but I missed Chi Cho, who rarely made an appearance.

On the weekends Chi Cho stayed at home, but he lolled in the garage, working with his tools. When we were young, he fancied himself a handyman, which helped when the plumbing failed or when Teto broke a back window with a rock aimed at me.

For the most part, my father didn't really discipline us, but his anger was worse than any ass licking. One time Chi Cho beat on Teto, after my brother had pushed Monique into a rosebush one summer afternoon. He attacked Teto so badly that Mona had to run into the living room and physically restrain Chi Cho before he killed his son. I still recall my brother yelling, my mother's tears and prayers while she pulled Chi Cho off Teto, and blood on the couch. Chi Cho pretty much left the physical punishments to Mona after that. For years, though, all he had to do was yell at us, and we'd run off to our rooms—I did because I couldn't forget that day he jumped on Teto.

Then there were the good days. Once in a great while, Chi Cho, fresh out of the garage, would join the rest of the family at the dinner table. Eating, telling jokes, and making us chuckle, he ignored Mona's pleas to let us eat. She wanted everyone to be quiet as we ate: You could hear forks on plates, glasses tinkling, and teeth grinding bread, salads, and meats. The only words were "Pass the rice." But with Chi Cho, the scene changed dramatically. We smiled and talked in between gulps of food. Sometimes, when a lively song came on the radio (we played the radio all day long and most of the night) Chi Cho would do a finger dance—two fingers on the tabletop, his thumb holding back the other fingers, and pretend to be a callus-fleshed Fred Astaire.

Chi Cho worked up an Irish jig or a jarabe tapatío. He added sways, marches, and kicks as his hand moved to whatever rhythm sprung from the radio.

And we all laughed, including Mona.

hen Chi Cho was in his garage shop, he didn't want to be disturbed. One summer, I joined a local baseball team at Obregon Park. Nearby businesses sponsored each team and paid for the uniforms, which mostly consisted of colored T-shirts with the names of the businesses on the backs. I was a member of Ortiz's Auto Parts Giants.

One Saturday, I ran home with my new green shirt and baseball cap. I was proud of being a baseball player, even if I didn't know how to swing a bat or to throw a baseball more than a few feet. As I walked up the steps to the porch, Teto rushed up from behind me, grabbed my cap and ran around the yard, yelping like a crazed puppy.

"Give it back," I yelled. "Give it back, or I'll . . ."

"Or you'll what?" Teto responded, looking at me hard with my cap behind his back.

"¡Ya, cabrones—dejen de pelear!" Mona hollered from behind the kitchen window. Teto ran to the driveway and then tossed the cap onto the roof. He walked calmly into the house, snickering.

At nine years old, I still felt vulnerable around Teto. At the moment I began to cry, Chi Cho emerged from the garage.

"M'ijo, why are you always the helpless one," he admonished. "Do you want to be this way all your life? Look, Tutti, you are either going to do, or you are going to get doo-dooed on. You need to choose."

Chi Cho grabbed a ladder from the garage, placed it against the wood-plank sides of our house, and climbed. He retrieved the cap, slapping the thing against his leg to remove the dirt.

"Papi." I began to muster some courage, trying to be one of those who do. "I got a game later today. Can you come?"

"Not today, Tutti, but maybe later in the week, okay?"

For a few weeks, I asked Chi Cho to come to a game. He always answered with the same line, "Maybe later this week."

My last game was a father-and-son affair. I really wanted him to be there. He said he would, and even got into the car. But, suddenly, he stopped, muttered something about some work he hadn't finished, and returned to the garage. I walked over to Obregon Park, in my green jersey and cap, alone. Many fathers were there. I knew some kids didn't have any fathers, but they seemed to cope just fine. I didn't do as well.

I had a father—he just didn't show up.

"Whatever you do, don't let Chi Cho drive you anywhere," I warned Celia, my wife and mother of my little ones. "Even though he's lost it, he still takes out that damn Fairlane. I swear to God, some day he's going to get killed—he's a stone maniac behind the wheel."

Celia and the kids had plans to visit with Mona and Chi Cho that weekend. By then, we had moved much farther east to Pomona where I had a teaching position in one of the high schools there. Needless to say, I didn't turn out to be a baseball player. But living so far away made it an excursion to get back into East L.A. to visit my parents.

The last time I went my father had insisted that he drive us to a Chinese restaurant in Monterey Park. He was always nuts about Chinese food and now appeared not to want to eat anything else.

Mona lost the argument about who was to drive. Chi Cho started to throw a tantrum, which bothered me to no end.

"Let him drive, Mama, he'll be okay," I foolishly suggested, trying to end Chi Cho's wild insistence. What a mistake that was.

Chi Cho drove fifty miles an hour down a residential street. Kids on bikes, mothers taking a walk, and workingmen standing on street corners were all fair game. He jumped onto the freeway and headed east, driving as if no other car existed. He pushed himself into lanes that other cars already occupied. A chorus of horns blaring followed us wherever we went.

"Chi Cho, *estás pasando la salida*—you're passing the exit!" Mona yelled, her fingers on the dashboard losing their color.

Chi Cho then did a miraculous thing; it made me believe in religion again. He stopped the car in the middle of the freeway. Other drivers swerving around him, cursing, brakes screeching. Nobody hit us, though. Chi Cho calmly put the car in reverse, backed up to the exit, and then pulled off.

As always, he came out of this without a scratch.

Another time, he almost struck an elderly woman trying to venture out into the street at a crosswalk.

Mona shouted, "Why don't you pay attention, *viejo*!"

Chi Cho took his hands off the steering wheel, with his foot still on the pedal, and exclaimed, "Okay, then . . . you drive."

I just about died.

But soon we had to keep close track of Chi Cho's daily activities. He would call insulation workers to come in and insulate the attic; they showed up in big trucks, with all the necessary material. There was no attic.

Or another time, he decided to turn in his ancient Fairlane for a new car. He came back with a brand-spanking-new Honda. Red even. Teto made him return the freaking thing.

Teto, especially, had it in for Chi Cho. While I ended up slighter in stature, closer to my dad, Teto was a larger, hardier guy, more from Mona's side of the family. He had a swagger, like many hard-hat people I knew, and a quick temper. I had my beefs with the old man, but for the most part, I got over them. He was my father after all. He didn't really mistreat us. And for all his preoccupations and not showing up for baseball games, he at least came home from work—more than can be said for other fathers.

But Teto was not so understanding—or forgiving. He wanted a dad who took him to the movies. Someone to play ball with. Someone to take him to Disneyland or the beach. He wanted a dad who held his hand and showed him the way of the world, someone to travel with him through the dense forests of life, man and boy-man, and to name and explain the mysteries and stories of the nature they trampled underfoot. Chi Cho was not that kind of father.

Teto's bitterness grew over the years; he never forgot the beating that Chi Cho had given him as a child. Even after my brother moved out, married and had children, he felt this gnawing emptiness cradled in anger, like he was owed something.

"Fuck that old dude," Teto often said. And every tale of Chi Cho's madness that rose from Mona's lips increased Teto's contempt.

"He ain't so bad, Teto," I once tried to explain. "I think he could have done better, but, dude, he made sure we had food on the table and a roof over our heads. In fact, you should be glad he wasn't always in our faces. Who needs that? Better that he work in the garage or sit in front of the TV than to have him watch over our every move."

"Yeah, well then where was he when I needed him, when I could have used somebody to help me figure out what to do, just to have someone to talk to," Teto began his litany, his voice rising with every point.

"Teto, leave it alone," his wife Lydia interjected. But once Teto got on a roll very little could stop him.

The whole predicament was sad really. I felt for Teto. I knew what he was talking about. I just didn't want to think about it anymore.

My father denied what was happening to him up to the end; he denied the blood in his stool, the pain, the times he fell down and was unable to get up, the memory lapses. He denied his dying.

Although healthy for most of his life, the years of industrial work, inhaling who knows what, had finally claimed the *viejo*. Chi Cho didn't drink too much, maybe a few beers. He didn't smoke. The cancer was a direct result of his work.

As the disease racked his body, Chi Cho's mental condition quickly worsened. I hate to say this, but when the cancer came, in one sense it was an act of mercy.

For most of his last years, there was very little to link my father with anything outside of his world. Oh, he had family that's true. He had friends. He once had work. But in the end all of this—family, labor, and purpose—collapsed into the stillness of a damp and asylumlike room.

Chi Cho denied death like he denied love. He played all the roles—father, husband, and friend—but never truly gave himself over to them.

He was an artist, who sometimes made exquisitely designed welded pieces for neighbors, although he hardly ever charged what they were truly worth. There were times he played dominoes and poker with a few work buddies, but mostly he hid out in his garage, not stepping out for hours. He argued with Mona and us kids when he would get frustrated, but he never bothered to address the real issues.

Chi Cho came home at night, paid bills, offered change if we needed it, but he never uttered the words, "I love you."

When the cancer struck, everything I wanted to forget or cover up welled up inside me. I felt not love, or pity, or concern. I felt hate. And too often when this happened, I saw Teto's face there.

"Die, Dad, so I can let this go," I said to myself when Mona told me the news of Chi Cho's worsened condition. Damn him. Damn Teto. Damn that I don't love my father—that he couldn't love me.

The family gathered at the house. The doctors had given Chi Cho only days to live, if that. He refused to go to a hospital. He claimed that the doctors would remove his insides and sell them to the highest bidder. I actually thought he might have a point, that maybe he wasn't so crazy.

My sister, Monique, was in tears. Although she looked like a younger version of Mona, unlike our mother she dressed in bright greens, pinks, and yellows. Monique and her husband, Clyde, a *gabacho* who worked as an orderly in a local hospital, helped clean Chi Cho up.

My father could no longer speak. Mona gave him morphine, left over from when her sister's husband died of cancer a few months before. There was no longer any need for doctors or nurses or expensive hospital beds. The only thing left was to make Chi Cho's final moments as comfortable as we could.

I waited until the last moment to visit Chi Cho. Mona called every day to tell me how he was doing. He was in so much pain. Celia finally told me, "You have to see him before he goes, Tutti. You can't forget he is your father. You have to at least hold his hand."

Celia was right, of course. I called Teto to find out when he was going to see Chi Cho. For all his ravings about our father, Teto visited Chi Cho as much as he could after work. We all agreed to take time off from work to spend Chi Cho's last hours with Mona and the rest of the family.

When I entered the house, the smell made me nauseous. It was the odor of decay like mold on days-old bread. My dad lay on top of a bed in the living room; his own room was too uncomfortable for him to stay in, especially now that he was at death's door.

His eyes were closed. He was wasted, emaciated, skin and bones really—cancer reduces everything to the barest essentials. Monique and Mona were there. Teto sat nearby in a rocking chair that my dad used to rock in during his better days.

In his sleep, Chi Cho's breathing was very slow, feeble, like a small animal's. Mona held a rosary by his side, whispering prayers.

"Hey, dude, what's up?" I greeted Teto.

He looked up at me, smiled a thin smile.

"Nothing but rockin' and rollin'," he quipped, always the smart aleck.

We waited for a few hours, stopping into the kitchen to fix a sandwich, make more coffee, or just to talk among ourselves. Aunts, uncles, nephews, and nieces came and went. But we were at the bedside constantly—Mona, Monique, Teto, and me—with our wives and Monique's husband taking up the rest of the space. Even Patas roamed into the kitchen once in a while, seeming to sense something was wrong.

Around midnight, my father opened his eyes. Monique called Teto and me in from the kitchen. We all gathered around Chi Cho, Mona holding one of his hands.

"Bendito sea Dios," Mona mumbled, thanking God.

Chi Cho looked at Teto and Monique, then me. Chi Cho appeared to smile with his eyes, although his mouth did not move. Just then, the radio in the kitchen began to play an up tempo song. Chi Cho uneasily maneuvered his other hand to the side of the bed, and without moving any other part of his body, he began a slow, limpid, finger dance on the blanket.

Monique placed her hand to her mouth. Mona ceased her whispers. I looked on in amazement. Teto didn't say a word, but I gazed over and saw a tear rolling down his face.

I leaned over, and with all I could muster, I spoke into my father's ear, "I love you, Dad."

He couldn't say anything, but his eyes watered, and I knew.

Just before one A.M., Chi Cho was gone.

BOOM, BOT, BOOM.

Raul and Stick prowled the back streets and endless stretches of mall roads for another watering hole. They were making the rounds, taking in as many bars as they could before they passed out. They ended up in a beer joint that sported a splintered wooden sign with faded lettering. It was covered in puke green stucco, somewhere in the wilderness of warehouses, cheap stores, and single-family homes in a place called Commerce. "A rootin'-tootin', shit-kicking bar," Raul exclaimed, with a massive grin that seemed out of place with his barely opened eyelids. There was nothing around for miles but buildings rife with graffiti, sun-starched streets, and bone-gray cement walkways—an exasperating sameness that sometimes drives people who live in L.A. nuts.

It's true parts of the city strut with the pulsing heartbeats of blast furnaces or a mechanic's air wrench. That parts of it, like downtown, fall into a *quebradita* dance dip toward a polished ballroom floor or are filled with the frenzy of people, a fugue of voices and car horns. There are fleshy beaches, interludes of palm trees and parks, and a jeweled skyline of multicolored glass and steel buildings. There's a skid row of lost dreams and spent realities, of fury—this is riot town, after all—and acid rain. There are hundreds of midnight images: black-uniformed officers with taped nightsticks, scrawled bus stops, spasms of gunfire, crowded jail cells, whirling helicopter blades, sidewalk Romeos and red-toed Juliets. You have Watts and East L.A., Hollywood and Dodger Stadium, movies and the garment district. But for Raul and Stick, there was only this—a sad, silly, and sometimes deadening symmetry called suburbia. And they thrived on it.

They were carpenters.

"You ever notice, man," Stick offered, after they had pushed aside the black velvet cloth that covered the door's entrance, "that most bars look different on the outside, but on the inside, they look like any other bar in the world."

The place was dimly lit, although there was daylight outside. It had gold-webbed mirrors and tacky glitter on the plastic coverings over the barstools, a couple of which were patched up with black electrical tape. Dark figures gathered close inside red faux leather–covered booths. Truck drivers in the Bronx knew these places; mill hands in Pittsburgh or South Chicago knew; oil riggers in Texas have been here.

Raul and Stick found this particular joint by driving for a block or two after leaving another place on Telegraph Road, one of the main drags. Stick pulled into a graveled lot in his pickup truck—you know the kind, with primer spots, tool chest, a ladder, and an air compressor chained to the truck bed.

Carpenters.

The two men passed the billiard tables—colored balls striking striped ones, scrambling toward side pockets. They moved directly to the long-handled spigots with beer brand logos sticking up from behind the bar counter. Different-size beer bottles were stacked like miniskyscrapers on tabletops. Bowls of mixed nuts on the side.

Around the place were dull-eyed beefy men. There were loud-mouthed young bucks who didn't give a damn about how loud they were, crammed into a corner. A couple of tight-jean-wearing women lolled through the swirling cigarette smoke. Someone who looked like a wasted regular—tie loosened, head almost on the table—sat alone at one spot; at another, a fine-looking lady in a low-cut blouse held court with some nervous dude who kept peering over her shoulders at the gawking men nearby.

Raul and Stick swaggered to the counter, no detours.

"Hey, bartender . . . slap down two beers and a good bottle of tequila," Stick yelled out.

Stick had shoulder-length brown hair, wraparound shades—which he didn't take off, despite the lack of light—a close-cropped beard and a flaming skull tattoo on his chest that showed through his opened flannel shirt. He was tall, lanky, and tanned. A biker. Owner of killer rottweilers.

The beers and Cuervo Gold were set down in front of Stick. He looked at Raul and joked, "Uh, Raul, my man, did you want anything?"

Raul was built like Stick's alter ego: bull-muscled and short—truth be told, nobody to mess with. A former prizefighter, he had deep-set eyes, short slicked-back hair, and a huge mustache that covered his upper lip. Tattoos swirled around each of his fore-arms: fine-line shaded women in Mexican sombreros and Aztec motifs. He was no biker, but a Mexican lowrider who normally couldn't stand bikers. Stick couldn't stand lowriders. But there they were, preparing to chugalug till their lights went out.

They quickly downed the tequila in shot glasses, followed by beer chasers. It didn't take long, no matter how tumbled-down Raul and Stick believed they already were, before they couldn't see the end of the bar.

Although it may have appeared otherwise, the men were not celebrating. They had both lost their jobs that day. An Anglo and a Chicano, who normally didn't get along, were standing there in the sawdust and in puddles of beer in the middle of nowhere, in the city of Commerce. Carpenters. And out of work.

Hot days, dog days—they weighed on Raul like tons of scrap metal at a junkyard. On those days, he rose at dawn every morning and braved the perils of L.A.'s spider-webbed freeways armed with black coffee and a Winchell's donut. Looking for work. During the frequent dry spells, he waited on busy street corners for cheap-labor contractors in trucks who pulled up to pick out a day's work crew. Every week he would end up at a parole office in Montebello. Until recently he had been serving a three-year prison term for acts that he blamed on immaturity. He had to declare felonies on every job application; most likely he would not get hired.

But Raul was determined to work and not return to the joint. For one thing, he had three children and an estranged wife who expected him to provide support. Her name was Noreen. A real stand-by-her-man kind of woman—as soon as Raul got busted, Noreen ran off with the babies.

Baby-faced and voluptuous, Noreen's beauty was only exceeded by her penchant for drama. The world revolved around Noreen. When Raul first dated her, she spread the rumor she was pregnant, although she wasn't. Once when Raul tried to break off the relationship, she broke his car windows and left a wildly written note on the windshield about how her world had been shattered like the windows. Raul finally decided to marry her when she really did get pregnant, and threatened to jump into the ocean from the Santa Monica Beach pier.

You'd think married life would cool down the emotions—but not for Noreen. Soon she was accusing Raul of having other women, of not being there for the children, and of never having a decent job. The last point was a nagging concern for Noreen. She expected a regular *signed* paycheck from her man—regardless of sun, rain, or economic downturn.

Raul responded by closing down emotionally. He tried to hang and ignore the theatrics. He dutifully signed over the checks and generally made it to work way before the shift started, hoping this would clear up any chaos at home. But another chapter in the Noreen soap opera would unfold, and he was back on front street. It didn't take long for Raul to tire of this stale game.

But instead of dealing with it directly, Raul took it out on others or himself—fighting in bars and dropping pills or drinking heavily to ease the pain. This eventually led to his last arrest.

For Raul, the jail term helped him get out of the line of fire for a while—although the last turn proved distressing: no visits, hardly any letters, and a taste for *pinta* food, jokes, scams, and noise that had become bitter like moonshine *tepache.*

So there he was, walking through the doors of an agency in East Los Angeles, fantasizing about the good job score that waited to be grabbed by his eyes only from a metal-and-cork bulletin board inundated with paper and colored tacks. Raul got the feeling things were going his way when the woman divvying out jobs threw him a smile that said, "Try me."

For the next few weeks, Tanya, the woman behind the smile, and Raul trekked from one construction site after another. She had wild hair on a heavily painted face, a small paunch for a belly and wide hips—the way Raul liked his women. He even managed a date with her, but, as fate would have it, Tanya turned out kind of *zafada*—a little loose in the head. She once answered her door, after Raul came over, with glazed-over eyes, shouting incriminations about other women, betrayal, and who-the-fuck-did-he-think-he-was. *Oh, shit . . . déjà vu,* Raul thought. That was the last time he saw her.

But, in spite of this, Tanya managed to get Raul a job as a carpenter's helper. Ernie, the Chicano subcontractor who hired him, built houses, restaurants, and warehouses throughout the L.A. basin. He mostly worked with desperate people—the undocumented, convicts, and homeless, those most other people wouldn't open their doors to. He did this to pay nonunion, minimum wages for ten to twelve hours a day. When Raul arrived on his first day, he saw many Mexicans, mostly young, mostly without green cards.

Raul worked as a framer, setting up the wooden skeletons of various steel and slab buildings for the drywall people. He also framed what were called "tilt ups"—the wood framing for concrete walls on large buildings or parking structures.

He traveled to towns he normally wouldn't visit, let alone live in: ritzy hills in Hollywood, beachfront slopes near Redondo Beach, and condo rows in the west San Fernando Valley. Raul labored under a hot-tempered sun. But he didn't mind, as long as some money came his way.

For the first few weeks on the job, Raul did fine. At least, he lasted—so many others came and went. Ernie was real cheap, though. Sometimes to cut costs, he would have his helpers raid other work sites at night for extra studs, cement bags, and "mud seal"—the foundation planks that were specially treated for termites.

But soon the ten-to-twelve hour days felt longer and unsparing. And the paycheck didn't extend too far into a week.

"*Ese,* Ernie, I need to talk to you, man," Raul said after cornering Ernie by the tool shed.

"*Orale,* Raul, what's the problem?"

"Look it, I've been putting in almost twelve hours every day in the *jale.* But the paycheck shows only eight. Come on, *ese.* What gives here?"

"Ah, Raul," Ernie replied, with a slight stutter mixed in with a heavy Chicano accent. "You know how it is, homes. I don't get full pay until the j-job is finished. I got enough *feria* to keep us going for a while. But if we finish faster, then the sooner I'll get the rest of the b-bread from the contractor. It'll be cool, man. Meanwhile, I'll get us some *birongas.* Okay with you?"

Raul had to agree, but it didn't take long for him to figure out that Ernie had no intention of paying for the extra time he'd put in. And Raul knew there was really no place to turn to when you work a nonunion gig with mostly undocumented help who were considered outlaws like him, even if they hadn't done any prison time.

So Raul continued to hang in there, and every Friday he asked Ernie the same question, and every Friday, Ernie sprung for a case of beer, and every Friday this cooled out some of the guys—but not Raul.

One day, Ernie hired a dude who wore shades and talked in Southern Californian white. You know: "Go for it." "Get my drift." "Fuckin' A." He was known as Stick, another con. Stick was particularly valuable as a forklift driver.

Stick lived with a heavy-smoking, round woman with blond locks, glasses, and a fondness for malt liquor. Unmarried and without children (if you don't count the rottweilers), they lived off sales of marijuana bags and whatever work Stick could muster up. When the day came to pay rent, and they were short, their main plan of action involved moving out in the middle of the night. Like Raul, doing time for Stick involved filling a need—risking a few bucks to get over until something more decent came along. But like many poor working-class *gabachos* in L.A., Stick and his "old lady" landed in mostly poor Mexican sections of town.

Isolated and broke, Stick's first focus of attack were the Mexicans he saw working, even for little pay, feeding whole families, while he barely made ends meet.

At lunchtime, Stick sat by himself against a pile of two-by-fours, away from the Mexicanos. So, Raul strolled by and later almost wished he hadn't. Stick had horror stories. About the time a Mexican ripped him off for some dope. The time some Mexicans jumped him in a parking lot. The times he and his biker friends had it out with Mexican *vatos locos,* gangbangers, at different carnivals. At one point, Raul turned around to see if Stick was really talking to him. Poor sucker, Raul thought. He hated Mexicans, but here he was, surrounded by them. Raul didn't leave, though. He listened to the tales, ate his food, and figured the *gaba* probably deserved to get his ass kicked.

But soon, they started to trade war stories—of failed crimes, failed relationships, and failed jobs.

"What'd you get pinched for this last stint," Stick asked.

"You don't want to know, man, it was stupid shit," Raul responded.

"Hey, I've done a lot of stupid shit—join the club, dude," Stick assured him. "So, what was the deal?"

"I got desperate—you know: no work, my wife on my case, a jones for any good high," Raul began. "I'm not into heavy shit; I just get desperate every once in a while. So, I dropped some reds to mellow out and went to rob a store in City Terrace. It was a matchbox of a building—real small, with two young people holding down the fort. I figured this would be an easy take. So I go in and start asking for the *feria*. But they panicked. I had a small handgun, and I didn't even know if it worked. The girl behind the cash register hands me a bag of coins . . . coins, man! But—you know—I took it. Then I heard police sirens; I figured they had pressed a silent alarm. So I'm running out the door when I drop the bag. As soon as it hits the floor, all kinds of pennies fall out. I shoulda' just left them there. But, for some reason, I stopped to put the pennies back into the bag. I think something in me wanted to get caught—I don't know. It's weird, *ese*, but sometimes I think that's it. When things get real bad, I kinda want to be *torcido* for a while. Three fucked-up meals a day, but at least I don't have to feel like shit all the time. Stupid, huh?"

"Yeah, real stupid—punk shit," Stick snarled, but he thought, at least he's not fronting like other cons he knew.

Raul, against his better judgment, began to like Stick. Beneath his smooth shades and muscled torso, Stick at least was up front.

Then one day while Raul sat near Stick by the stud piles, and as he jumped into a soaked sandwich of tuna and jalapeños, Stick stared at Raul through his shades and asked, "What's the matter, dude? You don't look so hot."

"Ah nothing, just me and Noreen, my ex, trying to get back

together," Raul replied, almost nonchalant. "You know, to give it another try. For the kids."

Stick looked straight at Raul for a while, then he made a face and, to Raul's surprise, said, "Don't do it."

Raul glared at the dude with one squinted eye.

"You're not happy about it," Stick continued. "I can tell. Don't do it. You'll be a miserable piece of shit if you do. I've been there. It's not even going to be good for the kids, believe me. You don't have to take my word for it—it won't work. Don't get back with her."

Raul became amused at Stick's concern for something that obviously had nothing to do with him or the job. But he knew in his heart, Stick was right.

One day, Ernie ordered Stick and Raul to frame roof panels. They had to hammer in eight-penny nails with no more than three whacks of a thirty-two-ounce framing hammer. This is what Ernie expected of his men. One, two, and in. Even sixteen-penny nails were pummeled in with two or three hammer blows. Boom, bot, boom. The key was to build up speed, get the wrists wailing, the arms in tight formation, the eyes focused, and then the hammer down. Boom, bot, boom. Anyone could get good at it. Boom, bot, boom. Each job demanded more speed. Hammers descended in rapid order. Nails pressed into wood. They had quotas of about four hundred panels a day. This meant some fancy hammering. Boom, bot, boom.

The ones who had worked with Ernie for some time were expert at doing this. There was one seventeen-year-old who Ernie had trained since the dude was a snot-nosed kid. Raul was twenty-five years old, a veteran in many other things, but a novice when it came to boom, bot, boom. For one thing, he had to unlearn while he learned. The panel building was not going to be easy for Raul, and Ernie knew it.

At first, Raul rushed into the hammering, but he did it all wrong. He used his whole hand instead of a fluid wrist movement to let the hammer do most of the work. His method, in turn, caused the hand bones to ache as if they had flames in the joints. But even worse than the aching, was when the hammer missed its mark and hit a thumb or a finger.

"*¡Puta madre . . . que chingadazo!*" Raul yelled each time.

Now this was torture. Raul's fingers turned into bloody stumps. He stopped long enough to wrap them in gauze and medical tape. But he still continued hammering.

Ernie made it a point to stop by once in a while and say stuff to Raul like, "Hey, *ese,* you swing like a girl," or, "Look at the young vatos, they're m-making you look bad."

Stick got wind of what was going on, Raul's humiliation, and he didn't like it. He knew it had to do with Ernie getting back at Raul for constantly demanding his proper pay. He also knew, because Raul was a con, and on "paper" as they say, Ernie held this over him so he wouldn't make any noise about things. But he also couldn't stand seeing what Raul was doing to his fingers.

"Why don't you call it quits, Raul?"

"No way, man. I'm not going to give Ernie the satisfaction. I'm going to get this thing right if it takes all my fingers to do it."

So they both banged away—boom, bot, boom—putting the panels down as fast as they could. The pain became intolerable. But Raul wouldn't quit. It was just as well. In time, Raul got the hang of it. He had to if he didn't want stubs for fingers. And it wasn't long before Stick and Raul had the most number of panels done in a week.

"You know what I like about you," Stick said one day, again to Raul's surprise. "You got heart."

But week after week, no matter how many panels the men did, how many sweltering hours they put in, Raul ended up with a short paycheck. Now Ernie was messing with rent, food, and child support. Who needs heart then? Raul thought. So the day came when Raul walked up to Ernie and told him straight up, "I want the money I've worked for, Ernie. I want it now."

"You cons are all alike," Ernie responded. "Well, you know what Raul? I've had it with you."

Ernie's shouts about lazy ingrates could be heard up and down the work site. Stick stopped unloading studs off a truck with the forklift and turned around.

"Hey, I don't n-need this shit," Ernie continued in a more pronounced stutter. "You don't like it here . . . then get the hell out!"

"Why don't you fuck yourself and the fuckin' tree you fell out of!" Raul said, an almost stranger's voice since he normally tried not to get so excited about things. It seemed like weakness to Raul, but he was so mad that if he didn't talk it out he was sure he'd grab a two-by-four and knock Ernie's teeth out. "You don't have to tell me to leave, *cabrón,* because I'm quitting!"

"Good . . . grea . . . great!" Ernie exclaimed. "Tha . . . that's . . . j-just fine with me."

Raul grabbed his leather tool pouch and hammer and walked out of the job site to the street. But as he did, he thought, *I need this fuckin' job. Now what am I going to do?* But he acted as if the job didn't mean anything to him.

Then, he heard more noise and shouting. Raul turned around and saw that Stick had jumped off the forklift's driver seat and began moving toward Ernie.

"Hey, you can't fire him," Stick yelled. "He's one of the best you got."

"Don't get into this, Stick," Ernie responded. "You, I need. Raul can jump into a lake, for all I-I-I care. This thi . . . thing has nothing to do with yo . . . you."

Those remarks really got Stick going.

"The hell it don't. If you fire him, I quit."

Ernie tried to stop Stick from quitting, reasoning with him. But Stick turned around and kept on walking.

"Go ahead then, leave—the both of you!" Ernie screamed after Stick. "You'll never work for me again, I-I-I can tell you that much. Just wa-watch. You won't work around here any . . . anymore."

Stick caught up with Raul.

"Why the fuck did you do that for?" Raul asked.

"Aw, forget it," Stick replied. "This ain't no big thing. This stinkin' job. Who needs it?"

"But you forget, *ese,* we got to face our POs and old ladies," Raul added.

"Fuck it then, we'll both be up shit's creek," Stick said. "Let's get fucked up."

That's when the two men climbed into Stick's pickup truck and drove to the nearest drinking joint. On the way, though, Raul kept thinking, *I lost a no-good, Mexican-slavin' job. So what! It was a fucked up* jale *anyway.*

Raul and Stick were in the bar, drinking like there was no mañana. And without jobs, there might not be. Raul looked around at the other patrons. They seemed like similar stories in flesh. A woman in a short blue denim skirt and large shirt tied in the front, displaying ample cleavage, stood at the end of the bar. She reminded him of Noreen. He had her story down—a single mother, on welfare, most of the time horny, tired, perfumed to make up for the lack of perfume in her life. And as he thought of Noreen he also thought, *Oh, God, my kids, my poor kids. Even if it was a lousy, stinkin' job, how am I going to face them? Damn . . .*

Stick finally took his head off the counter, his shades falling onto the countertop; he turned his turbulent blue-sea eyes toward Raul.

"You ever tore up a bar?" Stick managed to say, his hair covering most of his face. Outside, the daylight had already slipped into darkness.

"No, and I don't intend to, *ese*," Raul slowly replied.

"It's no big thing—I've seen it done plenty times," Stick said, in and out of a stupor, his head going down, then up as he continued his train of thought. "Funny as shit, just start tearing things up . . . chairs and bottles flying . . . people running out . . . bartenders not knowing whether to call the police or hold their dicks . . . I never got in on one, but I always wanted to . . . it'd be a hell of a rush."

"Stick, we're in deep shit as it is. How 'bout we have a few more *tragos* and call it quits for . . ."

But before Raul could finish the sentence, Stick had thrown a barstool at the mirror in front of them. Chunks of glass and wood crashed onto the floor. The woman in the denim skirt screamed. Others got out of the way. Two big vatos instantly rose from their seats. The bartender didn't say a word. He rushed to a phone beneath the bar and dialed 9-1-1. Then he grabbed a shotgun, held it in front of him, aimed at Stick.

Raul sobered up, mighty fast. He pulled Stick from where he

was still seated and dragged him toward the exit. The big vatos came toward them as Raul tried to get Stick onto his feet. Raul pushed through the velvet cloth, the night air striking him like a roundhouse punch. Everything was dark. Raul made the long walk with Stick to the truck. He opened the passenger side and pushed Stick in. Stick was surprisingly compliant considering his bravado of moments before. A few shadowy figures emerged from the bar—including the big vatos—looking to bust some heads.

There was no time to get away. Raul stretched down to beneath the seat and pulled out his trusty thirty-two-ounce hammer. Without a word, Raul walked up to the biggest of the two big vatos and laid a blow to his head.

It was a wall of sirens that Stick heard when he opened his eyes. He hesitated a moment, trying to clear his mind. He soon realized he was in the passenger seat of his truck and his shades were missing. Stick looked up and barely made out the commotion in front of the bar. Everything finally cleared when he saw it was Raul striking a large prone body on the ground—with the most musical swing of hammer he had ever seen—and several guys moving back through the doorway, a woman in hysterics.

For an instant, Stick thought about starting the truck and getting the hell out of there. He couldn't afford to get popped again. But instead, he revved up the engine and pulled up to the bar's entrance.

"Raul, quick—get in before the fuckin' cops get here," Stick yelled out.

Raul stopped what he was doing—as if awakened from a trance—and jumped into the truck's cab. Stick jammed the stick shift into unyielding gears and screeched out of the parking lot, gravel flying everywhere.

MECHANICS

Everything has to do with loving and not loving

RUMI

The furnace roared with the sound of perpetual thunder. The heat bellowed from its mouth as pit crews with shovels threw limestone and coke into its flaming belly. Huge hydraulic arms swung open the furnace roof. A large overhead crane dropped tons of scrap metal into the furnace. The roof closed, and massive electric lines connected to the roof drew thousands of volts into the bubbling mixture inside, the walls lined with fireproof bricks. A fiery monster, this furnace consumed scrap metal, iron ore, oxygen, and lives.

Enrique was the journeyman millwright on the night shift. He sat on a stained metal chair in a small corrugated-tin shack below the furnace floor. A large empty desk covered with grime filled up one end of the makeshift quarters; a row of dented lockers, a tool cabinet, and a chipped wooden bench graced the other end.

Next to Enrique a young "helper," Tobias, sat awkwardly on the bench with a metal coffee cup in one hand and his tool belt still clamped around his waist. Everything on the furnace floor had been running smoothly for hours.

"Why don't you take off your belt and hang it over there by mine," Enrique said. "Relax, man."

Tobias, who had only been working maintenance for a week with Enrique, promptly removed the tool belt and placed it on a hook by the lockers. The graveyard shift was usually slower than the day turn. For one thing, the pain-in-the-ass day foreman wasn't around, and the night pit boss was usually too laid back or drunk to be any bother.

Also, the night-shift guys on the furnaces usually did their own small repairs, calling on the millwrights only for the big jobs. Most of the time, this meant the millwrights could turn out the lights and cop some Zs.

Enrique perused the sheet of paper the day foreman had left him; it contained a list of things he and Tobias were to do while they waited for the customary five air whistles to sound, indicating a breakdown on one of the three furnaces, the overhead cranes, or major machinery.

Because lost time meant lost profits, the millwrights were supposed to repair whatever broke down immediately to keep production going. Sometimes this required improvisation, what they called a "Mickey Mouse" setup, until a repair crew could finish the job on the weekends. Sometimes this meant somebody could get hurt or killed if the setup didn't hold. In between emergencies, there were long-range projects to consider.

Enrique eyed the page in his hand with great interest, then threw it into a drawer.

"Let the day shift do it," he said. Tobias smiled on cue, hoping that Enrique was making a joke.

For days Tobias had looked eager but confused. There were so many things to remember working on the furnaces' maintenance team. Enrique and Tobias usually started the shift by making their rounds: checking valves and piping on the furnaces; the water pumps and motors on the cooling towers; oil and fluid levels on the cranes, hydraulic lifts, and slag cars; greasing all major gears, bearings, and pinions.

But as Enrique often told Tobias, "Don't try to learn everything all at once."

Later that night when things were quiet and the rumble of the furnaces diminished to a subdued hum, Enrique closed his eyes and reminisced. He had been working at the steel mill for twelve years. He started just two months after his marrying Espie.

Everything then—so long ago—seemed right; he was married to a beautiful woman and living in a small but pleasant apartment that he rented only a month before their wedding. On top of that, Enrique had just gotten a job at the steel mill as a millwright apprentice. Although the first level of apprentices were called "oiler greasers," which sounded derogatory to him, it was a job that promised up to fifteen dollars an hour within two years, all benefits paid, and a pension.

What more could a young, poor, married couple from East L.A. ask for?

Soon after he began to work, Espie got pregnant and the company health plan paid for the clinical visits, pills, Lamaze classes, and finally the baby's birth. In the end, the whole process would cost Enrique only $4.50 out of his pocket because his wife wanted to have a color TV and a phone in her hospital room.

Two days after his son's birth, Enrique went to work singing. That day, he didn't seem to mind the grease, dust, or noise. He passed out cigars emblazoned with "It's A Boy!" to everyone he met. Old Man Jake had a box full of cigars that he had gathered from new fathers over the years; he placed Enrique's cigar on top of the others and put the box back into his grease-caked locker.

It was a wonderful thing when someone in the steel mill had a baby; everybody celebrated. The mill gave many a man and his family a standard of living few could obtain. In return, these men sacrificed their days, their bodies, their minds, and often their limbs, to the mill. Alcoholism was so rampant that the company had its own recovery program. And many of the men talked often of the marriages and divorces they had been through during their tenure at the mill.

There was the case of Abel, one of the swing-shift melters, who didn't know what to do about his cheating wife. As a joke, a couple of the guys told Abel to shoot the lying wench and end his misery. Actually, they were tired of his whining. Abel, unfortunately, took this advice to heart and did just that. He was given a life sentence in Folsom for his troubles.

The erratic hours at the mill often kept the men away from their homes. Many millwrights and mill hands worked rotating shifts—daylight one week, nights the next week, and afternoons the following week. This destroyed any sense of a normal life. And sometimes a guy was so tired from the schedule changes that he rarely indulged in the loving things people do to maintain their relationships.

Gambling, hanging out with prostitutes or other men's wives, taking dope, or downing alcohol to drown one's pain—that was the lot of many of the mill's workers.

"The mill becomes your work, your home, your woman," Old Man Jake used to say to the young bucks that had just started in the "oil gang."

The mill workers could get tired and cynical after a while—but then a baby arrived, and all of it seemed worth it.

Enrique thought about this and looked over at his apprentice. He remembered when he had been like Tobias: anxious, in awe, and making too many mistakes.

Enrique recalled the impatience of the older millwrights who mostly didn't teach, but let the apprentice learn on his own—the hard way. If you screwed up and didn't make the grade, you couldn't blame anybody but yourself. No upstanding journeyman would take the responsibility.

"That ass wipe was just plain stupid," a journeyman millwright would say about a bungling apprentice. "I told him what to do and he just couldn't get it."

Enrique knew how difficult it was to learn the intricacies of the hydraulic systems—to repair, cut, and replace piping; to align and plumb the motors and shafts; to master the welding techniques and passes; and to manipulate the overhead cranes with the right signals, as they lifted the tons of equipment needed for various jobs.

And the veteran mechanics weren't much help; they had a different language, their own unique gestures and words that one had to know inside out to survive.

The worst part was that the old-timers played tricks on the young dudes.

"Go fill this bucket with air, pronto!" a journeyman had once yelled out to Enrique during a particularly tense repair job on one of the forges. Enrique had grabbed the bucket and run out, safety hat and glasses, steel-tipped shoes, and tool-laden belt rattling down a brick walkway before he realized he was being had. He had turned around and the other millwrights were splitting their guts with laughter.

The whistle blew five times, signaling a major repair. Enrique quickly rose from his chair, kicking the sleeping Tobias on the soles of his outstretched feet, hanging over the bench. Enrique grabbed his tool belt and rushed out before Tobias could shake off the sleep.

Enrique climbed to the furnace floor, to the dust and disorder, as a broken water pipe steamed its contents onto a section of the furnace roof. Tobias ran up behind him, still trying to fasten his tool belt amid the cries of the furnace helpers. A pit boss yelled, "Hurry up will you . . . we're on production!"

E nrique, who was also known as Kiki, waited by the curb outside Our Lady of Lourdes Church on Third Street. He was handsome in his crushed velvet black tuxedo, carefully styled hair, and muscular build. His face was *güero,* as they say, light-skinned, but with strong Mexican features. He looked up and down the street. He pushed up his sleeves to glimpse the watch on his wrist—Espie was twenty minutes late.

Father Alvarez, in his white, gold, and green vestments, pushing open the heavy doors of the church, spied Enrique. He declared that unless Espie arrived in the next ten minutes, he was going to bring in the next wedding party, which had already assembled at the other end of the church. Droplets of perspiration fell from Enrique's forehead.

"¿Dónde chinga'os estás?" Enrique said beneath his breath so the priest wouldn't hear.

Espie was a pretty dark-haired woman. Although she appeared thin and slight, she had a husky and confident voice that belied her size. Espie's real name was María Esperanza. It turned out that her three sisters and even her mother had the name María. There was María Encarnación, María Consuelo, and María Dolores; her mother was María de Los Angeles.

"The Many Marías," as Enrique's brother Gregorio often jibed.

So there wouldn't be any confusion, the girls went by their middle names—in fact, they went by shortened versions of their middle names: Encarnación was Chonita, Consuelo was Chelo, Dolores was Loly. And Esperanza became Espie.

Espie was by far the best looking of these Marías, though all of their hands were worth having in matrimony. Espie was the last to be wed. As Enrique waited on the curbside, his future sisters-in-law and their husbands were also milling about in their lavender bridesmaid's gowns and usher's tuxedos. The wedding party was made up of the Marías and their spouses. Only the best man and the ring bearer were related to Enrique: his brother Gregorio and Gregorio's seven-year-old son Ricardo.

"Where the hell are you, baby?" Enrique said to himself, almost abandoning hope that Espie would arrive at all.

Then, as Father Alvarez prepared to bring in the next group, a caravan of classic lowrider cars pulled up in front of the church. Out of the first cherried-out 1948 DeSoto in the convoy, Espie emerged in a white satin wedding dress with a long, ruffled train.

"She's here," yelled Espie's sister Chonita. Her other sisters pulled the rest of the wedding party together so the ceremony could begin.

Enrique didn't have time to argue with Espie about being late. He walked up the aisle, lined with pews decorated with artificial lavender flowers. He stood in his position on the groom's side of the chapel. The wedding guests, many of whom had grown rest-less, woke up dozing companions, gathered up kids, a few of whom were already running up and down the side aisles, and took their seats.

Enrique's wedding was a typical East L.A. affair—he had richly detailed 1940s and 1950s vehicles, custom-fit black and gray tuxedos, homemade bridesmaid dresses with large stitch lines, and a massive reception at Kennedy Hall, a well-known Eastside dance establishment.

And just like any other wedding, many things went wrong.

Espie arrived late because it had taken all morning to wash and wax the caravan of cars. The bride-to-be, a passenger in her cousin's lead lowrider, was literally held hostage as each car was lovingly wiped and sprayed.

But Enrique had also almost missed his own wedding when his future mother-in-law, the irrepressible María de Los Angeles, had him hanging the ribbons and other decorations for the recep-tion on the ceiling of Kennedy Hall until the last moment that morning.

As the wedding group prepared to enter the church, the bride's stepfather had not arrived. He was to give the bride away, though everyone guessed he was too drunk from hanging out at the cantinas on Chavez Avenue. So Espie's brother Beto, in denim jeans, ended up walking her down the aisle, while her mother openly fumed at her husband's absence.

On top of that, little Ricardo noticed that Enrique's wedding ring was missing. A local metalsmith was forging it that very morning. Enrique looked around at his guests, trying to solicit help about what to do. Loly, one of the Marías, came to the rescue—she pulled a plastic Cracker Jack ring from her daughter's finger and put it on the ring bearer's pillow, until the real ring arrived. As odd as this may have seemed, everyone accepted this as an adequate temporary solution.

So there they were, looking sharp—Enrique with his lavish suit and spit-shined shoes. Espie in her long gown, trimmed with white lace, a veil, and her bouquet. Nothing but the best.

It had only been a few months since Espie had dropped out of high school; she was all of seventeen years old, Enrique only nineteen. They had known each other for six months, which some might say was not a long time, but a lot had happened in those six months. Enrique felt he was ready to be married. Espie said as much herself.

Enrique thought about this as he knelt before the wall-length painting of a crucified Christ, preparing to take the host. He thought about everything that had brought him to this point as the priest spoke solemnly from an open text. Enrique managed to steal a look at his bride and feelings of love and pride welled up inside him. This is what he wanted, he was sure of it. At first, when Espie hinted at marriage, he had resisted. But now Enrique was convinced that this would be a life-long relationship, the way he believed relationships were meant to be.

Then the time came for Espie to place Enrique's wedding ring on his finger. She reached for the Cracker Jack ring on the pillow and gasped. At just that moment, the metalsmith's young helper was huffing and puffing up the aisle toward Gregorio—he must have been running for blocks. The kid handed Gregorio a gold band in a worn handkerchief, freshly cast, and still hot. So hot that Enrique almost jumped out of his skin as the ring went on his finger.

The rings were finally exchanged, and the vows made; Enrique vividly recalled the lines "to have and to hold from this day forward." So sure of themselves, Enrique and Espie repeated the words and kissed.

Later at the reception, things continued to go as they had gone all day. Gregorio fell on the cake while trying to take it from the car to the reception table in the hall when a small child dashed in front of him. He used his car keys to reshape the cake as if nothing happened—but this didn't quite work. The band failed to show up, so Chelo dashed home to get an old record player that spun 45s—of oldies and cumbias—instead.

Before the affair ended, wasted relatives were up on the stage singing old Mexican standard tearjerkers.

Then Gregorio and his wife, Perla, got into an argument, and she stormed out of the hall, jumped into her car, and sped off— but not before trying to run her husband over in the parking lot when he attempted to stop her.

Later that evening, the newlyweds took stock of the situation and agreed they should leave: the dollar dance was over, the bouquet had been thrown—along with the routine scuffle between the least-likely-to-marry single girls—the photos were taken, and the guests were beginning to pass out. Without telling anyone, Enrique and Espie left the reception, entered her house, removed their wedding clothes, put on their jeans and jackets, climbed back into the car, and took off, neither one having a clue as to where exactly.

Meanwhile, more people arrived at the reception, including characters no one in the family knew, and like any good East L.A. wedding, this one had its proverbial brawl—the smashing of tables, chairs, and glass—and the arrival of police.

But Enrique and Espie were already on the road, driving as far east as they could to find a decent enough place in which to enjoy their honeymoon, some bottled champagne they had kidnapped from the reception, and the seventy dollars Espie received from the dollar dance. Unfortunately, they ran out of gas in El Monte and ended up at a cheap motel.

Enrique couldn't help wondering if these mishaps weren't part of a blueprint for the rest of their partnership.

T here are few places in this world where there is true love," Old Man Jake remarked to Enrique, a day before the veteran retired from the mill after forty years of service. "And this mill, ain't one of them."

The older mill workers often talked like this about their relationships. Enrique never quite understood the bitterness behind their words, despite the years of hearing war stories from the love front. Enrique didn't feel that way about Espie.

"Just remember, 'romance without finance is a nuisance,'" said Bailey, the black mill hand, who recalled that line from an old Charlie Parker song.

"A lot of what people call love is nothin' more than economics," Bailey continued. "Marriage is like buying a prostitute for a night . . . only you've paid for her the rest of your life."

"That's bull, man!" Enrique countered. "You can't be calling a wife a prostitute . . . there has to be real love there."

"Just listen to what I say," Bailey said. "You don't think so now, but wait a few years. You'll find out."

Enrique didn't swallow it. He gathered his tool belt and left the lunchroom, located in the maintenance yard. This talk made him angry. He thought about that guy Abel—he wondered how anyone could be so ensnared by jealousy as to shoot his own wife?

Enrique's family—which included four children, counting a new baby daughter, before Espie began using a diaphragm—became the focus of his life, the rhyme and reason of his existence. The family was why he came to work, sometimes putting in double shifts and extra time on the holidays. It was why he came home.

Espie and the children were his only solace from the madness of the mill. He sought them out, selfishly. He expected them to be there for him. He expected them to accept his every mood and reproach. He became quite possessive.

Enrique grew to fear that the world would interfere with his homestead. He wouldn't let Espie go out with any friends or even with her sisters. Enrique considered Chonita, Loly, and Chelo too wild.

He figured if he could protect Espie from what he perceived to be an unpredictable and dangerous reality, he could avoid having a shattered life like many of his fellow mill workers—like all the men he ever knew.

Every other Friday, on payday, the men of the mill would go to the bars and drink most of their paychecks away. Or they would bet on the horses or visit the poker clubs in the cities of Gardena and Bell. The racing forms were piled next to the paycheck-dispensing hut and prostitutes rented hotel rooms for the night.

Enrique continued to seek refuge with his family.

"Let's go out to eat," he suggested unexpectedly to everyone one night.

"Yeah, *papi*—let's go to McDonald's," said Carlitos, his second-oldest boy.

"No, I mean a good restaurant, you know like Clifton's or Phillipe's downtown," Enrique said. These were far from classy joints, but going out was going out—and they put on their best clothes as if they were hitting the streets big-time.

"Oh, Kiki, it makes me happy to break from all the routine," Espie said while reaching for Enrique's hand as he moved the car into the street. "I just wish we could do this more often."

"What do you mean, babe?" Enrique asked.

"I mean, to be honest, most of the time we stay home, share a few beers, and watch videos. I like this better."

"Oh," Enrique responded, without another word.

Enrique, despite his handling of Espie, considered himself a modern man. Unlike many others at the mill, he sometimes helped clean around the house. He even took care of the children, changing the new baby's diapers and getting up to feed her when she cried late at night.

So he didn't understand when Espie began to withdraw, to avoid him—she hardly spoke to him the night they went out. As it turned out, it was a long time before Enrique asked the family to go out again.

"What's your problem?" he asked Espie one day in the kitchen.

"I don't have a problem!" she yelled and walked away, but not before dropping the dish she was washing into the sink, breaking it into several pieces.

Enrique found himself carefully taking out the jagged sections from the sink when he heard Espie walk out the door, get into the car, and race out the driveway, tires peeling—the noise seemed to mock him.

The arguments escalated. Many nights he wished things were different, but he didn't know what to do. The more he tried to extract explanations from Espie, the more she withdrew.

One day, Enrique was driving the family to Elysian Park for a picnic. He had gotten onto the freeway, when an argument ensued. Espie wanted to see her sisters, two of whom lived near Hollenbeck Park in Boyle Heights with their families.

"Look it, Espie, I don't think this is a good idea," he said. "I don't trust your crazy sisters."

This remark got Espie going. She told Enrique to stop the car and let her out.

"Are you nuts?" he asked. "The kids are in the back—what am I going to do with them when you go?"

"That's all you care about, isn't it?" Espie said. "How much work these kids are going to be? What about me, huh?"

She then tried to open the door and jump out of the moving vehicle. Enrique swerved, hit the brakes, and pulled off onto the shoulder.

"What is wrong with you!" he yelled.

Espie didn't say anything when she opened the door and walked toward the off-ramp.

He waited a short while, seeing how nervous the kids were getting. Soon he drew up next to Espie, who had made it to the street.

"Okay, we'll go to your sisters," Enrique said.

Espie got back into the car without looking at him. All evening long, she didn't say a word to Enrique.

Another time, Enrique and Espie were in bed, when Espie told him that she and Chonita were going to see a movie the next day.

"I don't think so," Enrique said. "Besides if you want to go to the show, you can go with me."

"When? You never take me to the show," Espie said. "Besides, I'd like to go with my sisters sometimes. It doesn't always have to be with you."

They argued a little more before Espie screamed and smacked her fist against the wall, making a small hole. Enrique exploded in return, hitting the same wall with his fist; he made a larger hole next to Espie's. The holes remained in the wall, never fixed, always gaping.

Something was gnawing at Espie, and Enrique couldn't deal with it. He didn't understand why Espie made everything so difficult. She used to be so easy to be with, he thought.

To Enrique, Espie was everything and everywhere. The birds sang out her name in the morning. The machines in the mill appeared to repeat it. The trains steam-whistled it syllable by syllable as they passed by. He even tattooed her name on his right arm. She once asked him why he was obsessed with her—why couldn't he be more trusting. He said because he loved her; he didn't think he needed any other reason.

Some nights, Espie cried. Most of the time Enrique didn't hear her.

For years, company officials threatened to close the steel mill; they claimed it was largely unprofitable. And for years the mill workers broke their backs to keep the mill going. Rumors circulated, new production quotas were established, and the men continued to keep the furnaces and forges running day and night, spitting out beams, rebar, and wire rope.

But, finally, none of this did any good.

Enrique was on the furnace floor, working as quickly as he could on a busted pipe that carried the water that cooled the furnaces. Working at Enrique's side, Tobias got parts and tools as they were needed. The intense heat burned through the thick leather of Enrique's shoes. Moisture gathered on the small of his back and on his forehead. In minutes, though, the new pipe was in place, and the furnace continued melting scrap without shutting down.

After Enrique climbed down from the furnace roof, he heard the word about the mill's fate from Jerry, the lead melter.

"So, she's closing, huh?" Jerry said.

"Who? What?" Enrique asked.

"The mill, man," Jerry continued, looking incredulously at Enrique. "You mean you don't know—I thought you millwrights would be the first to find out."

"The mill is going down? Who told you?" Enrique asked.

Jerry handed Enrique a folded piece of paper, smeared with dirt. The Steelworkers Union's letterhead graced the top of it. Ironically, the union people were the first to tell the employees about the company's plans to shut down the plant, even though they were usually the first ones to push pay cuts to keep it alive.

"¡Que pinche desmadre!" Enrique said, disbelieving. "How could this be—we've been doing good here. This plant has been producing beyond all the quotas. We've done everything the company wanted us to do and more. I can't believe this."

"Well, it looks as if we've worked ourselves out of a job, compa," Jerry responded.

The steel mill was history. The company's spokesmen blamed foreign steel producers, unions, lazy workers—everything but the kitchen sink, Enrique thought.

Many smaller bucket shops and rolling mills that surrounded

the plant were moving south to Mexico or to Taiwan, where labor was much cheaper. To compete, the mill had to move as well.

Times were indeed changing. This particular steel plant had been in operation in Los Angeles since the end of World War II. Much of the machinery was brought in from the massive steel facilities on the East Coast. Some of the forges and dies went back to the turn of the century.

There were fathers, grandfathers, and in some cases, great-grandfathers who had worked there. When the company first established the mill, the mostly Mexican families brought in to do the menial labor lived in old barracks established for them. There were people who still remember the flakes of steel that fell like snow on the hanging wash.

Other people ended up here as well: Southern, mostly skilled, white workers; black manual laborers; Cherokees and Hopis; Poles and Yugoslavs.

Soon other industries were established, then more housing, stores, and schools. Decade after decade, the mill's furnaces roared its monstrous song. It fed families, allowing some to buy their first homes; it sustained whole communities.

Enrique's family had come from Jalisco, Mexico, a generation before and ended up in the mill. His father had worked there, his uncles, and even his brother Gregorio managed a stint before he took a job with the local phone company.

Now, this would be no more.

The mill's employees were given a couple of weeks to clean out their lockers, their tool sheds, to apply for unemployment benefits, and prepare for retirement or a new job—if they could find one. A small maintenance crew remained to dismantle the machines, furnaces, and forges. Enrique did not have enough seniority to be on this crew.

After Enrique was laid off, he and Espie argued even more—but now they argued about whether they could keep the house, about selling one of the cars, about not saving up for the kids' futures.

The arguments were also about Espie going to work.

"*¡Nel pastel!*" Enrique insisted. "You ain't getting no job. If I have to work two jobs flipping hamburgers I'll do it, but you ain't working. What about the kids, what about the baby?"

"*El mismo pinche rollo*—will you stop it!" Espie said. "It's time for me to work, Kiki. We're going to need the money and I have to do more with my life. I can't just be home all day and night. I'm tired of this. Damn, maybe the mill's closing is the best thing that could happen to me."

Enrique grew even more confused.

For once in his life, Enrique felt he had no control. He hated this feeling. He had lost his job, and he felt he was losing his wife. Espie no longer accepted his solutions, his ideas—his view of things. She never used to be like this, and it bothered him to no end. Thinking about the children, the baby, so soft and beautiful, kept him going. The children loved their parents without reservation, whether a steel mill existed or not.

Once, after a particularly hard time with Espie, Enrique walked over to the kids, who were watching TV in the living room. He hugged them, and they hugged him in return. He hadn't felt as safe, as wanted, in a long time.

"Espie, Espie," he pleaded with her one day. "What's wrong? *¿Qué te hice?* Why don't you love me anymore!"

Espie didn't respond to his pleas.

Espie started to go to night school determined to get a high school diploma. Enrique agreed to baby-sit the children on those nights she attended classes.

By then they had been married for twelve years, as many years as Enrique had in the mill. Junior was eleven years old; Carlitos was nine, Sonya four, and the baby, Darlene, a year and a half.

During the day, he waited in unemployment lines, wandered from warehouse to warehouse, factory to factory, seeing the same "No Help Wanted" signs until his eyes strained, his feet ached, and his head pounded. In the evening, he came home, prepared dinner for the children, and sat with them in front of the TV before bedtime.

On Sundays he attended Mass, sometimes twice, which he had not done in years. He prayed and he prayed. And still he felt his life slipping out of his grasp. He sensed it in his bones. And he didn't know what do.

One day, at dinner, before Espie ran off to her classes, Enrique told her, "Espie, I know things have been rough lately. But they're going to change, I promise you. I'll get a job. We can save money and hopefully keep the house. Just don't give up, baby, don't give up on me."

Espie tried to smile, reached for his hand, and squeezed.

"Kiki, I'll try, okay?" she said. "Let's just say I'll try."

One evening Enrique came home after stopping off at the local bar to grab a couple of beers. He had been pounding the sidewalks all day in search of work.

The door to his house was slightly open. Enrique pushed it open further. The living room was nearly empty. The TV was gone, the stereo, the photos on the mantel, the kids' toys—just about everything.

And so were Espie and the children.

Enrique panicked. He called Chonita, who lived a few doors down. Almost a year had passed since the mill closed. Enrique and Espie had lost the house. They had moved closer to Espie's sisters—a compromise Enrique made with his wife.

"She's gone, Chonita," he said. "I have a feeling you know where she is."

"Enrique, I may have a lot to say to Espie about her life, but she makes up her own mind," Chonita said. "I don't know where she is."

"She took the kids, man," Enrique responded. "Okay, she can go, for Christ's sake, but don't take the kids."

"Listen, don't lose it, okay?" Chonita said. "I'll make some calls. I doubt she's gone very far."

"Help me out, Chonita, okay?"

"Sure, Enrique, but don't beg, please," she said. "I'll call you as soon as I find out anything."

In a half hour, Loly, Chelo, and Chonita were at Enrique's apartment.

"What's missing?" Loly asked.

"Her things, the kid's things—look around—almost everything," Enrique said, sitting on the couch, the only major piece of furniture in the almost empty living room.

"I can't see Espie getting a truck and loading all this stuff," Chelo said.

"Yeah, maybe you got robbed," Chonita added.

"Sure, that's all I need—to lose my job, my family, and get ripped off, too," Enrique responded.

"Worse things have happened. Did she leave a note?" Loly asked.

"A small one on the refrigerator."

Enrique pulled the crumpled paper from his back pants pocket. He gave it to Chonita, who read it: *Kiki, I know this is a bad time, but I can't stay here anymore. I'm going crazy. I'll be gone for a couple of days with the kids. Don't worry, we'll be fine. I'll call you in two days. Amor—Espie.*

"A couple of days!" Enrique exclaimed. "Does this look like she's going to be gone for a couple of days!"

That night, Enrique couldn't sleep. He walked into the kids' rooms. Junior and Carlitos had a bunk bed surrounded by posters of wrestling personalities, baseball stars, and comic book characters. Their favorite toys were missing. The room where Sonya and Darlene slept was stripped clean, including the crib; although many of their clothes and toys were gone, a row of stuffed animals graced the top of a carefully made-up bed.

Then Enrique walked into the bedroom where he slept with Espie. Anger rose from some deep, dark place he couldn't name.

The night seemed endless. He paced around the room. He opened a can of beer, then another. At one point he lifted the weights he had against a wall of his room. Loads of energy rushed over him. He just couldn't sleep.

Terrible thoughts flashed in his mind—thoughts of Espie with another man. The more he lingered in their room, the more real these thoughts became. Then he went to Espie's top drawer, opened it, and picked up the few items still there. Espie's diaphragm wasn't there.

"Why the hell would she take that!" Enrique yelled out. "Who's she fuckin', man!"

He paced throughout the house. The blood simmered in his veins. He became frantic. He staggered outside. He ran down the street. He came back.

"God damn it, Espie!" he yelled. "You said you would try. Why the fuck did you give up?"

Then the thought crossed his mind to check the .22 rifle he had in the closet. He had bought it for shooting practice at the suggestion of his steelworker buddies. He never used it. He went to the closet, paused at the closet door, then opened it. There behind some hanging clothes, still in its original box, was the gun. Good, the robbers missed this, Enrique thought, while pulling out the box.

He held the weapon in his arms and looked at it for a long time; thoughts darted in and out of his mind about what he was going to do.

The flange on the six-inch diameter piping was hard to take apart; for years heat and rain and toxic chemicals caused the nuts and bolts at the refinery to corrode shut. Enrique placed a large pipe wrench on one of the nuts, then maneuvered a piece of pipe over the end of the wrench as a "cheater" so he could gain more leverage to turn it. After several hard pulls, the nut began to shriek, than it moved a little, and, finally, the pipe wrench rotated freely as the nut and bolt unfastened.

"*Híjole,* that was a hard one," Enrique said, wiping a brow with the back of his hand.

Enrique worked at a small refinery on Medford Street. He had been there for three months, hired as a pipefitter. With twelve years experience at the steel mill, he made it without a hitch into the maintenance department. For once he had more time on a job than the others looking for work.

He had a steady day job; the pay was only a few dollars below the hourly rate he received at the steel mill. Most of all, Enrique was elated to be on full time again. The day the plant manager called his house to have him come in for a physical, Enrique got on his knees right there in the living room to give thanks.

A year after the mill shut down, Espie had filed the divorce papers. And although she had taken many of their things when she left Enrique, it was also true—as Chonita suggested—that he had been burglarized.

Espie apparently left in such a hurry, she forgot to lock the front door. Somebody walked in and cleaned out whatever else of value was left in the house.

There was other sad news. Old Man Jake had died of a heart attack, less than a year after he retired. In fact, most of the old steelworkers died within two years of getting out of the plant. They couldn't even enjoy a few years of retirement before their hearts gave out on them.

After Enrique started his new job, he found a small studio apartment for a hundred dollars a month in an old beaten-up hotel that housed many single men, mostly undocumenteds from Mexico. A bar on the first floor opened up onto the street, just like in Mexico. He spent many a long evening there.

The room was sparsely furnished, but clean. Just the essentials. It was about five minutes from the job. Enrique settled into it quickly. After getting hired, he started to get his sense of humor back. And although he had a few drinks at the bar most nights, he wasn't drinking as much as when the mill closed. He came home and felt good, even if he was lonely there.

The night Espie left, Enrique contemplated loading the rifle he held in his hands, putting the muzzle into his mouth, and pulling the trigger. He also considered going after Espie, and shooting her—the stories among steelworkers actually helped him see how stupid this was. Through it all, he kept seeing his children: Junior's crooked smile. Carlitos's hyper personality. Sonya's funny way of saying "nilk" instead of milk. And the baby, Darlene, chubby-cheeked and big-eyed. He couldn't do it—shoot himself or Espie. He put the rifle away, and fell asleep.

On the weekends, Espie brought the kids to visit. They were always eager to see Enrique, even in his tiny place. No matter what happened, the children were wonderful; they seemed to understand. They were his one constant, his one comfort.

"I hate what we put them through," Enrique once told Espie. "Even when we don't come through for them, they're always there for us."

Sometimes Enrique would wake up at around three in the morning and feel almost sick with grief, an emotional vortex taking away his breath. He would sit up in bed, inhale deeply. He didn't want to feel this way anymore. He had to get on with his life.

The next morning, he'd get out of bed as usual and prepare for work.

Enrique rested his arms on the back of the park bench as he watched his children run and holler around the play lot. Soon his thoughts rushed back to Espie, as they had done many times before—how she was no longer in his life. At first, he didn't accept this. Already two years had gone by, fighting, hoping, and turning over events in his mind, haunted by his mistakes, pleased by his victories. Now, it was all done, he thought, sitting there as the sun's rays danced lightly on his skin, yellow hues swimming around him. The dark green waters of Hollenbeck Park lake gleamed beneath the afternoon sun as slices of light and shadow cut across its surface.

He repeated the words to himself: *It's over.* And this was good. Although there were days he loved her so much he thought of nothing else—and there were days he wanted to get as far away from her as possible.

There were days he wanted to yell out his fears, stupidities, and hurts, and there were days his voice felt trapped as in a concave room. There were days when he'd lie for hours on a bare bed with cobwebs floating on the corner of ceilings. Days he'd straddle along the rain-soaked streets. Days caught in an almost endless threshold between the death of a love and the birth of another. Days obese with argument and life; father love and woman touch; empty rooms and bar nights.

Sometimes he wasn't sure of anything. But he was sure of this: He never loved her more than at the moment when she finally left him.

Now, finally, he could rest, take a break, and sit on a bench by the lake. He was tired of fighting, of disrupting his waking hours with schemes to win her back, to convince her, to overwhelm her. Everything he had tried was another way to avoid the inevitable. Now, he was free from all this. Now he could consider other things—perhaps the mountains or shooting his .22 rifle or fishing—just to go fishing for blue gill at that lake, for example, like he used to do when he was younger. He was free. And he thanked her.

"When you're empty, you start to fill up," he remembered from a Sunday sermon. This was how he felt now. He thought about what he had been through these past two years—out of work, hungry, insane, in love, out of love, working. Now that he was in the refinery, he felt strong, almost strong enough to risk another relationship, to go out on dates, to open up his heart again. For too long, he had been too frightened to try.

The court finally approved the divorce. It took a few months, but he had received the final round of papers the week before. And somehow, in a funny way, when those papers arrived at his room the bitterness began to dissipate.

He felt relief. He didn't have to fight for Espie anymore. He didn't have to live with her outbursts and emotional changes. He didn't have to spend excruciating sessions in his mind trying to figure her out or go out of his way not to enrage her. And, by then, he also realized how much he contributed to their break up—the rages and his clawlike hold on Espie's life. At a certain point, they were just not good for each other. It's over, he said to himself. Good.

That morning, when Espie came by his building to drop off the kids, he looked out the window and noticed a young man in the driver's seat of the car. Espie got out and opened the back door to help the children out. She wore a long skirt, a slit up the side, prepared to go out on the town. Espie looked good, Enrique thought.

Enrique walked down the stairs and out to the sidewalk. Espie nonchalantly pushed the sleeping Darlene into his arms. She then gave Junior and Carlitos a bag of clothes and blankets and took a few seconds to brush Sonya's hair. Enrique looked closer at the stranger behind the wheel. The stranger said nothing, but he appeared uncomfortable as Enrique's figure stood near the passenger side. Enrique, on the other hand, didn't feel as bad as he thought he was going to feel seeing Espie's new companion.

He started back into the building with his kids. He turned around and saw the car pull away. At that moment, a pervasive serenity entered him, a peace he had not felt for a long time. It seemed odd but he knew then: This is how it ends, this sensuous and tumultuous alliance, barely glued with promises echoed in churches and whispered between sheets, and which had crowded his thoughts and emotions for years, as if nothing else could slide in edgewise.

With Darlene hanging over his shoulder, he entered his apartment and kept the door open until the rest of the children were inside. Then without much thought, without aches of regret, he slowly closed the door, shutting out a baffling but sweet part of his life forever.

Waiting. I'm stuck here waiting—as if I was a piece of chewed gum on a church pew. I'm always waiting for this, waiting for that. *Como pendeja.* As if somebody said, "You will wait. And you will be good at it." Somebody like a nun with a face of crumpled paper.

Chingáo, this is my lot in life—to let the world's time run past me, like lightning bolts *uno tras otro* in the summer sky, while I sit and wait. And wait. *Y otra ves . . .* wait.

I'm going through the five stages of death here. I'm in this revival, *oiga,* beneath a tent not far from downtown's Skid Row. You can see the rusted fire escapes on faded hotels and the tall buildings west of here that have windows like eyes, looking down on us. There's poor people everywhere. *Hijole*—it's funny how people who have nothing just love Jesus. I mean stone homeless, no place to take a . . . well, *ya sabes.* But, we saved.

My name is Ysela. Not your normal name. It's Mexican, pronounced e-SE-la. When I sing, I just get up and tell the world my name is Ysela. *¡Andale!* Say it right. The "y" sounds like an "e." And when you say it fast, *a la bravota,* it sounds nice. Ysela!

Inside the tent, there's a microphone up top of a wooden platform, fold-up chairs spread all over the place and people getting wound up like tops while others begin to talk. Somebody should know I'm still here, all alone. *Pinche* waiting.

What do I have to do, man!

So what am I waiting for? For somebody to hear *my* story. Everybody else's had a chance. They've all gone on up to the mic, *como dicen—test-i-fying*. They've all done their thing, had their fifteen minutes, boring us to pieces. Now it's my turn, *oiga*. I've been waiting a long time to tell my story. And I have a good one, too.

You know, I'm descended from an important family. My family's been in California for generations. I mean hundreds of years. My family came from the original settlers. The Californios. That's right. They owned all this land, *oiga*. They had ranches and horses and field hands. They had fancy clothes, stiff-brimmed hats, sashes, swords. They were handsome, brave too—true vaqueros, the original cowboys, the ones who named these lands.

But it was sad, what happened to them. *Pobrecitos*. They got ripped off after the Anglos came. They fought them—even stopping Anglo soldiers just outside L.A. more than 150 years ago. In the battle the Californios beat them with lances, *oiga*.

But the Anglos still came and forced them to sign a treaty. It was supposed to guarantee some rights. They got to keep their language, their land, and even some power. But that didn't last long. The Anglos found gold, *oiga*. Thousands came from the East for gold. Gold changed everything. They took the land. They killed people. Treaties mean nothing.

One of these last Californios was my great-great-uncle, or something like that. His family originally owned Griffith Park, *oiga*. When the Anglos took it, they let the family stay in parts of it. The park got built up. Roads. Trails. Then the damn zoo. Tourists and visitors came by all the time. Soon all these people had to do was clean up the place. My great-great-uncle, the last of his clan, at the very end was an old stick of a man, *oiga*, beaten down, roaming the park, picking up trash.

He died doing that. Working for someone, cleaning the land that used to belong to him. Now, not even his house—or that story—is 'round no more. It's all gone.

You might have figured, though, that I'm not all Californio. I'm real dark, see. Somewhere along the line, some members of the family got hooked up with the poor Mexican migrant workers and railroad hands who were living here building this place, L.A.

I got a lot of Indian in me, *oiga*. Along the way, somebody from Jalisco hooked up with somebody from Durango, who hooked up with one of my Californio family, and others came along, more Mexicans, more Indians, and then I came, born in a small room of a small house in La Kern Mara.

There used to be a brickyard by the Floral drive-in theater where I grew up. I lived near there until all of it got destroyed, *oiga*, the brickyard, the houses, the drive-in. They built a freeway. Then new streets. Then new houses. Soon there wasn't much of Kern Mara. Pushed out again, I s'pose.

If you haven't figured it out, I'm a churchgoing woman. This may be hard to believe, but it's true. I've been singing gospel since I was a little girl, the darkest Mexican in the choir. I almost look black.

Fíjese, when I did the rounds through the southern part of the state, visiting churches, carnivals, rodeos, hoedowns, and ja-maicas, doing gospel songs and things like "Bill Bailey, Won't You

Please Come Home" for good measure, most people who'd never seen a Mexican thought I was black. Once even, some *hueros* followed behind me. They yelled out "Hey, Aunt Jemima." *Mira nomas.* I looked at them white boys and told them in pure barrio Spanglish—*comen caca, pinche huevones,* slime balls and sons of *putas sagradas.* They took off running, *oiga.*

I'm a big woman, too. Real big. I don't mind, really. I've been big so long, I don't know how else to be. My family called me Chata for years, *oiga,* till I wouldn't answer to it no more. I wear big dark dresses, my hair short, curly and bouncy top my head. When I started singing, God took over my tonsils. He invaded my throat, and now all I hear is an angel, and it's me. But, sometimes, I'm not so sure.

For now, I'm alone. In a trailer behind a row of small, unpainted wood houses in Montebello, not far from the Los Angeles city line. Years ago, this area wouldn't even be considered East L.A. When I grew up, East L.A. ended just past Atlantic Boulevard. My mother, *que en paz descanse,* said that other people, mostly whites, but sometimes Japanese, lived on this side for years. But now—nothing but Mexicans.

I know what I'm talking about because I grew up *en el mero* East Los—*en* La Kern Mara, *te digo.* When I was small, I remember the family gatherings in our dirt yard. You know what I mean—dogs barking, roosters strutting, and hens pecking at the ground. What a mess they made, *oiga.* We'd have birthday parties, *sabes,* where everybody brings kids, but no presents. Whatever your name was, the adults always called you *m'ijo* or *m'ija.* There was kegs of beer and then a fight. You had the *tios* and *tias,* a *monton* of cousins, and 'buelita propped up on a metal chair under a tree. And the *morrillos* running *a donde quiera* like nobody cares.

Finally, like clockwork, *oiga*, mami and papi would get into their *pleitos*, and everybody would leave before the fists start flying and mami runs to hide in the bedroom.

But lately, I hear people call all this area east of where I used to live, for miles into the county, I hear they call it East L.A. Like I say, Mexicans took over everything, *oiga*. Mexicans moved east of Atlantic, and kept on going, man—eating up Montebello, Pico Rivera, La Puente, Bassett, Whittier. *Ajúa*—you know it! So I tell folks that I live in East L.A., but for reals, I live in Montebello, *oiga*, in a small trailer tucked behind a clump of old houses.

I got a daughter and a son. They don't live with me. Not for years, *oiga*. They're going to school and living with my mother. They're only part Mexican. Their papi was a cowboy buck rider from Oklahoma; ended up here once, doing the rodeos, and he kinda' fell for a chubby young girl singing gospel in a wide dress.

I never liked that cowboy, *oiga*. Got drunk all the time. Gave me babies, then split. I hardly saw him . . . then I never saw him. He stopped coming 'round, and I was alone with the kids, Juana and Toño, who the cowboy used to call Two-Tone, partly because of the name, but also because of his white-brown color, *sepa yo*.

The kids keep growing, too. They come and visit and never really get into any big trouble. But I know they've suffered. I know they sometimes aren't sure about who they are—white or Mexican, or both. I tell them it don't matter none, *oiga*. That to God, it don't matter. And they listen. And they know. And they laugh. But they leave, and I keep thinking, I'm not so sure.

Mis padres got rid of me real quick with all this. Even got the church to refuse me singing there. But I never stopped loving my God, *oiga*, my Jesus. I never stopped.

I got real fat and ugly then, but now I think I'm okay. There are men still hanging 'round me. I even had an affair going with a rich married *gabacho* who liked his women big, but he kept me in this trailer, in a hard-to-find place, waiting. He paid the bills for a while, as long as I didn't tell nobody who I was seeing.

Fine with me. That Doudy—he was Mr. Doud, but I called him Doudy—helped me get singing gigs in parks, at fiestas and dances. I did my gospel thing, but people wanted some up-tempo modern songs, so I'd throw in "Bill Bailey."

Doudy ended up getting away from me. He just stopped coming 'round. Then he stopped paying the bills. I tried to get him at his house, *oiga*. I even walked up miles and miles to Hacienda Heights, to his fancy ranch-style house there, walked up to his door, but in the end I got real sad, thinking about who I was— this fat, ugly woman with curly short hair and dark skin, who nobody can possibly love, and I just turned back and walked away. My tears feeling like broken glass.

I also went out with a Chicano police officer over in Santa Fe Springs. A big man, *oiga*. Real big for a Mexican. He liked his women big, too. In the beginning he was *muy de aquellas*—real sharp looking, *oiga,* in his uniform, shiny black gun, and chrome-like handcuffs at his sides, making noises of leather and steel whenever he moved around. Man, I liked that. He used to say, "I'm the white man's worse nightmare—a Mexican with a badge." A real *tripeaso*.

Pero that *cabrón* also scared the shit out of me, pardon my French. A lot of anger in his blood, that one, like boiling all the time. He was good to the kids, but I always worried. Like maybe he'd pull a gun on them, *oiga,* the way he sometimes did with me in drunken rages—pushing the gun hard against my cheek, my heart going a thousand miles a minute, and me praying that I wouldn't be shot there and left to rot, *oiga*.

I had to get away from that one!

Anyways, God gave me a voice, and it's my blessing. I have never had no money. But I have this voice. To sing. To tell my story. Once, after Doudy stopped paying the bills, I came across a dude who heard my voice, singing and talking, and said he had a proposition to make. He wanted to know if I would do sex tapes, *oiga*. Tapes he would sell through mail order, you know, in porno magazines. I didn't like the idea at first, but man I needed money real bad. So I did a few tapes. Just my voice, talking dirty. On Sundays, I went to church and prayed for God to forgive me. I sang extra hard in the choir. I believe Jesus knows why I did them tapes. I believe He understands, so I don't have to 'splain to nobody. I only did a few. Anyways, it kept food on the table, *¿qué no?*

I got a story all right. But I'm not the only one, *oiga*. When I get my chance to talk at this gathering, I'm going to talk about my brother, Pompi. I don't know where the name comes from. Pompi was older than me. He even had a different father than me.

Pompi I remember well. Especially back in 1990. It wasn't so long ago, but it seems like it was. I was a teenager then. I sang all the time at revivals. I was kinda' round, and I know I was cute. All dark, with red blush, and thick curly hair, and singing like an angel.

Pompi was a Marine, *oiga*. A proud Chicano Marine. But he came out of the corps all messed up. Yelling all the time, and drinking. *Híjole*, could he drink! He started to get gray hair. He stayed quiet for a long time, sometimes. Then, he wouldn't come home for days. Then he would show up again, not saying nothing, *oiga*, sometimes not even hello. Man, he was *mírame, no me toques:* Look, but don't touch.

Something terrible happened to Pompi. He saw something.

He didn't talk about it to no one. But one night, *oiga,* he told me the story.

See, Pompi was a Marine who got sent to Panama in 1989. They were there to get that *vato* Noriega, or whatever his name was then. Marines stormed the country and set up shop for a while. Pompi was a new recruit. What Pompi saw, *oiga,* nobody should see. He a Chicano, a proud one at that, to see what he did.

One night he tells me what happened to him, with water in his eyes and his lips shaking. Drunk. Angry. His face was red. He tells me, "We were on patrol in a rundown part of Panama City. The place had just got the shit bombed out of it. There was a lot of wreckage, man—fires, debris, and a *chingo de* bodies. I mean blown to bits. At one point, I was standing next to a sergeant, some guy from Michigan who was our squad leader. We heard a noise and checked it out. Inside one of the tore up houses was this tiny Panamanian kid, about five years old, crying. He was full of dust, and his foot was bleeding. The guy next to me got angry all of a sudden. He screamed about these damn 'mud people,' and what a lousy job we did not destroying them. The vato put his weapon to the side of the kid's head, then blew his brains out. Just like that, man. I didn't know what to do. I wanted to yell, but the sergeant looked at me, telling me with a look that I'd better not say nothing. So what if the *morro* was brown like me—I was a Marine, and Marines stick together."

Pompi wasn't ever the same, *oiga.* He kept what he saw inside of him. Chicanos are used a lot by this government against other Latinos—like on the border or in Nicaragua. Some don't mind, I s'pose. But Pompi minded. He was a good Marine. He never said nothing. But he never forgot that Panamanian kid, *oiga.* He never forgot the expression then as his head exploded when that bullet hit him.

Maybe this was what Pompi saw the rainy night he put a shotgun into his mouth—the kid's face, his terror, his beautiful little brown head splattered everywhere. They found Pompi in his father's garage. It took a few days. Nobody knew where he was. The garage started to stink, *oiga,* and they found him, bottles of tequila all over, and his own head blasted open.

I felt bad for a long time. I got even fatter after Pompi's death. I knew what he knew. All I could do was pray. That's why I'm here, why I've been saved, *oiga,* and why I go to church. I'm in Jesus' hands. Pompi didn't have a chance. But I pray Jesus is taking care of him and that little Panamanian kid, too.

So here I am at the revival. Waiting for my turn to speak. I'm tired of waiting. Everybody's already had their say. I also got me a story to tell. I know I can tell it good, too. I'm good at stories. I'm good at singing. I'm good on those tapes. God gave me a voice, *oiga.* He gave me this, and I still can sing like I was a cute, dark little girl in the choir, singing like an angel. All the way to the Californios. All the way to Pompi. All the way to heaven, *oiga.*

CHAIN-LINK LOVER

I grabbed the balled handle on the stick shift and pushed the 1967 V-Dub past several other cars along the industrial stretch of Santa Fe Avenue. The car had a yellow hood, gray door, and maroon fenders, body parts from auto wrecking yards along Mission Road's junkyard row. La Pancha sat—actually more like folded up—next to me, her sleek legs pulled back close to her body, giving me a view of the turquoise panties beneath her shorts. She was long-limbed—I don't believe this is quite what the makers of VW bucket seats had in mind. I turned the volume up on the stereo player. A cassette tape blared as we navigated a particularly shredded up section of street. The singer's voice boomed out of the speakers, hitting me in the back of the head like a baseball bat.

"Baby!" I sang back to the *sonidos,* "Baby!"

The guitar growled its feedback and the organ bellowed and the V-Dub rocked past warehouses, foundries, and shuttered factories.

"Well it won't be long till the next party," I said to Pancha.

"I hope not, Serf," she said, making my name sound like a Beach Boys' tune.

It's short for Serafín—Serafín Ramos.

"That place we just came from was hellified boring," Pancha continued. "But I know Rita most of the time throws a mean *borlo*. And I'm, like, ready to 'pardey' . . . oowwwww!" she screamed. Pancha knew I liked it whenever she did that. Something about a woman screaming in delight changes everything.

Pancha ran the small office of a photo studio on Whittier Boulevard. I visited her after the photographer and his darkroom technicians had gone home. On the outside windows and on the walls were posed pictures inside different-shaped frames. Pictures of *quinceañeras*—the large coming out parties for fifteen-year-old barrio girls—immense wedding parties, baptisms, graduations, proms, and families with kids for days—only the beautiful people. You'd never see any of *my* photos on those walls.

Well, maybe, I wasn't *that* bad looking. I didn't have a double chin or zits. I did drive a truck, though, and I looked like I should. I mean that I wore old T-shirts, tired jeans, and a tattered baseball cap. I was in okay shape—beer belly not yet fully formed. Not ugly, man, but nothing to crow about.

When I visited Pancha at the photo studio, and no one was around, we'd sneak into the darkroom, fogging up the mirrors over the sinks with angst-driven giggles and sex-potent barbs. Sometimes I leaned between those honey stretch of legs as she sat on the counter next to the chemicals, careful not to spill any of the foul-smelling stuff, and talked that good young I'm-lonely-let's-get-together smack.

She pretended shy, pretended no interest—and I got interested. I drove her home a few times, once almost making off with a kiss, but she turned her head as I closed in. No play from Pancha. *Please, Serf,* she'd say, *not now, Serf.* No matter. I became the Don Quixote of love, a glad gladiator, a Jaguar knight with an arrow aimed at her heart—jiving, conniving, and frustrated as hell. Giving up—the mature thing to do—was not something I could pull up from my worn-torn bag of tricks. And tricks they were. All puff and smoke. Nothing behind the illusions. But I persisted, the prerogative of most annoying jerks.

Okay, I'll admit it. I was one of *them* guys. The kind that keeps asking the same woman to dance even after she turns him down several times—and who only stops when the cutie pie grabs her drink and moves to a secluded corner. I'm the kind of guy who drags his two small nephews he's baby-sitting to a woman's apartment, someone he only met the day before at the doctor's office. It should all be that simple. I'm the kind of guy who keeps walking up the steps of a great love's house with umbrella in hand, even though he passes another dude, also with umbrella in hand, leaving the house of the great love—it doesn't matter, I keep on going.

Did I need a piano to drop on my *coco*? You bet I did.

So despite weeks of her hard-to-get routines, I planned my next move with Pancha. I strategized—like in a game of love chess, warfare of the heart. I racked my brains for something romantic (but nothing came to mind). Then a friend handed me a flyer: There was a deep-sea fishing excursion off the coast of San Pedro.

Cool.

I could see the romance blossoming as we meandered over an ocean wave in the middle of nowhere: sweet tropical drinks in hand, the meeting of sea and sky in front of us, no land in sight.

What was I thinking?

I invited Pancha, who foolishly accepted this desperate offer. I blamed her for that. She didn't have to go. I was a jerk, *órale,* but they picked 'em. So we got up early and drove a good half hour or more to the L.A. harbor. There was an unusually cold breeze inside a fog thick as cotton, which should have told me something.

The boat seemed small, heavy bottomed, and barnacled with a salt-worn wood cabin in the middle. We were going rock cod fishing. Whatever that was. Like a true fool, I didn't know what I was doing. Pancha was polite, perhaps opened to giving me a chance to prove myself. I was nervous thinking about that long-awaited kiss while being gently rocked in the arms of the ocean blue.

A group of people flocked on the dock waiting to get on the boat, including friends of mine. They gawked at my beautiful companion—and wondered the wonder of wonders: How the hell did this guy get dates like this? One of those inexplicable mysteries, I supposed, which tended to surround all dweebs, perhaps contributing to their blasted longevity in the world.

Despite that, we're off into the gray abyss, the gates of Hades, the great unknown. We each had long fiberglass fishing poles with a row of hooks on the line. We didn't start thrusting these into the water till we had gone about an hour into sea. Meantime, everybody was rockin' and reelin', bobbin' and weavin'. Stomachs were churning. Heads spinning. Hardy men were seen with their necks across the bow, throwing up like babies. Landlubbers. Me included. Pancha was on her last legs. She climbed on top of the cabin and refused to come down. She lay there, moaning. I also thrust my head over the boat's edge once or twice. I didn't care how this looked. All prettied-up faces, all tough veneers, all smart-aleck remarks went overboard that day. We were all sick. The one or two alleged sea dogs in the group vomited and just smiled.

"You'll get used to it," they blathered.

Pancha was dying on the cabin's roof.

"Come down, baby," I managed to say. "We're throwing in the fishing lines."

Neta. When we reached the "spot" (how they figured this out was beyond me), the boat's engines were turned off. We got our lines baited and tossed them in. *Fíjese,* the fish were boundless there. We picked up the fish lines and a dozen or so got hooked. We tossed the bucking creatures onto the deck and threw back the lines. We caught some other kinds of fish as well, including one species that had poisonous scales. The people who ran the boat knew how to fillet them without getting any of the poison on their skin. Every once in a while someone caught a small shark— they infested these waters. They were not baby sharks, just "Mini-Me" sharks. We tossed them back, since we weren't licensed to bring these creatures to shore.

After ridding my stomach of everything, I continued to fish— nothing else to do. Baiting the fish lines, throwing them into the water, and looking out toward the farthest reaches of ocean helped. Believe it or not, I was having fun. Pancha didn't say a peep. She was done, had it, gone to nausea purgatory. I felt bad for her. When we returned to the dock, she didn't smile, didn't say anything. She slow walked to the car. Pancha's brave, though. She hung in there and didn't whine. I apologized profusely. She just stared past me.

"Take me home, Serf," she muttered through a dry mouth.

P ancha eventually forgave me for that fishing fiasco. That's how we ended up in my VW, pushing the dust around this corrugated steel jungle called Vernon, below the East L.A. barrio where Pancha and I—in separate *cantones* mind you—lay our heads.

It was party time. And I was glad, too, especially with Pancha—a beam of joy in an uptight and confusing world.

We entered an intersection. I swerved around an eighteen-wheel tractor-trailer and made a right-hand turn. The semi wanted to turn, too; it had pulled over to the left-hand lane for a wide right. I knew I shouldn't have cut in front of the semi. Although I handled a much smaller truck at work, I knew those rigs can't make these turns without moving into the farthest lane.

You've got to be careful about such moves on L.A. streets—people get wasted for lesser affronts.

But there I was, thinking only of the music, Pancha's long legs, and the feel of the stick shift in my palm. Pretty soon, I felt something big, really big, breathing down the backside of my Bug. La Pancha looked behind her and exclaimed: "*Híjole,* there's a big-ass truck on your tail—and, man, who's ever in it is pissed."

I spied the truck in the rearview mirror. It was the same one I had passed moments earlier. Hell, I figured I could just pull to the right lane and let it go by—which I did. But it didn't.

The truck pulled up to the side of my car; I could see some dude in the cab giving me the finger and cursing, most of which I couldn't hear but surely understood. Then a beer bottle hit the top of the Bug.

"*¡Pinche!*" Pancha yelled. She got that right.

I downshifted to gain more power and boosted the V-Dub, hoping to get far enough ahead of the truck to make a turn at another intersection and get the hell out of there. But a red light forced my hand. The car in front of me stopped behind the cross-walk, and I braked behind the car while the truck pulled up, this time to the right of us.

"You ready for *pleito,* Serf?" Pancha asked, more mischievous than curious.

I just smiled, or hardly smiled, and waited. Sure enough—you just know about these things—a heavyset, flannel-shirted dude—real *macizo*—jumped from out of his cab with a tire iron in his hand. He walked around to the front of my car and stood there, daring me to get out. I threw a look over to La Pancha, who appeared to be enjoying all this. I knew I couldn't pull no chicken-shit groveling there in the middle of the street. It was just the trucker and me—man to man, *mano a mano,* multicolored Bug to shiny semi (but, damn, I wished I had a "nine" with me).

L a verdad es—I needed to hang out, to have a good time, to let my worries hang out to dry on a clothesline, and leave them. They're called "hang-ups," no? Too much stress on the job, *ese.* Every day, several times a day, I checked in at a warehouse with a bobtail truck full of new lamps. I drove that freakin' truck from the lamp plant on a side street off Bandini Boulevard to the main warehouse in Carson—back and forth, back and forth.

The *jale* didn't pay a whole lot. But it kept me from having nothing to do, although I fucked up something fierce when I first started.

First of all, I had to double-clutch the truck while driving—pushing in the clutch to move to neutral, then letting go, and pushing in the clutch again when I changed gears. I tore up a lot of gear teeth trying to get the hang of it. But I also had to learn—

the hard way—how to get that truck around narrow streets, gas stations, low bridges. Once I toppled the credit card stand at one fill-up joint when I backed up without looking. Man, I couldn't apologize enough to the manager of the place, who was practically in tears when I pulled out of there.

Another time, I scraped the top of the truck's trailer 'cause I didn't pay attention to the height limits on a train bridge. With all the trucks around here you'd think they would build higher bridges (yes, I'm blaming others for my own *pendejadas*). I sure felt like one of those fishes that I had caught that time. Hook in my mouth kinda' feeling.

But perhaps the scariest thing I did was to forklift heavy boxes of lamp parts to the right side of the trailer. I thought it would make things easier to take off. *Pero*—all the weight fell on that side. So when I got off a freeway ramp, I turned into the curve and dumped the damn truck over.

Before I could say *pisto*, I was lying sideways in the cab. Even at fifteen miles per hour, I slid the truck a ways after it had hit the ground. Inside it was terribly uncomfortable—seat belt tight at my waist, my upper body toward the ground. A sorry sight when the fire trucks, ambulance, and truck removal people arrived. Although unhurt, my ego took a creaming.

My boss—Mr. Grossmueller—really got on my case. He yelled at me for every little thing as it was, I mean outside of those incidents. Once I came twenty minutes late after talking to Pancha from a phone booth. It was just innocent talk, me trying to break down Pancha's defenses with a smooth delivery of words—okay, I'll be honest here, they were more like stones being lobbed at a fortress wall.

"It's about time we kissed, don't ya' think?" I implored (more like begging—I had no shame, I tell you).

"I'd like to hang out with you some more," she responded. "Serf, I like you—except for that stupid fishing trip, you've been nice and kinda' fun. But let's see more of each other first."

"Pancha, you're driving me nuts, here."

"Oh, you can handle it, *¿qué no?*"

"Yeah, sure, no problem—but I'm talking about a kiss, not having my baby."

"Don't be silly, Serf. . . . Listen, I like having a good time like anybody else. Let's just go out for a while. Be patient."

Be patient—that's the phrase that's demolished many a relationship. But like I said, I'm not one to give up. I keep going and going, like that goofy pink bunny in the Energizer battery commercials. Ding, Ding, Ding.

After I hung up, I jumped into the truck and pulled into the warehouse. Mr. Grossmueller came at me, cursing like I had just killed somebody. He went on about me taking too long getting from one place to another. I wanted to punch the *puto,* but I needed the job.

"Sorry, sir, it won't happen again, sir," was all I could say. Man, I just hated saying sorry to this dude.

"You bet it won't, Mister *Ray-mos,*" Grossmueller continued to berate. " 'Cause you won't have a job here, *com-pren-dee.*"

A real asshole.

But other than Grossmueller and the calamities on the road, I liked this job. Every morning I'd negotiate the truck—barely able to scrape by the parked cars along the narrow street—onto the loading dock. I'd get out and wait as a small army of dudes hauled boxes of the finished product into the truck's trailer. To kill time, I joked around with the pretty office women. This was the best part of the day, bar none. There was Luisa, who always wore wraparound skirts and bright blouses that caressed her mighty fine physical attributes. Another was Ana La Loca, as I called her, with a smile edged in silver fillings. She was young, eighteen like me, and we talked regularly, mostly playful nonsense about pretend love and pretend dates, only she had a six-foot football-playing hunk from East L.A. College for a boyfriend. It was just pretend. And there was Claudia, an older woman from Veracruz, around thirty, dark and shapely, who loved to go dancing. Although she's had five children from five different men, dancing was an elixir for her, keeping her in top form and fun to be with. I tell myself that one of these days, if Pancha doesn't work out, I'll be out dancing with Claudia.

Luisa, Ana, and Claudia—they kept the place jumping.

In time, I got the hang of the truck, avoiding low bridges and watching whenever I backed up. And the office women liked it when I showed up in my truck, ready to be loaded up with newly manufactured lamps.

Grossmueller never stopped his yakking, though—he just had no other way of getting anything done.

"What happened here?" he screamed one day to no one and everyone at the same time.

Some oil had fallen onto the dock area. He always tried to keep the docks clean, picking up ice-cream bar covers and newspapers that I had dropped. But the oil—now that was serious. Who would spill oil? It didn't matter, nobody was going to come clean or rat on anybody. But for Grossmueller it was an issue of grave importance. He went on about it for days. He just couldn't believe anybody would spill oil on his precious docks.

If it weren't small things like the oil spill that got him going, it'd be something else. He yelped all the time. I'd pull in my truck to his yells—at the lamp assembly workers, the guys who loaded up the trucks, and even at my pretty friends in the office, only they knew how to take it in stride, making fun of Gross-mueller's unpressed pants and shirts, and sweaty underarms.

Yeah, it was *firme* working there, despite the *jefe*.

So this large dude was standing in front of me, weapon in hand, smoke appearing to come out of his ears. What a drag.

I stepped out of the car, giving him the hardest look I could muster. I'm no gangsta', but I figured if I had to go down, I was going to look like I was *cagando un palo* doing it.

First thing I noticed was how much smaller I was than the trucker. People in other cars took in the whole scene while we faced off. All I could see was streetlights in their windshields. The trucker bounced one end of the tire iron into his other hand while my hands emerged out of my pockets, empty and vulnera-ble, curled into fists.

"Fuck you, you puny son-of-a-bitch!" growled the trucker.

"You want a piece of me, then come get some!" I yelled back.

I just about had it—I thought about my job, my *pinche* boss, and how this dude was ruining my one moment of *descanso* with Pancha.

The trucker just stood there, eyes pushed into deep sockets, mouth tight as a gasket.

You really want to know what was on my mind: Yadira—a fe-male, yes, but not like Pancha or the office women.

Yadira was a fourteen-year-old mentally disabled girl who lived across from the lamp factory.

One morning, this awkward-looking adolescent rushed up to the rusted chain-link fence that surrounded her house and stared at me. So I waved hello. She smiled something fierce and waved back. After that, without fail, Yadira ran up to the fence, smiled and waved madly at me. I responded in like fashion, not knowing that I was reeling the poor *muchacha* into a snare of childish infatuation.

Yadira never stopped repeating the motions, eagerly anticipating my smile and gesture. *¡Qué fastidio!* It got worse when she started to yell out her love for me in broken English: *I loov ju.* That was fine as long as I kept my distance, but then Luisa, Ana, and Claudia got wind of the situation.

"You've got quite a filly looking at your tail, Serafin," Luisa commented.

"Don't start—I'm just trying to be nice here," I responded.

"That's Yadira—she don't know about nice. Nothing in between. It's black or white. Up or down. Love or no love. For Yadira, there's no such thing as nice," contributed Claudia.

"What do you want me to do—ignore her?"

"What we're telling you, *bobo,*" Ana chimed in, "is once Yadira thinks you have even a slight interest in her, she's never going to let you go."

"And you better treat her right," Luisa added. "We're watching you."

"Oh you guys, just leave me alone. I know what I'm doing."

The words of a desperate man. Yadira started to wear long pleated skirts with white socks to impress me. Once she placed an old white chair by the fence—she'd sit there for hours, rocking away, scanning my every move as I helped load the truck. If I so much as looked over her way, even for a negligible interest in some noise, she stood up, smiling like a simian in heat. I really didn't know what to do. I had to find a way to extract myself from her adoration, her focused attentiveness to my every move, her excruciating dejection whenever I didn't respond.

I knew one day when I left this job or she'd tire of me not returning her love, I'd break Yadira's heart. It was one of the many things that weighed heavily on my already battered *mente*.

ou don't scare me, shithead," I told the trucker. "I don't care what you got. You going to just stand there or what?"

He kept staring. I kept mad-dogging.

"What? Take a swing at me then. Go 'head. You think you tough enough, then go 'head—what?"

I knew a lot of this was scared talking—I talk a lot when I think I'm about to get my ass whupped.

Inside the cars the onlookers kept looking, Pancha kept smiling.

The world stood still for that moment. The whole thing could've ended with my brains splattered all over the place. But no matter how scared I was, I wasn't going down begging or crying or nothing. If he was going to get me, I was going to be looking him straight in the eye, defiant, angry, and stone cold crazy.

"You want me, come get me!" I prodded again, much braver now since I figured he didn't have the *huevos*. I knew most people didn't. It was something I counted on (but the day will come when I meet the vato who has what it takes to do exactly what he intends to do).

No one blinked. No one backed off.

About then, some of the crowd got bored—the light had

turned green or something. I saw a couple of them open their car doors; one guy yelled out, "Shit or get off the pot—we got places to go here!"

At the same time, a police car moved rapidly in our direction from the other side of the street. The trucker dude glanced over, then turned around, rushed over to his cab, and climbed on, but not before calling me a "fuckin' asshole." The semi then sped through the intersection.

I stood there in the street, following the truck with my eyes as it squealed past me. The police car pulled over to the side, but the officer just sat there. He musta' seen enough of these face-offs to not do anything until they got out of hand. I heard horns sounding and other voices, including Pancha's, yelling, "Serf, get back inside, will you?"

To put it plain, I was never good with the womens. It's true I tried, as my forays with Pancha demonstrated. But love was a fleeting thing—mostly because I was oblivious to my own failing attempts at being interesting and smooth. That's what makes jerks, right? We're not really bad people. We just don't pay attention. It's hard for us to accept a clear unequivocal "no." So we always seem to be out of earshot when that dreaded word roams around a room. I know as I get older—and mind you, as I finally leave my teenage years—this is something I'll have to gain a little bit of *clecha* about. This knowing what women want, what they really mean, what they are truly looking for. Jerks, to be honest, are just self-centered . . . well, jerks.

Then along comes the mental case, head over heels. Where's the justice?

I know I shouldn't be mean. But after weeks of Yadira's un-waning fascination with me, I became embarrassed. It started to affect my sleep, man. I had dreams of Yadira climbing the fence and chasing me down the assembly line of lamps to plant a big smooch on me.

I became self-conscious. Yadira sought me out, intense long-ing in her gaze. It showed in the way she grasped the fence, in her meticulous efforts, I believe, to put on the best clothes for me to behold. Once she actually fell on her face trying to get a bet-ter glimpse. She got up to resume her spot at the fence, didn't even wipe the dirt from her clothes or the blood from her mouth. She had tears; I saw them. She hurt. But this didn't stop her vigil.

An intense feeling of pity washed over me that day. Man, this was worse than death. I'd rather be hit by a tank than to ever feel that way again. It's a complex emotion, pity—mixed in with car-ing and hate and . . . guilt. And, man, did I feel guilty.

Yadira. Poor Yadira. What cruel deity brought you into this world to love so much—and not know a similar love in return.

Eventually, though, I will admit, Yadira's zeal had its appeal. I dreaded going to work after a while, but there was actually a day or two when Yadira didn't show herself by the lemon tree in her front yard, where she often situated her sorry self to catch my eye. And you know what? I missed her. This is strange, I understand, but even the loving passions of someone who's not the sharpest pencil in the box pulled at me. To be so loved, I mean in a pure sense because Yadira was simple enough not to have any other grades of love but the purest one. It was a curiosity, an allure-ment, something that began to tug at my own heart.

'Cause even lamebrains like me have heart, you know.

I became mixed up inside. First off, Yadira made my life miserable, measured by the wisecracks that the office women made about me.

"Love makes the world go 'round," Ana would say to no one in particular as I entered the office.

"All you need is love," added Luisa.

"Love the one you're with," Claudia, my dancing Claudia, would throw in.

· It wasn't funny anymore.

But Yadira—and I want to be careful here—also made my day. That's right. I could hardly believe it. I hated to be diminished in the minds of the office women, but I also started to look forward to Yadira's unselfish and absorbing affection. Where else would I find this kind of love—I suppose with my mama, but then as the song goes, even I'm not sure about that.

Punk-ass fool," I said as I climbed into the V-Dub. "All that posing for what . . . for fuckin' nothing. Fuck that *puto.* If he didn't have the guts to do something, he shouldn't have even tried."

"Well, you stood up to him, *ese,*" Pancha said. Then she did something totally unexpected—at least for idiots like me. She leaned over and planted a warm tender kiss on my frothy lips. Damn, there was a God—the same one who also protected me from that nutty truck driver.

I pulled out of the intersection and turned onto another street, in the opposite direction from where the truck was going. Were we standing there for an hour or just a few seconds? I couldn't tell.

As I drove, Yadira's smiling face came to mind—I mean even after Pancha's kiss. I saw Yadira standing beneath the lemon tree, in her boundless joy, her fingers tight around the chain-link fence as I back up out of the lamp factory docks in my truck and double-clutch my way out of there. My heart jumped when I thought of this. It really did. If just for a second.

"Fuck it then . . . how about that *borlote?*" I exclaimed while pushing the Bug farther up the splintered streets—wailing guitar notes over a samba beat on the tape deck, La Pancha placing her slender, brown forearms around her knees to get more comfortable, after surviving yet another night in another street of this city, mad city, fuck-it-all-and-blow-you-away city—to the next party up the road.

PIGEONS

While pulling and twisting at a couple of long, curved balloons with his hands, Monte looked down at the instructions booklet he had placed on top of a wooden table in front of him. The booklet showed him how to make balloon animals. He peeked at them every few seconds as he wrenched the balloons into the vague form of some animal inspired creature. Somehow an image of a giraffe emerged, and he handed it to the first child in front of him.

Arroyo Seco Park lay opulent and green on this warm spring Saturday. Groves of compact trees collared the mowed grass around the picnic area, where numerous families were celebrating birthdays or just enjoying a day out in the sun. Monte and his live-in girlfriend, Berta, were throwing a birthday party for Berta's ten-year-old daughter Betina. Most of the family was there, including all the children, ranging in age from still in diapers to the rambunctious prepubescent. They were the offspring of Monte's and Berta's siblings. Monte wanted to particularly impress Berta's mother, Socorro, who reluctantly came to the party; her father, on the other hand, refused to make it because Monte and his daughter were, in his words, "living in sin."

So far, so good, Monte thought, after contorting another set of balloons into a misshapen poodle.

Earlier that day, Berta's family seemed cordial and open to Monte, who was painfully aware of her father's feelings toward him. They were quiet though, not like his own family, who was often too loud for most people's tastes.

"All right, kids, now line up so we can play a game of freeze tag," Berta suddenly announced.

Monte sighed as the children gathered around Berta, abandoned balloons falling to the ground around him. The things I do for love, he thought, while eyeing Berta's behind inside well-worn jeans, cut off at the thighs. Beyond her shapeliness, Berta was also sensible and bright. She gave Monte a stability and coherency he had not previously known. Monte had dropped out of high school and worked as a foundry worker for much of his twenty-seven years. Berta attended church on Sundays and worked with preschool kids during the week. She was home for dinner and made sure Betina was watched over and read to at night. Monte's days, on the other hand, were marred by a varied work life. Varied in that most times, there was no work.

Monte stood up from the park table, disrupting a group of pigeons pecking at the ground nearby. He walked toward his brother, Miguel, who had piled black nuggets of charcoal onto a grill for the hot dogs and hamburgers. They looked as opposite as two brothers could: Monte, rough-hewed and stocky, had mounds of tousled hair beneath a black-and-gray Raiders cap while wearing a matching Raiders jersey shirt. Miguel was tall with long burnished locks, tied into a ponytail; he had on a light-blue guayaberra, embroidered in front with dark-blue thread. Monte removed a cold bottle of beer from the cooler and walked over to Miguel.

"*¿Qué hubo, carnal?*" Monte greeted.

"Nobody here but us hot dogs," Miguel said, looking over at his brother. "What's this—didn't think of bringing me a *chela,* too? *No seas gacho, carnal.*"

"Get your own," Monte said, but then backed up a few steps and grabbed another brew from the cooler.

"So what do you think of Berta, *ese*?" Monte asked, while handing his brother the bottle.

"What do you mean, what do I think? It's about time you found somebody, even if she does come with a ready-made family."

"She's good to me—that's all that matters."

Just then their sister, Flora, who was heavyset and mocha-colored inside a loose yellow blouse and matching culottes, walked up.

"*Estos escuincles*—these kids get on my nerves," she said.

"Everybody gets on your nerves," the brothers answered at once, then laughed.

"Stupids," Flora replied as she stomped off.

Miguel, Monte, and Flora Duran were small children when their parents moved to East L.A. from the tin-roofed, plywood-and-chicken-wire shacks they had been born into on the hillsides of Tijuana. When their father left the family, his wife, Delia, and their three children eventually settled in the Aliso Village housing projects in Boyle Heights. At one time, Aliso Village and the neighboring Pico Gardens were the largest public housing developments west of the Mississippi. These projects were also the spawning grounds of the Primera Flats and Cuarto Flats barrio gangs, some of the oldest street associations. Over the past two decades, newer and smaller—and often deadlier—gangs arose, making this one of the most violent areas in the country.

The LAPD's Ghetto Bird helicopter routinely scoured the

projects at night. Numbers were painted on the rooftops for easy location should police have to raid an apartment or chase suspected gang youths. There were nightly spasms of gunfire and countless family crises. Despite this, the Duran family did fairly well—none of the siblings got involved in gang life, in heavy drugs, or major arrests. Work, work, work; that's all they knew.

Monte glanced over toward Socorro, his possible future mother-in-law, alone on a knife-scarred bench. To Monte, Socorro looked like an old Indian from pictures out of *National Geographic* magazine, only she had on a secondhand purple velvet blouse over loose brown pants. She didn't say a word to anyone; her thoughts lost on some distant shore of memory.

Monte felt there was something strange about Socorro, as if she was a temporary guest wherever she went. Socorro came to L.A. in her early twenties while pregnant with Berta. Her husband, Manual, started a new life for them here, although she was quite happy in her Sinaloa village where her large family worked the land and helped each other out.

As a little girl, Socorro loved the desert breezes that swept past the windowless opening in the room where she slept. She loved the way she could run for miles and never leave the dirt and vegetation of her backyard. She loved the freedom, like that of a wild horse, a horse with wings and a purple mane, as she imagined, able to traverse the tallest mountains and sit on a throne of clouds in the sky. She recalled her mother once yelling from inside the mud and wood hut: "Socorro, it's time for dinner—come home." Socorro looked up from behind a row of cactus. She held a dry ocotillo branch that she pushed into a slow-crawling tarantula, which recoiled from the point of the branch. Her barefoot and naked two-year-old brother, Marcos, squatted next to her and the dust-covered tarantula. "I'm coming," Socorro answered, then turned to her brother. "See, Marcos, it's time to eat." Socorro grabbed the boy's hand and they both walked toward the house, rocks and debris beneath their feet. On the way, Socorro pointed out for Marcos the bear, lion, and pig forms she saw in the mass of white and gray clouds in the sky—she made sure to locate the winged horse sitting on a throne. She always seemed to find one in the clouds.

Years later—and after many dangerous forays to *el otro lado*—Socorro tried to settle into her new environs, although she mostly felt alone the times she cared for Berta and, later, Berta's younger siblings, Gilberto, Guillermo, and Bonnie (La Bonifacia), despite her husband's efforts to help make ends meet.

Manual, who started off peddling fruits and nuts on freeway off-ramps, eventually opened up a successful carneceria specializing in Mexican-style meats: beef, pork, poultry, goat, lamb, and cow's brains, tongues, and guts . . . *res, carnitas, pollo, birria, cordero, cesos, lengua,* and *tripas.* He added Mexican products such as moles, picantes, chocolates, candies, and a variety of freshly squeezed drinks: tamarindo, Jamaica, orchata, piña, guava, limón, champurrado, mango, atole, and others.

The Lujan family ended up in a part of L.A. County where Mexicans hardly resided at the time: West Covina. Although Mexicans were now all over the L.A. basin, there were still streets and neighborhoods with only fairly well off Anglo families—who lived in much more secluded and sterile households than Socorro was used to.

Manual was happy—he was living the American Dream, despite his traditional ways and manners. Socorro kept silent, gritting her teeth, bearing it all.

As Monte knocked back his beer, he noticed a group of other children, dusky in ripped and dirty pants and T-shirts, about seven years old, hitting something on the ground behind the bushes. He couldn't tell what they were striking at; he didn't think twice about it. Monte was relaxing, celebrating Betina's birthday with the family and woman he loved, beer in hand. It didn't get much better, he thought.

At one end of the park, a well-built tall man in a white suit wearing a pearl white Lucha Libre wrestling mask sang rancheras from a CD boom box and Mic amp. A crowd of people surrounded him. Several children held on to *paletas,* purchased from a peddler with a brightly painted cart, who repeatedly pushed on a bicycle bell to attract customers. Another masked man—smaller, less well built, and pudgy around the waist—held CDs in the air to sell, renditions of Mexican classics from the masked ranchera singer.

Monte chuckled at the scene. He then turned to look at the family, which included a number of Anglos. Berta's siblings had all married one. This was okay with Monte; he prided himself on not holding grudges against white people. The Anglos in Berta's family were usually aloof except for Gilda, Guillermo's wife, who spoke perfect Spanish and was very close to Berta. Kids' games seemed to be her great joy—she was also a preschool teacher.

Living in a mostly Anglo community forced a few changes on the Lujans—like Guillermo becoming Bill; Gilberto, Gil; and Bonifacia being called Bonnie. Only Berta, the oldest, stayed with the original sound of the name, although everyone knew her daughter Betina as Betty. They talked without accents and with limited Spanish. The Spanish they did use was to communicate

with Socorro, who held on to her mother tongue despite the almost three decades of living in the United States. The Lujan children, even with their darker skins, seemed to do well with their
neighbors and in school. The more they interacted on their
terms—in other words, the less Mexican they were—nobody
seemed to act like there was anything different about the "lujans," as people called them.

Monte's family was *puro* East Los—maintaining a presence in
the Aliso Village apartments for years, although more often than
not filled to the rafters with three or more other families. The
area, however, had recently undergone major redevelopment—
the Aliso Village had been torn down, leaving only rubble, which
eventually became a vacant lot. New subsidized apartments were
being built where the projects once stood.

After his mom moved out of Aliso Village, Miguel went to U.C.
Berkeley to finish his schooling. Flora found a home in El Monte
with her husband, Simon, taking their mom along with her.
Monte first moved into a basement apartment on State Street
near First, then into a small but well-kept dwelling in Highland
Park with Berta and Betty.

Drinking his beer, Monte watched the masked singer and the
crowd that gathered around him. Tied to a tree near the group
was a red-and-orange star piñata—something that Monte insisted
Berta should not bring to Betty's party.

"Man, look at all the *tijuaneros* hanging around this park."

Miguel looked up from the grill at his brother. He was now an
active Chicano trade union member and he didn't share Monte's
growing resentment of those from "the other side." Miguel noticed how over the years, Monte became increasingly annoyed
with the city's Mexicanness—and therefore his own. He saw how

his brother stayed away from anything remotely tied to the old country like it was a bad rash.

"Oh, I see, you are so much better than them, being mostly out of work," Miguel responded.

"Well, I would've been working, but these Mexicans are taking up all the jobs—and don't tell me they only take jobs nobody wants."

"Why not? The truth hurts, don't it?"

"I want to work. You think I like Berta at the preschool while I sit around the house! I'm telling you, *ese,* I've been a foundry worker for a long time, and so far I've been unemployed for most of the last five years. Sure, I may be a *pocho* to the Mexicans . . . but I was born here. I speak Spanish *and* English. I should be working, not the *tijuaneros.*"

"The problem is you're prejudiced against your own kind," Miguel argued. "You forget, you're named after Montezuma, a proud Aztec name—which you never use any more. You think Americans are better than Mexicans. Tell that to some of these white people. They can't tell the difference if you were born here or not—and they don't care."

"Hey, don't talk so loud—there are white people in Berta's family."

"You know I'm not antiwhite—but I am against people who hate us no matter what we do. I'm not saying nothing new here."

"Yeah, exactly, the same old story," Monte countered. "Chicano this and Chicano that—that's you, bro'. *A poco creas que esta gente te tiene respeto.* Far from it. Mexicans don't care about you. Don't be so naïve, *ese.* They only care about themselves. Can you imagine the quality of life we'd have if they'd all go home."

Miguel stopped poking at the meat on the grill and aimed a fiery eye at his brother.

"Don't you mean the 'quality of life' we'd no longer enjoy if Mexicans weren't around to sew our clothes, mow our lawns, clean our homes, or take care of our kids. If they didn't get pushed around and hounded for the little pay they got. You ever think how we'd be if *esta gente* didn't do all they did so you could have the kind of life you have now?"

"*Hijo,* you're a stubborn ass. . . ." Monte tried to interject.

Miguel had been in a foul state of mind for some time. After graduating from Berkeley, he returned to the barrio, to Boyle Heights. That year almost sixty people had been killed by gunfire within a two-mile radius. Several of them were teenagers and even children, caught in street warfare by stray bullets. To Miguel, a kind of madness had blanketed the area. He sensed it—of loss, displacement, of being pushed around and forgotten. Some residents took it in stride. Others organized marches and community events for better housing and to curtail the violence. Those who were forced to leave the projects ended up in South Central L.A. or another part of the Eastside. Rival gangs would return at night from some far-flung area to carry out their deadly missions. Their neighborhood—several generations old, from the old pachuco days, generations of people killed, hurt, addicted, and imprisoned—continued as a killing field, even after they no longer had homes there. It was a last gasp. The last stand. The cholos were caught in the insane weblike hold of La Vida Loca, and even losing their barrio could not change that.

Miguel saw the destruction of Aliso Village as another example of Mexicans being pushed around, without a say-so, without the respect afforded anybody needing to change their community. There were many other such examples—the Chavez Ravine barrios that in 1950 were destroyed when poor Mexican families were forcibly removed from their homes so Dodger Stadium could be built. Also when the freeways were constructed—the western section of East L.A. had several freeway interchanges to accommodate the suburban commuters driving into downtown, although whole barrios were removed to create them. Miguel conceded that something had to change, that barrio warfare had claimed too many lives and that the poverty in the area was only getting worse. But "change from the heart of the people," as he called it, is different from urban planners, city officials, and major developers meeting in plush offices to carve up the barrio so they can profit on the renovations.

Miguel felt betrayed by the razing of Aliso Village. Even though new subsidized homes were being built—with new rules that said families with known gang members would not be allowed back—and there were plans for well-to-do town houses, things would never be the same. The banks of both sides of the L.A. River here were long filled with warehouses, small manufacturing plants, and scrappy homes. It was an area ripe for revitalization. Downtown's skyscrapers loomed large over the people of Boyle Heights, although their eyes and interests were facing the other way, to the more lucrative Westside and beach areas. With proximity to the greatly improved Little Tokyo area, an artists' warehouse district, and the downtown banks and stores, Boyle Heights could now be seen as too valuable. In Miguel's mind, getting rid of the projects was phase one in plans to remove most or all the poor Mexicans from this neighborhood.

To Miguel, Monte's attitude was a brainwash, a cultural cleansing of the indigenous Mexican-Chicano identity he was most proud of.

"Listen, little brother, you have a short memory," Miguel barreled in. "You remember when we first went to school and couldn't speak English? How some vatos chased us down the streets, calling us 'TJs.' All because of a made-up thing called a border? Come on! God didn't create borders; men did. You remember how we played over at Pecan Park? How the people made fun of us. Our own people. Our own skins. We're family at war with family. This doesn't make sense. Nobody should get treated this way. Nobody should have to go to sleep feeling less than a full human being. Now look at you—you sound just like those *tapados* who put us down. Not me, *ese. Soy Chicano. Soy Mexika.* My roots are as deep as anyone's on this land. Not only that but we helped build the roads, houses, schools, and industry that keeps this country going. We've fought in all the wars and proved to be more *bravos* than the rest. We belong here."

A long pause followed Miguel's words. Monte recalled as a youngster the derision he felt being Mexican, even in East L.A. How many of the kids used to laugh at him because of his broken English. He also hated the burritos and tacos his mother made for his lunch bags; he would throw them into trashcans on the way to school. On the big screen, he saw Mexicans only as *banditos* or poor cowardly slobs. He wondered why no Mexicans ever seemed to do anything important. As far as he knew, Mexicans were not among the more well-known war heroes, TV characters, movie greats, or inventors. Mexicans were barely a second thought, less important than other people, hardly warranting a footnote in history books or glamour magazines. So for years, Monte wanted to forget he was Mexican. For a short time, he told a few people he was Italian. Once he considered changing his last name from Duran to Durant.

Just as Monte began to mount a substantial reply to Miguel, a commotion broke out among the children playing games with

Berta and Gilda. Betty ran to her mother from the nearby girl's rest room.

"They're killing them!" she screamed.

"They're killing who—what! What's going on!" Berta yelled back.

"Pigeons . . . lots of pigeons!" the girl exclaimed.

Monte and the others rushed toward Betty to calm her down and find out what was happening.

"Mama, those kids in the bushes, they're using sticks to hurt the pigeons," Betty explained between sobs.

"Oh, no!" Berta responded. Gilda and Flora pulled the other children close to them. Monte looked up and again saw the same boys he had seen earlier: They were Mexican, in worn clothes and barefoot. They were carrying plastic bags with dead birds in them.

"*¡Oigan!*" Monte yelled at the boys while sprinting in their direction. "*Vengan pa' ca. Les quiero hablar.*"

The boys looked up and saw a bear of a man moving curiously fast toward them.

They looked at each other, then ran.

"*¡No se vayan!*" Monte yelled, but they were too far away for him to catch up.

"See, what did I tell you—those damn Mexicans, they ain't like us, man," Monte exclaimed in strained breaths as he walked back toward the family, still assembled around Betty.

"You would do the same thing if you were hungry," Miguel offered.

"Hungry! That's no excuse to kill birds and frighten all the other kids here!" Gilda yelled back.

"Miguel, those kids should be put away for doing this," Berta added. "You don't kill pigeons in America. You just don't do that. This is not Mexico."

"Well, not too long ago it used to be," Miguel continued, trying to be patient. He knew people expected him to react wildly whenever a subject like this came up. "Besides, Berta, you still got family in Mexico, don't you? Listen, these people are hungry. It sucks when barefoot kids have to kill pigeons in the park so they can eat. Instead of getting mad about the damn pigeons, what about those kids?"

"Sure, bro', but I got my own problems," Monte said, his breathing returning to normal. He swaggered toward the cooler, then continued. "I'm sorry, but they're going to have to learn to be American or get the hell out—that's just the way I feel about it."

Miguel paused for a minute, then turned toward the meat patties and wieners on the grill. He turned them over and remarked, "My brother . . . a real *engabachado*. An America-love-it-or-leave-it kind of guy."

Monte ignored his brother, sat down on one of the benches and grabbed another bottle from the melting ice. He again noticed Socorro, staring off into the distance, quiet, unobtrusive. Out of place.

"Señora, you want a beer?" he asked.

Socorro didn't turn around or acknowledge Monte's question. She glared straight ahead, into the trees, into someplace else, among the heart-shaped faces of another land. As Socorro's mind wandered, she drowned out the arguing between brothers, Berta's worried tones, and the children's cries—beyond Arroyo Seco Park, beyond the din of freeway traffic, beyond the dead pigeons.

MISS EAST L.A.

My place is too small and cramped to even light up a cigarette. It's a single room on the first floor of a two-story house in a place called the Gully, on Bernal Street just below the Fourth Street bridge. This is the White Fence neighborhood, one of the original barrios of East L.A. There are a lot of longtime residents here—I'm talking four or five generations. I've seen grandmothers with old pachuco tattoos up and down their arms, screaming after their grandkids to come home on time.

A lot of the men here work construction. They've built skyscrapers, freeways, roads, and houses all over Los Angeles—with not much to show for it. So, with all the skills they've gathered over time, they stucco their wood-frame homes or dry wall an extra room or whatever—most of the time without permits or inspectors.

That's how parts of East L.A. got built in the first place. The Mexicans moved into the most undesirable areas like the ravines and hills and set up their own housing, sometimes without plumbing or sewage. Eventually, the city and county provided basic services. So it's not unusual for small, dilapidated homes to be torn down, added on to, undergo a metamorphosis—like butterflies. If there's anything Mexicans are known for, it's hard work and creativeness.

I've lived here all my life. Not far from downtown is General Hospital—now it's the University of Southern California–Los Angeles County Medical Center. A lot of Chicanos inhaled their very first breath there—and exhaled their last. It's the cheapest and the most overworked hospital in the city. Our hospital. East L.A.'s.

I was born there.

One thing about me is that I've always wanted to be different. I don't want to end up like my *jefito* who worked as a laborer all his life. He worked hard, I give him credit for that, but I want to do something else with my life.

If you can believe this, my goal is to become a writer. I know this sounds crazy. My family thinks so. When I used to be in the *clica,* the White Fence Termites, I got into some trouble and even did county camp time as a juvenile. My dad and mom got mad and everything, but they never threw me out of the house. Later, when I told them I wanted to quit work to be a writer, I was out in the street like a flea-sick dog.

"Writing is for bums, for *chuntarros,*" my father yelled, while watching me leave the pad, duffel bag in hand. "You should work like a man—with your hands."

The thing is I wanted to be a writer even before I knew what writing was about. I wanted to carve out the words that swam in the bloodstream, to press a stunted pencil onto paper so lines break free like birds in flight—to fashion words like hair, lengths and lengths of it, washed with dawn's rusting drizzle.

I yearned for mortared-lined words, speaking in their own boasting tongues, not the diminished, frightened stammering of my childhood—to shape scorching syllables with midnight dust. Words that stood up in bed, danced merengues and cumbias, that incinerated the belly like a shimmering habanera. Words with a spoonful of tears, buckshot, boners, traces of garlic, cilantro, aerosol spray, and ocean froth. Words that guffawed, tarnished smooth faces, and wrung song out of silence. Words as languid as a woman's stride, as severe as a convict's gaze, herniated like a bad plan, soaked as in a summer downpour.

I aspired to walk inside these words, to manipulate their internal organs, surrounded by blood, gray matter, and caesuras; to slam words down like the bones of a street domino game—and to crack them in two like lover's hearts.

Wanting and doing are two different things.

ama has her own doubts. She doesn't mind that I want to write. She just doesn't know any writers, and she wonders how writers can live without a constant paycheck, which is a good point. But one day, fairly desperate, I didn't go back to my job loading boxes of fruit and vegetables off trucks at the downtown docks; I decided to get a writer's job, no matter what.

I had taken night writing courses at East Los Angeles College. In high school, my English teachers said I was good at writing. And, like all writers, I read all the time. So I figured, I could do this.

There is a free community newspaper sent to our home every week. It's called the *Eastside Star*. Besides pages and pages of ads, the paper actually has articles about local things: people who get married, divorced, or dead. It even has an advice column by a "Tía Tita."

The newspaper is on the first floor of a renovated warehouse on Brooklyn Avenue (now called Cesar Chavez Avenue—but I haven't quite got used to this yet). One day a few weeks ago, I walked into their office. I just pushed in a large wooden door, me with a white shirt and tie, which made my dark skin and thick wavy hair stand out—my family is from Puebla where *prietos* abound. A plump but pretty Chicana sat behind a desk stacked with papers on the other side of a wood partition.

"I'm looking for a job," I exclaimed, confidence pouring out of me like sweat (actually, it was sweat).

The woman stopped what she was doing. She threw me a look, you know, as if I was El Cucui come for her firstborn child.

"What kind of job?" she haltingly asked.

"I want to be a reporter—I can do feature stories or hard news. I can even take pictures."

"Hold on a minute."

She picked up the phone and whispered to someone on the other end of the line. I scanned the place—it had character. There were a few certificates on the wall, dusty, but impressive. Stacks of newspapers in one corner. A handful of desks, all weighed down by boxes, typewriters, phones, and papers. Just like a real newsroom, I thought.

"Mr. Galvan will see you," the woman said. "He's the publisher. Through those doors, *por favor.*"

My nerves jumped like drunken crickets. I went through the doors, which suggested a bigger suite than the one I had actually entered. There was hardly room for the massive desk against a bare window. Mr. Galvan, a graying, full-head-of-hair dude, like Cesar Romero, looked up at me with a faint trace of a smile.

"You want to be a reporter . . . have you ever done this kind of work before?" Mr. Galvan inquired.

"Yes, I mean, I worked for the high school newspaper, and I wrote some articles for the college paper," I replied.

Then I added, with pride, "I even had a letter to the editor printed in the *Daily News*."

"Well, it just so happens that I'm looking for someone to fill a position," Mr. Galvan said, rather casually. Before I had time to take a breath, he continued.

"But we can only offer you a hundred dollars a week, no benefits, and you also have to sweep the floors, take out the trash, answer phones, solicit ads, and paste up boards. What do you say?"

I was making $250 a week, with overtime, on the docks.

"I'll take it."

I said I was crazy, didn't I?

W orking at the *Eastside Star* barely provides for cigarettes, booze, and rent. The room I'm staying at is only a couple of blocks from my parents' house, even though I hardly visit them, except to get some of Mama's great mole. I feel I have to prove to them and to myself that being a writer is the best thing I can do.

The problem is you can take the boy out of the barrio, but you can't take the barrio out of the boy.

"You gotta leave now," I'm explaining to my *jaina*, a P.Y.T. named Sunni Lopez.

"Why? There's still some time left, *ese*," Sunni responds, in her usual gruff manner.

"Look, I have a lot of things to do so if you don't mind."

"But I don't want to leave just yet."

"I don't care what you want—I want you out of here!" I raise my voice.

"That sounds good, but I'm not going till I'm ready," she responds, her hand on a hip and a I-dare-you-to-yell-at-me-again look on her face.

"Oh, did you forget? This is my place."

"Well, let's just see if you're man enough to throw me out."

"What is it with you? You always want me to push you around or something."

"Be a man then." People around me seem to bring this up a lot, don't they, about being a man.

"I don't have to hit you to be a man."

"Then stop sniveling—you don't want me around, then make me leave . . . I'd like to see you try."

This is Sunni and me going through our standard routine. She is constantly pushing my buttons so that I will smack her and prove, in her eyes, I'm a man. Most of the time, I just ignore her or tell her this is stupid, all this arguing. Once, though, I must admit, I did hit her. Not hard. It was more like a push. I didn't feel good about it afterward, but then Sunni curled up next to me, called me "baby," and stroked my chest. What a life, huh? What a relationship! My mama taught me never to hit a woman or a child. And here I am kicking it with somebody who wants me to knock her around. Sometimes, though, I feel like really letting her have it—like right now.

But no, I walk out the back door for a smoke. After a few drags of a cigarette, I reenter my room and try again.

"Okay, Sunni, let's make a deal," I say. "You leave now and I'll pick you up after work. We can go out. Get *pedotes*. And come back and make crazy love. What do you say?"

"Benny, you really are a pussy," Sunni says, gathering up a large leather bag.

Sunni is an extraordinarily good looker, which is why I tolerate so much bullshit from her. A homegirl originally from the Aliso Village housing projects, she is part black, part Mexican. She joined the White Fence gang while we were in high school. She's always been tough. That's where the "be a man" stuff comes from.

Sunni's assets are her large hips, thighs, and breasts; she's what they call "big boned." But this also makes her a hard lady to knock down. I actually think she can kick my ass if we ever have a real knockdown, drag-out. She tries to get me there, getting close to my face when we argue. But nothing comes of it. One thing I learned, though, is that Sunni likes it when people stand up to her.

Sunni was the only one who stuck it out with me when the rest of the homies considered me too "out of it" to hang with. She was the only one who *wanted* me to be a writer.

This particular day, I'm eager to get to work. After weeks of carrying out trash, pasting up ads, and taking phone calls, Mr. Galvan finally wants me to come up with a feature story idea. His newspaper runs news and other information only when it will sell advertising space. The popular bilingual advice column from Tía Tita is actually written by a man, Genaro, the only Spanish-speaking staff writer on board.

The *Star* has tons of ads for used cars, furniture (with deals almost as bad as borrowing money from crooked shylocks), and supermarkets. Its thriving classified section also carries small announcements for *curanderas,* fortune-tellers, and "under the table" house rehab crews.

But every once in a while, Mr. Galvan will run an original researched piece of some interest to the community. This is what

I've been waiting for—I didn't want anything or anybody, including Sunni, to make me blow it.

"Drop me off at my crib, then," Sunni says, still angry as we head outside.

We go to the backyard where I've parked my lowrider 1975 Toyota Corolla. It's actually a rusty blue number with overhanging tires, encircling chrome rims so that it looks like I'm cruising all the time—although the Toyota doesn't go too fast as it is. Sunni is pissed off at me all the way to her home, but I don't worry. Tonight she'll be back to her old loving self.

"*Hola,* Benny, you're on time today, what gives?" asks Amelia, the receptionist who greeted me the first time I'd entered the newspaper's office. Over these past weeks, we've become friends. For one thing, she's good for the *chismorreo*—which, as anyone knows, is what good reporting is really all about.

"Hey, Benny, you missed some fun already," Amelia begins. "Galvan found out about Dario."

"What . . . that our dear managing editor has been humping the publisher's wife," I say.

"*Simón,* and on top of that, Galvan came in and fired Dario this morning—on the spot."

"*No me digas.*"

"Not only that, after he fired him, Galvan had the nerve to punch Dario in the mouth. *¡Un chingaso, pero bien dado!* Dario fell down, then got up, and Galvan hit him again. *¡Zas!* Then Dario went down and everybody, including Genaro and me, kept telling him to stay down, stay down, but he got up, and Galvan walloped him again. Finally, Dario stayed down while Galvan stormed out of here. Genaro had to walk Dario to his car so he could go home and take care of his fat lip. *¿Que escándalo, no?*"

Like I say, Amelia is good for the *chisme.*

As I move toward my desk, Genaro, a middle-aged, heavyset, wire-haired man, and the only experienced journalist among us—he wrote political commentary for a newspaper in Mexico before receiving death threats and exiling himself to Los Angeles—wants to know my opinion on something.

"Benjamin Franklin Pineda . . . *¿cómo lo ves?*" he says, knowing full well that I hate to be called by my birth name (my father had a sense of humor, *¿qué no?*).

Genaro displayed on his desk a photo of a man's beaten-up head, without a body, its eyes painted open, and a bad drawing of a bow tie where the neck should be.

"It looks sick, Genaro," I respond. "Where do you come up with these things?"

The decapitated head was discovered behind a trash bin in an alley off Soto Street. The police asked the newspaper for help in identifying the victim. So Genaro figures he can place the photo—with its goofy additions—on the front page next to a cutline that reads: "Does anyone know whose body this belongs to?"

"Genaro, I think you should stick to just doing Tía Tita columns," I say.

"*¡Ay, Chihuahua! No tienes la menor idea de como ganar lectores,*" he replies.

There's never a dull moment at the *Eastside Star.*

I'm not sure what I'm going to write about for the feature. I've picked up the morning editions of other newspapers to see if anything strikes me. But it's a slow news day. No mud slides, no corruption cases, no major exposés. Before this day I had tons of ideas; now that I have a chance to actually pull something together, I'm at a loss.

Then Rigoberto, the *Star*'s layout guy, who used to work in the production department of a newspaper in Guatemala—another exile—comes down the stairs from the layout room.

"Benny, how you doing, *vos*?" he says in his heavily accented English.

"Cool, Rigo, just looking for some story ideas—you got any?" I ask.

"Well, I saw something that may interest you," Rigoberto replies, stopping by my desk and rifling through the stack of newspapers. He picks through a few and then takes out the weekend's *Los Angeles Times*. In the Metro section there is an important item, something I had missed, which is not hard to do after I've been partying with Sunni for a couple of days. The article has a photo of an attractive Chicana face and a headline that reads, "Miss East L.A. Found Murdered."

The story begins: *Police say the 18-year-old recently crowned queen of East Los Angeles was found stabbed to death Saturday night at the Central City Hospital where she worked as a nurse's aide.*

According to the account, Emily Contreras, a recent graduate of Wilson High School, was discovered during the night shift with numerous stab wounds, lying on a hospital bed in an empty room. A twenty-one-year-old orderly, Daniel Amaya, was also stabbed a few times but survived. Contreras was selected Miss East L.A. only a couple of months ago after a controversial race.

It seems incredible, but somebody has offed our queen!

"You know, I think you got something here, Rigo," I say.

The Miss East L.A. pageant was actually an entertaining affair this year. At first a rather unattractive, plain-looking teenager won the crown. This brought up more than a few eyebrows—the *comadres* with their *veri veri* had a field day. This vision of unloveliness turned up on TV and everything. Most people just couldn't believe she was the one selected, which is okay, I suppose, if you consider how sexist these contests are to begin with.

But later it's revealed that the winner was the niece of one of the judges, who apparently rigged the voting. Looking at the judge's pock-faced mug in the newspapers, you knew they were related. So *la reina* had to resign and the runner-up, Emily Contreras, was declared the new winner.

Only now she's dead.

Mr. Galvan had designated Genaro temporary managing editor of the newspaper before the incident with Dario, so after apologizing for not seeing the thoughtfulness of Genaro's dealing with the bodiless head, I ask him for permission to follow up on the Miss East L.A. murder case.

"Esta bien, ya lárgate," Genaro exclaims.

The police are not much help to reporters. And since the *Eastside Star* is not considered a "legitimate" newspaper, like the *Times* or the Spanish-language daily, *La Opinión,* my chances of getting information from them is . . . well, *olvídate.*

But I have an ace in the hole—a cousin of mine is a detective in the homicide division. It's good to have family in key places.

I decide to jump into my blue "Toyot" and visit him.

"I came to see Detective Davila," I say to the desk officer.

"He knows you were coming?" he asks.

"Well, not exactly . . ."

"Then I don't know if you can see him. He's really busy," the officer replies. "Why don't you tell me what you want, and I'll see if he can talk to you."

Telling him I work for the *Eastside Star* did not make this any easier.

Finally, after what seems like an hour, a young Chicano, in a suit jacket, blue jeans, with badge and gun on his belt, and carefully combed hair, approaches. It's my *primo,* Detective Raymundo Davila.

"*¿Qué hubo,* Benny?" says Mundo, which is the shortened version of his name. He has an outstretched hand and a distrustful rise in an eyebrow. "What in the world brings you here?"

"I guess you haven't heard; I work for the *Eastside Star* now," I say.

"Oh, I heard. I also heard how you broke your mother's heart taking this job."

"Man, not you, too," I respond. "Listen, being a writer is a good profession . . ."

"Save it, *ese,*" Mundo interrupts. "I went through the same thing trying to be a cop, remember?"

Mundo has a point—he was also expected to work in the construction trades like my dad and Mundo's father. Hard-ass work with one's hands was the only kind of business allowed in our families. Being a cop just didn't compute—neither did a writer.

"*Simón,* I remember," I ease. "Well, I came for some help. You know about the Emily Contreras murder—Miss East L.A.?"

"Sure, we're working on it right now."

"I'm looking for information on this case, what really happened. You know, whatever is available as far as suspects and motives . . . that kind of thing. I want to do a big story."

"Well, you ought to know, *primo,* that we normally don't give out 'that kind of thing,'" Mundo says, walking away.

"But I understand you guys will be helping us with the decapitated head case," Mundo turns toward me, and smirks. "So let me find out what I can do for you, all right?"

Genaro, I think, you're an angel with that headless story. Oh, and did I mention it's also good to have family in key places?

Mundo gestures for me to enter his office, a cluttered, small cubicle with wood paneling from top to bottom.

"According to the coroner's office, Contreras was found with seventeen stab wounds in her neck and chest," Mundo explains, getting right to business. "One puncture went directly through her heart. The perpetrators apparently entered the room where Contreras was taking a nap. She worked late. The orderly on duty at the time told her to rest while he kept watch. The perps apparently also attacked the orderly, who was found in the corridor with minor stab wounds to his arms and chest. He says there were at least three attackers, men with masks. They killed Contreras and ran out. There are no other witnesses at this time."

I wait for a few seconds. Mundo looks at me with a tired expression.

"And?" I finally say.

"And what? That's all there is."

"No suspects? No idea of why anyone might want to do this? Nothing?"

"It's under investigation," Mundo says, putting the paperwork away into a file that he casually throws on top of a stack barely balancing on his desk. "That's all we got for now. You should be glad I gave you this much. One thing, *primo*, you can't mention anything about the number and location of the stab wounds. We need this information to help confirm a possible suspect. You understand what I'm saying?"

I nod.

"Now if you don't mind, I have a lot of work to do," Mundo says, rising to his feet. "Say *qué hubo* to your mom and dad for me, all right?"

That night, I tell Sunni about the story, and she's intrigued. As always, she has a number of theories on what may have happened.

She paces back and forth.

"I bet you it was a contract hit," she proposes, her imagination getting the better of her. "The queen contest was a fix, right? Maybe there was some money involved. And having her get the crown was blowing it for some people in high places."

"Too farfetched," I counter, while I sit immersed in an old, mildewed bathtub a few feet from where Sunni is pacing. "But it's strange that three men would come into the place and kill her, almost in plain sight. I know it was late, but it is a hospital. Where were the nurses, the doctors, or the patients? Something's fishy."

"I got another idea," she says, excited about the prospect. "Maybe, just maybe, she was snuffed out by the uncle of the girl who had to resign. You know, hire a few vatos. Get the queen. He'd be pissed off, right?"

At this point anybody could have killed Miss East L.A., even Sunni. I realize I have to talk to the one witness in the case, the orderly who was also stabbed. Knowing the police, and especially Mundo, I didn't think I would get much help from them on this.

The next day, my Toyot is parked in front of Central City Hospital. Using my skills as an investigative reporter, I forage through the employee file box while the receptionist is talking to the nurse's supervisor, asking if I can discuss the incident with her. So far the hospital has been hush-hush about the killing. I know I won't get any statement from them, but I do find an address for Daniel Amaya, the orderly.

Amaya lives in Maravilla. This is rough territory. Maravilla has a bunch of rival gangs—the biggest is El Hoyo Mara, after the "hole" the residents found refuge in a few generations back. Amaya lives in the barrio known as Marianna Mara. Still, being White Fence, despite my inactivity, I'm *trucha* about where I go and with whom I talk. But I'm a reporter. Somehow I have to get the story.

I wear a long-sleeve shirt to hide the *clica*'s tattoo on my arm from coming up in the 'hood. I'm not into "the life" anymore. But like a lot of old homeboys, I still carry the "tats" and scars.

I park in front of a tiny shingled house. There is a wooden archway over the sidewalk outside the front door. A grapevine with small buds of new black grapes curls around the archway. An unpainted wooden fence surrounds the place. Colored flowers and ornate ceramic pots are scattered around the yard, suggesting the hand of a Mexican gardener.

An old woman gently opens the door after I've knocked for several minutes. In Spanish, I ask if Daniel lives there and if he's available for a few questions. It turns out this woman is Daniel's grandmother, small and thin-boned, with deeply creviced brown skin on her face and hands. Daniel lives in an even smaller place out in back. I follow the woman through a walkway surrounded by intense gardenias, roses, and cactuses.

Daniel answers the door quickly as if he's been standing near it. He looks at me intently, suspiciously. His arm is wrapped and in a sling. Despite the alleged ferocity of the attack, there are no bruises or cuts on his face, which is boyish except for acne scars. His grandmother returns to the front house. Standing in the doorway, Daniel is reluctant to talk.

"I've already told the police everything," he says, with a slightly nervous tone in his voice. Otherwise, he's calm. "Why do I have to talk to you?"

"You don't have to talk to me, Daniel," I say. "But I'm doing this story and it would be good if I could get some comments from the one witness. It's up to you. How about it?"

Daniel contemplates this for a while. I'm thinking I have to concoct some scheme to get him to talk when, to my surprise, he opens up.

"I was working the late shift. It was around two A.M. There was only Emily and me on that section of the floor," he says. "The nurses station is around the corner by the elevators. I could see Emily was tired. She had been real busy since she was named the new queen. I told her to rest for a few minutes in one of the empty rooms.

"There's a back stairway, which is only available for employees. I think the three men broke in there and then walked up. Probably on the stairs, they changed into dark coats and masks. Nobody downstairs saw anybody with those coats on in the waiting area. Anyway, I come out of a patient's room; before I know it a masked man is stabbing me with a knife. He is cutting me on my arm and on my chest. I fall down. I'm hurtin', and I don't know what's happenin'. The man drops his knife and leaves; he meets up with two others, who come out of the room where Emily was sleeping. Then all three of them run down the stairs. It happened so fast. The nurses come running; one of them screams. I didn't realize until later that the two other men had already killed Emily. She was asleep and I didn't hear any noise from inside the room."

I ask Daniel a few questions: Why didn't he yell for help? Did the men say anything? Did any patients hear the noise? What happened to the knife that was dropped?

I don't get much more out of Daniel. I then ask him: "Who do you think would want to kill Emily?"

At this, Daniel looks at me strangely, as if he's trying to read my mind. He then says he has to leave now, that he's had it with these questions, and he would appreciate it if he weren't bothered again.

"Listen, I'm afraid they might come back to get me," he adds as he closes the door.

T he next day I visit Mundo to find out if there is any more on the investigation. I had just come back from downtown doing research at the library about the Miss East L.A. pageant. I'm really getting into this story. For some reason after I enter the police station, Mundo is standing there, as if he's been waiting for me. He again invites me into his cubicle.

"Yeah, we definitely got something," he says, only in not so helpful a tone as the last time. "But I'm pissed off at you, *ese.*"

"Why?" I ask, although I already know the answer.

"You went to see Daniel Amaya," he looks at me, more as cop than cousin. "What did he say to you?"

"Now, Mundo, you know as a reporter I have the right to talk to him," I respond. "And you also know that I have the right not to tell you what he said. So what's up? What's the latest on this?"

"Well, you're my cousin, *ese*, but I also have the right not to tell you anything," Mundo says. "The thing is we have a pretty good idea about what happened and why. But I can't tell you just yet. Check with me later. I would appreciate it, though, if you let us deal with this case. We don't want anything to mess up our investigation. Can you do that for me?"

I agree and excuse myself from Mundo's office. I walk fast toward the exit. I can feel Mundo's eyes on my back.

I go home. I should go see Sunni, but I'm not sure I want to. She gets me angry and confused about most things.

After a few chugs on a tequila bottle, I begin to calm down. Well, I wanted to be a writer, didn't I? I just can't seem to piece together what happened to Emily—although I feel I'm at the entrance of a big door where just beyond it lay all the answers. I'm just so new at this that I can't see a way to get through that door.

I lie down on a pile of blankets on the bed. The tequila is loosening me up. I begin to think. By then I had interviewed more people, including the pageant officials, a couple of the princesses, and even the crooked judge (in case he had a guilty look—which he didn't). I also talked to Emily's family—her mother, father, and younger brothers. Although Mundo says they have a break in the case, I still haven't pinned down why someone would want to kill Emily.

I find out that Emily was a good student at Wilson. She was active in student affairs, particularly the Chicano student group and the school newspaper. If she had lived, she may have been a writer, too.

She was extremely beautiful. Photos hang on the walls of the living room and kitchen of her house. Emily had honey-brown skin, elongated indigenous eyes, and a full perfect mouth. Her hair was thick, black, and long.

There is a photo of Emily in a black mariachi outfit, playing violin with other young mariachi musicians. Her mother shows me a newspaper clipping with Emily demonstrating for immigrant rights. She was a budding journalist, musician, and leader—she could have run for office, even become the first Chicana president. Everything I saw and heard emphasized her special nature, and how her death seemed so wrong, so unjust—just plain out of sync with the calling she apparently had in this world.

"She really cared about people, especially those who couldn't defend themselves," her mother states in between sobs.

It appears Emily also lived a decent home life. Her father works as an airplane mechanic; her mother is an involved member of the community, holding school-related meetings at her home. And the brothers are soccer and baseball stars in school. The family resides in a large, Spanish-tiled stucco house in El Sereno, moving from the Happy Valley neighborhood only a few years back when Dad first got the job at the airlines.

As a child, Emily grew up near Lincoln Park. A tomboy, she played rough with other children, throwing stones into the Lincoln Park lake, and running up and down the small grass slopes there. Her mother is the most articulate about her daughter's life. She wants to talk, to reminisce, to let Emily continue to live through her memory, her words. Her father, on the other hand, doesn't say anything. I can tell he's feeling terrible, but it's so personal and deep; I fear he will dissolve if he opens up to the tragedy.

I close my eyes; maybe if I sleep I can get beyond the facts into the real story.

Soon enough, I'm dreaming. I see the unmarred face of Emily Contreras. She is directing me toward a door with those dark eyes of hers. I open it slowly. Then I'm at the *Star* newsroom; Genaro, Amelia, and Rigoberto are there, laughing at me. I start to run. The streets are drenched; everywhere there's moisture, dripping from lampposts, from neon signs, from billboards. Soon I'm in the police station. It's dim and empty. I walk through a wood-paneled hallway. Mundo looks out from his office, staring at me. "We know who did it," he says, then he laughs. Now I'm in a hospital corridor. Sunni stumbles out of a room wearing a hospital gown, bleeding from her chest. "They stabbed me," she screams, then falls. Out of the room, behind her, comes Daniel. In one hand, he's got his grandmother's head.

Talk about cold sweats! I woke up soaked.

I've been working on the piece for the *Star* for days now. It's my first feature, and I want it to kick butt. This is East L.A., and nothing is as simple as it first appears. Questions of who, what, and when continue to accumulate around Emily Contreras's death.

Emily didn't seem to have any enemies; she was respectful, endearing. But in a place like East L.A., where almost everyone is from some part of Mexico, lives are entangled, rumors surface: Emily's dad smuggled diamonds on the airplanes. She had had an affair with a prominent businessman who wanted to end the relationship. A close uncle, doing time in San Quentin, may have flubbed a drug deal, resulting in Emily's sacrifice. Then there was the rumor that the police were trying to cover up a police shooting of an unarmed teenager near Emily's home, which she may have witnessed.

I want to provide more about Emily than a short newspaper item and photo. I want to breathe life back into Emily, so she appears to stroll through the living room of whoever reads about her.

So far, I'm the only one writing anything about Emily

Contreras. The *Times*'s story is weak; "their" Emily is just a face on a cardboard body.

Sunni continues to be belligerent, but when she reads what I've written so far, she says something she has never said to me before—"you're good."

Doing this story has got me thinking a lot about Emily, about the sweetness of her life and the tragedy of her death. It's got me thinking about all the various ways people can die in this town. Here death stalks us like a sullen figure over upturned sidewalks, like a sleepless guest that fades in and out of dreams—between the solid world and something fluid inside. I had an aunt, for example, who died in a diabetic torture—her eyes failed her and they removed her legs before her kidneys finally gave out. I had a neighbor who owned a taco stand and lost a husband to an armed robber, only to lose a son in another robbery sixteen years later. And there was a whole family—including a six-year-old and an eight-month-old—killed by rivals in a drug deal gone wrong.

Death is on the faces of small children and in the sage advice of old people. It lingers around every card game, converging at every corner, as part of every beer run, next to every family argument, behind every street encounter, and a likely result of every drug overdose or schoolyard dare. Death is like a shadow beneath the body, pulling us down toward its own ground, toward its own mouth, and articulating us in its own measured verses.

Whew . . . I think this story is really starting to get to me.

I'm lying in that ancient tub of mine, with cracked tiles surrounding me, letting the warmness of the soapy water seep through my bones, when it strikes me, this idea, preposterous and reasonable at the same time. It comes to me first in a flash. I try to think about something else, then the idea returns, refusing to go away.

What a dummy I am! I know now what Mundo was trying to keep from me.

I pull myself out of the tub, dry off quickly, and put on a pair of jeans, a loose shirt, and a denim jacket. I'm going to see someone who I believe holds the key to Emily's death. Before I do, I make a phone call.

I jump into the Toyot and take off like a mouse with a cat on its tail. I don't care about pedestrians, other cars or *nada*. This notion about who killed Emily is gnawing at me.

I drive a few miles to Maravilla. My mind goes over all the facts, the rumors, and the personalities surrounding the murder, and it all comes back to this—this one house, this one face.

I enter through the wood gate, walk beneath the archway, and swing around to the back. There's a light in the window of the small building there. Out of the shadows, someone emerges; it's Mundo.

"You may as well be in on this, *ese*," Mundo says, two uniformed police officers at his side. "But remember—you owe me."

Just like before, one knock and the door opens.

When Daniel sees Mundo and the officers, his face drops. He knows what they're here for. He tries to close the door, but Mundo rushes in, holding it open with his foot. I follow behind the other officers.

"Daniel Amaya, you're under arrest for the murder of Emily Contreras," Mundo says. He then proceeds to read him his rights while the officers turn Daniel around to cuff him.

Daniel has this look of incredulity, like if all of us have gone over the edge. But then his demeanor changes. He glances around the room, as if looking for something, a way to get around this. Then he drops his head and begins to cry.

I just stare at Daniel; everything is sharp and clear around him. His voice breaks through his sobs, loud and intrusive.

"Oh, I loved her so much," Daniel says, without looking up. "I tried damn hard to please her, to get her to see how much I cared. But she wouldn't even look at me—as if I didn't exist. I wrote her notes. I left her presents. But she didn't care. Then that contest, that *pinche* contest! She was getting all this attention. People would call. She would get visitors and compliments. All these guys started talking to her, flirting with her. I was just beginning to get her to notice me, and then this queen thing happened. I knew then that I had lost her."

Daniel looks up, a pained expression on his face.

"I just couldn't stand it," he continues. "I tried to talk to her, but she was cold. Being Miss East L.A., why would she bother with me, right? I told her this couldn't keep going on. I told her. I warned her. But she brushed it off. I just couldn't let her slip away from me, not when I was so close. . . ."

"So how did you do it?" Mundo interjects.

"Man, it was easy," he says, confidently, as if coming to terms with something. "After a while I began to see how I was meant to take Emily away from here. I was doing her a favor, you understand! She wouldn't know real love without me. There are only liars and manipulators out there. Schemers all of them. So that night I told her to take a rest. I knew she was tired. I even had the room ready for her. At first she wouldn't listen to me, but she finally said okay, that she would rest for a few minutes. I said I would keep a watch out for the nurses. It was a slow night. There were no patients on that side of the floor. I waited until Emily lay down, waited until I knew she was asleep; she fell out fast that's how tired she was. Then I went into the room. It was dark. But I knew where she was. I put on surgical gloves. Then I took out a knife that had been held by rubber bands on my leg. I walked up to her and without saying anything, I stabbed her—hard, and as many times as I could. I remember feeling the knife enter, how soft her body was, how easily the blade went in and out. I hardly hit bone. I just kept stabbing, placing my hand over her mouth in case she woke up to scream. It happened so fast, I didn't think about it at all. Then I ran out of the room, and I stabbed my chest and arm."

"That's why the wounds weren't deep," I say. "Because you'd done it to yourself."

"I almost had everyone fooled, didn't I?" Daniel continues, suddenly as if he were talking about a prank he may have pulled on a friend. "I threw the knife on the ground because I couldn't get rid of it after stabbing myself. I took off the gloves and hid them in my shoe. I could see blood everywhere. I knew it was Emily's and mine—our blood together. You see I needed Emily so much. She should have listened to me. She should have loved me."

Daniel stops, closes his eyes and sobs. The police officers pull him outside by his arms, followed by Mundo. As they prepare to leave, neighbors gather behind fences and parked cars; the only sounds are their whispers, police radio dispatches, and the din of insects. I look up—a slight woman with webbed lines across her face peers through a window in the front house. She sees me, then rapidly closes the curtain, which look like the wings of a ghostly angel turning away.

A má, you make the best mole," I declare.

Sunni and me are celebrating—my story's on the front page of the *Eastside Star,* with pictures from Emily's home and everything. And where else would we be celebrating but at mama's house, eating her poblana-style cuisine, guzzling down some brews, and enjoying the good life in the White Fence barrio.

"That's right, ma'am, this is *soo* good," Sunni adds.

My dad is quiet, but every once in a while he gazes at the newspaper spread across the table. I know there's a *grano* of pride in him somewhere. He won't say it, but I believe my writing life has hit a high mark in this family.

The article appeared the week following Daniel's arrest. It was better than any other news piece on Emily. I was even offered a chance to enroll in a journalism program for emerging writers at the University of California, Berkeley. Nobody in the neighborhood has ever had such an opportunity.

"You did a helluva story, Benny," Sunni chimes in. "Only if you had listened to me sooner, you would have long figured out that crazy orderly'd done it."

"What you clamoring about now," I respond. "You didn't know he had anything to do with it. You were going on about contract hits and judges out to get people and all that nonsense."

"Now don't start with me, Benny boy, I was giving you the general direction to look—you were just too dumb to figure it out."

"*I'm* dumb . . . the one who has the front page story, who's being recruited to U.C. Berkeley. Yeah, sure, I'm the dumb guy."

"Don't throw that at me—you may think you're so damn smart but I'll have your ass all over this street, *ese,*" Sunni shouts—while Dad gets closer to his food and my mother practically runs into the kitchen to heat up more tortillas.

"Talking tough and doing nothing—that's all you ever do," I say, stuffing a tortilla full of mole and chicken into my mouth.

"Come on then, punk," Sunni stands up. "I'll take you out right now—in front of your family, God, and the whole barrio. I'll show you who don't do nothing."

I get up, wipe my mouth with a napkin, and step outside for a smoke.

LA OPERACIÓN

Más vale ser cabeza de ratón y no cola de león
(It's better to be the head of a mouse than the tail
of a lion)

MEXICAN SAYING

Four sweat-drenched men quietly examined the door of a
flatbed truck that had been almost pulled from its
hinges. Moments earlier they had pushed the truck back
away from a cinder block wall where it was parked. The plan had
been to move it toward a nearby car, use jumper cables to attach
the truck's dead battery to the good one, and charge it. But Julio,
in his midtwenties with unruly hair, had left the door on the
driver's side of the truck open: He forgot about the dirt-rimmed,
cast-iron bathtub that lay on the ground next to the truck. The
driver's-side door was snagged by the tub then bent back as the
men pushed harder. Only Julio's pained yells stopped them from
tearing the door completely off.

The men assembled around the crumpled door, staring at it

for a considerable spell. Wicho, Julio's younger brother, whose hair was just as wild, wanted to say something, but he looked up at his brother and brothers-in-law, Domingo and Rafas, and realized this wasn't a time for words. So he leaned back on his heels, crossed his arms around his chest, and also contemplated the damage.

Wicho and the others just stood there, without a need to get excited or try to fix anything. Perhaps, also, a solution would present itself from inside the men's silence, a kind of "country" rumination that they had brought with them from Cerro Espinoza, their village in southern Chihuahua, Mexico. Even so, Wicho went through the possible fallout from the fuck up in his head, including the firestorm of his father's wrath that was sure to come.

Not a pleasant thought.

The truck was an income provider. Wicho's father, Carlos Padilla, had bought it from a neighbor soon after they had settled in the East L.A. hills. Rusty and unused for at least a decade, Carlos and the other men worked on the truck day and night. Somehow they got it running. They also put in the wood railings so the truck could haul large items and people.

For a fee, the men used the truck to carry trash to the dump from deep in the hills. They also moved furniture for their neighbors when needed. And sometimes they transported the women and elderly from their isolated homes to the bus lines on the main drags of Gage Avenue, City Terrace Drive, or Chavez Avenue. Although Domingo and Rafas worked at day labor jobs to complement their meager pay, the truck was the main breadwinner.

Carlos, his sons, and *yernos* were part of two families from Cerro Espinoza—the Oronas and the Padillas—that had recently arrived in the United States. Several members of these interrelated families lived in makeshift shacks behind other homes on De Garmo Street. The local *pandilla* called this barrio La Juarez Mara. The families built their homes out of wood planks, corrugated steel, drywall, and chicken wire; and they tapped into the electrical lines and pipelines of a few houses that lined the street.

The brothers, Julio and Wicho Padilla, lived in two of the shacks with their father as well as their respective wives, Juana and Marta. Their sisters Laurina and Josefina along with their husbands, Domingo and Rafas Orona, also brothers, and a small brood of brown children lived in two other shacks. Exposed wires hung from household to household and linked them to a nearby utility pole. They had no phones or hot water, but they were able to use the facilities in the front houses, home to U.S.-born and naturalized families, who rented them the empty back lots next to a dirt-and-stone bluff.

The jobs for the family truck also spread over to the other side of Gage Avenue where there were more hills speckled with homes—some makeshift like theirs—in the Gerahty Loma neighborhood. As they drove through the winding roads, the names of the local vatos like Thumps, Woody, Froggy, Scooby, Surdo, Sharks, and Payaso graced many a wall.

People around here got to know the Padillas and Oronas quite well for their services, the sweat of their brow, and the horsepower in their truck's engine.

As it turned out, the Padillas and Oronas were among several million Mexicans in the United States who every day sent significant portions of their salaries to their former villages and ranchitos. Hometown social clubs "on the other side" have sprouted all over—more than five hundred such clubs existed by the end of the twentieth century. The clubs represented many home states and villages. They hailed from Oaxaca, Guerrero, Nuevo Leon, Chihuahua, Sonora, Guanajuato, Sinaloa, Michoacán, Zacatecas—from almost every state in the republic. Most of their villages did not have running water or electricity—something the official government had been unable or unwilling to provide for years—until the clubs started the flow of funds. Most recently, some state governments have matched, peso for peso, any support sent from abroad.

On this unusually clear smogless Saturday, Wicho looked up from where he and the other men were evaluating the truck's condition. He liked to take in downtown's multilayered skyscrapers that crept up over a hill, shots of the sun's rays gleaming off the steel and glass. Wicho felt that the neighborhood, despite the seclusion and poverty, had its charm. Around a corner was a broken camper, boarded up; a small lived-in shed lay below street level next to it, surrounded by poles with carved horses that had probably been part of a merry-go-round.

Below them lay a massive ravine where countless houses, melancholy roofs, beaten woodsheds, and other structures cluttered the terrain. Roosters crowed, dogs howled, and children yelled from inside the scenery, saturated with sun.

Despite the distance from their village, and being removed from a much slower routine life, Wicho felt good about being here. As long as they worked.

Work was all these families had ever known. First as dirt farmers in Cerro Espinoza where they once owned a milpa of corn—what their ancestors had done for thousands of years. But over time, with the unstable fluctuations in the grain markets, the price of corn fell and they lost everything. Soon the families had to leave the pueblo to find work elsewhere.

After following the crops and construction projects—for pay between two to four dollars a day—they eventually ended up in Ciudad Juárez on the Texas-Chihuahua border. The Oronas and Padillas tried and failed at numerous moneymaking ventures in Juarritos (what the locals called their city)—such as selling wares, digging ditches, and fixing leaky roofs.

Carlos finally convinced everyone to risk the arduous trek to *el otro lado*—this was the only choice left if they were to survive. Carlos knew they had to make it to Los Angeles or Chicago, the big cities, where many paisanos found their way to labor, to hide, protected by sheer numbers, if nothing else.

To Carlos, *la frontera* was a living, breathing flesh of earth, cut deep by conquests, lies, politics, and racial interests, a festering sore that had never healed, had never closed up or scarred over. Here things changed often—*colonias* on both sides came and went; neighbors who put down what looked like strong roots would be gone by daybreak. Love could hardly ever last—it was mostly fugitive love, undocumented love, migrant and momentary. Women were particularly vulnerable to predators here—including the killing kind, as hundreds of women's bodies were found buried in scattered sites in and around Ciudad Juárez.

The border spoke a special language, a refugee tongue, written on scabbed and broken feet. It spoke on darkened faces and the age lines around the eyes of young people. And what it said was death. Hundreds have died crossing the border. Many were struck trying to traverse newly paved highways and interstates. Others drowned in the fast moving waters of the Río Bravo—or beaten in parking lots, shot by vigilantes or robbed by area gangs. Sometimes they were killed by border patrol officials, police, or in one infamous case, by Marines (who actually shot a local sheepherder in the Texas side of the border by "mistake").

In the Arizona desert, the sun feels like it's squatting on top of the land, blistering the ground and rooftops and skin. Even weeks before summer charges in, the temperatures can hit a merciless 125 degrees. In an area bigger than Connecticut and Rhode Island put together, there is nothing but sparse inferno— interrupted in parts by low mountains, bone-dry arroyos, saguaros, greasewood bushes, twisted ironwoods, and the occasional paloverde tree. Yet thousands of migrants trample through here every year. And many have succumbed to exposure—there were several highly publicized deaths of migrants left by thieving smugglers in locked boxcars or tractor-trailers—or simply stranded on the scorching landscape.

This is what the Oronas and Padillas, with their wives and children, had to face if they went along with Carlos. For his part, Carlos relied on his border experiences, although limited, to help. When he was younger, Carlos had come across a few times to work the fields in California's Imperial and Coachella valleys.

So for a couple of days, Carlos entered the pieced-together cardboard, plastic, and particleboard homes of newly arrived refugees. He talked to the desperate waiting to cross after dusk; he caught up with the latest info about tears in the border wall, about trustworthy *polleros*—the people smugglers—many of whom, as mentioned already, were unreliable or crooked.

It was a Salvadoran man—Hector Calderon—who turned out to offer the best assistance. Lean, wiry, and full of energy, Hector told Carlos he was an expert border jumper—"three times *mo-*

jado," he declared with pride—having gone across the Salvadoran, Guatemalan, and Mexican borders numerous times.

"I only take small numbers, people whose faces I trust," explained Hector. "And I'll tell you—I've learned to trust faces more than words."

Carlos, too, had learned this, and he believed Hector could be trusted.

When the deal was struck, the Oronas and Padillas put together five hundred dollars per person—all they had left over after several months work away from Cerro Espinoza. This was far less than any other group of *pollos*—or chickens, as the migrants are called—would be expected to pay. But Hector had long-range relationships with his "clients"—his real profit came when the migrants sent U.S. dollars back home. Hector also helped arrange this—people to the north, dollars to the south.

"By night we go," Hector told Carlos. "By day we rest."

Hector had everyone dress in dark colors, to blend with the opaque of night and terrain. He led them to muddy paths along a metal fence that had chunks already pulled off. Without a flashlight or written directions, he walked them several miles, with no food or drink, to small structures in the middle of nowhere where Hector kept supplies. In a couple of stops, he had friends with well-traveled vehicles they borrowed to cover more miles.

Hector was good all right—allaying the families' concerns that he would leave them in the desert to die. Hector had a system, which was the best way for anyone to get over to the United States and avoid the Border Patrol stops and their roaming vehicles, helicopters, infrared sights, and heat-sensitive equipment—the most militarized border in the "free" world, Hector said.

Tired, hungry, kids crying in the back of closed vehicles,

sleeping on concrete floors or parched gravel next to cactus plants and rock formations, fear their daily bread, the Oronas and Padillas crept closer to their destination: the sprawling, glistening, and green-laden place—including palm trees and the most amazing bougainvillea and jacaranda plants—known as the Angels.

Before pulling into L.A., they stopped in Riverside. They were then stuffed into another vehicle. In an hour's time, Hector brought them to a Chicano family on the Eastside.

Carlos, by then, had run out of money. But Hector offered some relief.

"As long as you work, you'll be fine," were Hector's last words. "Just pay the people who are setting you up here. And if I ever need your help in the future, I'll know where to find you. *¿Estamos de acuerdo?*"

So the Oronas and Padillas tried everything they could to work, including with the flatbed truck. They tried the best they could in a country that always seemed to be looking over their shoulders—as if their failure would only be a matter of time.

All right, Teresa, please sound out the vowels for the class," requested Pascual Sotelo, a fifty-five-year-old dense-eyed man in jeans and long-sleeved Western-style shirt who stood in front of a crowded classroom in a nearly finished renovated schoolhouse.

Six-year-old Teresa, a thin long-haired dusky girl in an orange print dress, kicked up her legs from beneath a small wood desk, and recited a memorized refrain:

"Ma, me, mi, mo, mu."

"Very good, Teresa," Mr. Sotelo exclaimed. "I see you've been practicing."

The school was in various stages of repair—there were still unpainted walls, glassless windows, and missing sections of ceiling. It had been slated for closure only a few months earlier. But with so many families from Cerro Espinoza working in the United States and sending back cash, the school was eventually saved—helping many of the remaining children to get an education they otherwise would not have. Little Teresa, who had no schooling until then, was one of these.

The village's former residents—forced to leave when their means of support got pulled from under them—had contributed money not only for badly needed school repairs, but new roads, a well, a garden, and new huts for the teachers to live in. Plans were also in the works to rebuild part of the old church. They were creating a parallel economy—and a highly structured parallel government to maintain it.

Cerro Espinoza was a small village of mestizos, Rarámuri Indians, and displaced transients in the Copper Canyon country of La Sierra Madre—the Mother Mountains.

Mr. Sotelo left the school building that afternoon to return on foot to his mud and log hut. He walked past tall pines, mesquite trees, and cactus drying in the yellow sun. Past small fields of corn, including some with furrows but no seed. Walls made of piled stone, no mortar, separated a field from another. Along the way, he came across a small boy on top of a horse on a two-lane highway, also built with support from the social club in Los Angeles. As Mr. Sotelo and the boy passed each other, they waved.

A group of young women, several carrying baskets on their heads, approached Mr. Sotelo from a dirt side road.

"How are you, *muchachas?*" he asked. "A hot day, no?"

"Oh, yes, Mr. Sotelo, but we have to keep washing our clothes regardless," one of the women responded.

"I understand," Mr. Sotelo said. "I suppose I can't stop teaching children just because it rains."

He continued his stroll until he noticed a Rarámuri man—wearing the loincloth, red bandanna, tire-soled sandals, and cotton shirt with fluffed sleeves of the tribe—watching him from behind a narrow tree.

Mr. Sotelo stopped and said *"kwira va,"* the Rarámuri greeting. But he also knew the man—a true *gentil*—would not respond. The dark and hardy Rarámuris lived in the deep recesses of the canyons, most often in caves, but also in scrap homes of stone, wood, or adobe. They were reticent, untrusting of any *chabochi,* or outsider, even if these "outsiders" were of Indian skin and sentiment—if they weren't traditional Rarámuri, they were *chabochis.*

As it is, Pascual Sotelo was not from these parts. He was the son of a railroad worker who aspired to go to school and become a teacher when he lived in the city of Chihuahua. Pascual first arrived in the Sierra Tarahumara, as this area was called, in his mid-twenties. The first day of his life here—which was supposed to be a temporary sojourn to recapture some of his own family's lost Rarámuri roots—began when he stepped off the brightly designed train of the Chihuahua al Pacifico Railroad line in Creel, the largest town in the Copper Canyon.

He took a short walk from the tiny sparse train station to where an ancient pensive church and a small plaza centered the town. Here whole families, single men, seductive females, the elderly with crooked canes, and tourists gathered in peaceful repose.

Little girls, with pretty slanted eyes, and the most insanely beautiful brown skin, in colorful embroidered dresses and head-scarves greeted Pascual with small wooden dolls that were black-faced and costumed, like the girls who carried them.

He gazed at the girls, almost in a trance, as they tried to sell him the dolls. They were maybe nine or ten years old. He came out of the spell when one of the girls said in a sweet-song voice, *"Tengo hambre. ¿Un peso, por favor?"*

She was hungry. Her words were pleading, dejected, rehearsed, and manipulative—all simultaneously displayed on her face.

Pascual stayed in Creel for a short time. One day a poorly compensated teaching position among the Indians opened up in the village of Cerro Espinoza. He decided to take it. Cerro Espinoza was several miles into the canyon country, just as the land rises up to eight thousand feet. Unlike other villages around here with Rarámuri names such as Guachochi, Uruáchic, and Norogachic, vaqueros, miners, and small farmers founded this village more than one hundred years before.

In time, Pascual fell in love with the village, which had a bustling two hundred families, mostly wood-shack poor. Cerro Espinoza was a major stopover before hitting the treacherous and majestic mountains, which consisted of five canyons, most of which were deeper than the Grand Canyon. He loved the grandeur and natural diversity of the area, how the volcanic rock formed mythic shapes as if peopled by those from another world—he loved the Rarámuri games and ceremonies, including the corn beer celebrations known as *tesquinadas* that many non-Rarámuris have also adopted.

But more importantly, Pascual fell for a young part-Rarámuri girl named Angelica. Raised along with her siblings by Jesuits from the local church, Angelica became his wife and was Pascual's anchor for staying and working in Cerro Espinoza. He's been there almost thirty years.

After a good forty minutes, Pascual ambled up a rocky knoll.

On the other side was the tiny settlement where Angelica, their two teenaged boys, and a baby resided. In Pascual's back pocket was a letter that a courier from Creel had given to him earlier that day at school.

"Angelica, I'm home," Pascual announced. "And I got a letter from your brother Carlos."

"Carlos—from Los Angeles—oh, Pascual, what does he have to say?" Angelica said emerging from one of the two rooms in the place, a small brown child in her arms. A handsome woman in her late forties, she wore a long cotton skirt below a faded Chicago Bulls T-shirt that came from the pack of donated clothes at the local church.

"Good news—everybody is working. And apparently that truck of theirs has turned out to be a real moneymaker," Pascual offered while handing Angelica the letter. "They'll be sending the pueblo more funds."

"I'm so glad—I worry about them being so far away," Angelica said. "But Carlos is smart and hard-working—he always has been. I understand he's made the club better organized."

"Yes, you're right, they're really working together now," Pascual said as he pulled up a stool to sit down.

At that moment, Pascual's tall sons—Mauricio, sixteen, and thirteen-year-old Tomas—entered the hut, followed by a scraggly golden-hair dog named Cantinflas, after the legendary Mexican comedian.

"*M'ijos,* your Tío Carlos wrote and says that pretty soon you'll be old enough to join him and your older cousins in Los Angeles," Pascual stated while taking off his dust-covered brown shoes and tossing them into a corner of the dirt floor.

"I can hardly wait, *'apa,*" Mauricio replied. He kicked Cantinflas slightly to indicate he should go to his designated spot near the *caleton*—an old-style wood-fed stove.

"It'll be hard," Angelica interjected. "But you'll have family there—and I understand there's plenty of work."

"It's something I've been looking forward to for a long time," Mauricio added.

In a few years, it had become the custom for most healthy young men of Cerro Espinoza to end up in the United States with their family members. Mauricio wanted to be among the next group of villagers to leave. To live in East L.A.

icho turned away from the truck and its door, leaving Julio and the others to figure out their next move. He strolled casually to his place, the closest to the dirt bluff, where his wife Marta was warming tortillas on a hot plate next to a skillet of eggs and chorizo.

"Can you believe those *pinche güeys*—they almost tore off the door from Papa's truck," he said.

"They're more brawn than brains, *esos brutos*, especially that *carnal* of yours," Marta responded.

"Well, I don't want to be around when Papa gets home and finds out what happened."

"Are you guys going to get some work in today?" Marta asked.

"If we can get the truck going, but I don't think that door is going to be an easy thing to fix. We'll just have to tie it down with rope and hope it holds."

Wicho stepped into the one bedroom in the place, separated from the front room by loose Sheetrock held by wires on a sloppily framed wall. He went to several carton boxes that had been nailed to the drywall, serving as shelves, holding underclothes, towels, and bath items. From out of one of the boxes, Wicho picked out a T-shirt with Tupac Shakur's face on it. He put it on after removing the wet one he wore. It was hot already, even though it was still early morning.

Suddenly, Wicho heard a ruckus outside; he looked toward Marta, who shrugged her shoulders. He stepped out the door and saw Domingo, Rafas, and Julio being escorted by green uniformed border patrol officers.

"Marta, hide or something—it's La Migra."

"¿Cómo? La Migra here, on De Garmo?"

"What do you think, I'm making this up. I'm telling you, hide."

But, before he could exit out the back, officers surrounded the place as a Chicano border patrol official announced in Spanish that this was a raid by the U.S. Immigration Service, and that everyone was to come out.

Wicho did, then winced when Marta followed behind him. But, really, what could she do. There was nowhere to hide.

The immigration officers pushed everyone toward the street, away from the shacks in the back. A bulldozer lingered there in the narrow sidewalkless road. Wicho realized they were about to lose their homes, which he knew had been built without authorization. Somehow the word got to the authorities of how the Oronas and Padillas were living.

Grace, a curly-haired, middle-aged woman in a blue house robe, who was also a U.S. citizen and one of the people who lived in the front houses, ran outside to confront the officers.

"What's going on here?" she demanded to know. "This is private property—you have no right to come in here."

One of the officers, accompanied by a sheriff's deputy, stepped forward.

"We have a federal court order to remove any illegal housing units as well as detain any illegal persons who may be living here," the officer stated, hiding behind mirrored glasses. "Over there is a county housing official, Mr. Miner. What we have here, ma'am, is a number of federal, state, and county law violations—violations for which you may be liable. Where do you want me to start?"

Grace looked at him and wondered what movie he thought he was in.

Meanwhile, various members of the Oronas and Padillas were being herded into pale green vans, with their hands behind their backs in plastic thumb cuffs. Their children were also rounded up and placed in another vehicle. Two of them were crying softly as a female border official squatted down to talk to them.

Two gruff-looking Anglos searched Marta and Wicho and asked them a slew of questions. Wicho opted not to say anything; Marta only nodded. Julio and the other men also remained quiet. Already in the back of Julio's mind were the beginnings of schemes for making his way back into the country.

Several neighbors gathered around the blinking lights, loud voices, and footsteps. Four cholos stood at the corner but then moved farther up De Garmo when a sheriff's deputy eyed them. Still, one of the young men—who had JM, the barrio gang initials, tattooed on his forehead—walked up to a van that had a wire mesh window. He offered his cigarette to Wicho, who had his head closest to the opening.

"*Gracias, hermano,*" Wicho said with the *frajo* hanging from his lips. He was unable to use his hands to remove it. The young man took the cigarette out of Wicho's mouth, took a drag on it, then placed it back between Wicho's lips.

"No hay de que," the youth remarked.

Grace talked to more officials, trying to figure out what she could do to stop what was going on. Mr. Miner told her this was part of a new national Border Patrol operation, aimed at destroying the illegal housing, bars, and dance clubs that had sprung up in neighborhoods where there were large numbers of undocumented people.

"We call this Operation Clean Up," he said, with a tinge of pride.

"You mean like Operation Jobs or Operation Better Streets— just ways to win people over to another disgusting thing that the government does," Grace added. "An operation is supposed to cure sickness, no? Is that what you mean?"

"Ma'am, these people are breaking the law . . . this housing is against the law," Mr. Miner responded. "We are only upholding the law of this land. Now, if you don't mind, we would like to do our job."

Moments after the Oronas and Padillas were taken into custody, Mr. Miner gave the signal for the bulldozer to proceed along the steep road toward the back. Wicho and Marta watched helplessly as the bulldozer tore into the walls of their tiny, but comfortable, home. They saw their few possessions being thrown up into the air along with the drywall, wire, and carton boxes. From there, the bulldozer leveled the other houses. The neighbors standing nearby gasped at the crunch and crackle of wood, tin, plaster, and cement that accompanied each thrust of the bulldozer's shovel. Dust swirled around them, swallowing everything—the greenery, the power lines, and the hints of downtown structures in the background. Some people turned away, angry, unable to witness the destruction.

Then, to Wicho's surprise, several of his neighbors began to move toward the officials. A few yelled for La Migra to leave. One threw a bottle at the bulldozer. The couple of sheriff's deputies who were there tried to restrain the group, but the yelling continued. One deputy ran to his radio to request assistance. This was not a good place for immigration authorities—or rival gangs, for that matter—to get stuck in.

Wicho saw all of this from inside the sweltering van. He felt intensely uncomfortable as perspiration surged from every pore. But he didn't want to show the *gabachos* that he couldn't take anything they gave him.

He looked over to see if his young nieces and nephews were okay. They had already been taken away in green station wagons. Wicho then watched the people get more agitated; one woman yelled out, *"¡Justicia!"*

"No human being is illegal!" exclaimed another resident.

Wicho didn't know about this; he only knew about not eating, about not working.

Soon more sheriff's units arrived. Deputies in helmets stepped out of the vehicles. They pushed back the crowd, which had swelled to around thirty. Some deputies scuffled with residents. A couple of them were on the ground, handcuffed. A truck backed up onto the dirt road. The bulldozer piled debris onto the back of the truck to be hauled away. The county officials started to exit. Only the deputies stayed to make sure no more residents interfered. A helicopter hovered above the trees. With the officials gone, and as deputies with blackjacks swaggered down the street, the crowd began to disperse.

Finally, the vans pulled out. Yet, as all this unfolded, Wicho couldn't help but feel a measure of relief. At least some people tried to do something, he thought. And he wondered about his father Carlos, and what he would think when he came home to find nothing. Would he still be mad at the truck's broken door?

For four days, Moises and another Rarámuri man bulldozed trees, rocks, and bushes from the edge of one of the mountains. No roads existed here before. A well-known businessman from Creel, Alejandro Quintero, had deployed the Indians at ten pesos a day for the strenuous and seemingly impossible task of creating a passageway to the top.

But not long after the men reached the level ground, trucks with materials and construction crews pushed up the pass. Mr. Quintero was building a hotel, literally in the middle of nowhere, overlooking a deep canyon that the Río Urique had carved over millennia.

Moises was a short, quiet, and tireless man who did most of the major construction work around this part of the Sierra—he had many years' experience working in cities like Chihuahua and Ciudad Juárez.

And Moises knew more than he would let on—he knew Mr. Quintero had connections with the drug lords that have forced many Rarámuris out of their ranchitos and cave dwellings. One village near here was abandoned when an Indian leader was found tortured and hanged alongside the main dirt road into the village.

Moises knew, too, that Mr. Quintero was building the hotel to capitalize on a potentially more lucrative business—tourism. For years, the government was touting tourism as the future of the area. Several millions of dollars had already been allocated for hotels and other accommodations (when this kind of money was never available for electricity, potable water, or paved roads). The aim was to make the Copper Canyon area more enticing to tourists than Arizona's Grand Canyon.

However, the already isolated and suspicious Rarámuri would have to give up more of their ancestral lands—and Moises did not like this. Besides drug lords and developers, the Indians had long battles with lumber companies, miners, and cattle ranchers. Everybody wanted La Sierra Tarahumara, but they wanted nothing to do with the people who gave these mountains their names, their mystery, their soul.

One day, Moises knocked on Mr. Sotelo's door made of short logs.

"*Si, pásale,*" Pascual Sotelo responded so Moises could enter. But Moises did not move. Pascual realized he would have to open the door and physically bring the man into his house.

"What's going on, Moises?" Pascual inquired.

"Just like you said—they're getting ready to make the hotel."

"This is a shame, a real shame," Pascual muttered as Angelica entered the room.

"We have to call a meeting of the *ejido*," Moises said. "I had to make that passage, but we're going to have to agree on how we can stop this development."

The *ejido* was the territorial indigenous governing body, run mostly by the Indians but including mestizo farmers and ranchers. Their meetings were generally held outside the churchyard, mostly in the Rarámuri language.

"I know—I don't blame you for the work you did," Pascual

added. "But it seems like no law or official is going to be on our side. Even the construction we've done with funds from the other side is now being challenged. They want campgrounds, hotels, and stands for trinkets. Like the priest said, 'whenever commercial development occurs, cultures are destroyed.'"

Angelica looked worried as the two men walked out of the hut to talk to the *ejido* chiefs. She worried that Pascual, who was becoming a vocal community member and friend to the Indians, would be spotted, and possibly hurt.

¿Mujé chuiri chi'lébari? Angelica asked in Rarámuri—where are you going?

But Pascual did not respond, concentrating on what he was going to tell the *ejido* chiefs.

Since most people did not have any vehicles, they walked for miles on end in the roughest topography—something the Rarámuri were known for, which explains the meaning of their tribal name, the fleet-footed people. But as soon as Pascual and Moises reached the paved road—the same one the L.A. club had helped finance—two men with baseball caps, white pants, and jackets approached them. Pascual saw that each man had a large six-shooter pushed through his engraved leather belt.

"Hello, *compas,* what brings you *tarahumaritos* out this way?" asked one of the men, using the diminutive mestizo word for Rarámuri.

"We're just passing through," Pascual answered, eyeing the weapons. Moises looked into the distance, away from the men's faces.

"Sorry, this way is closed," the other man responded, blunt and to the point. "You have to go back the other way."

Pascual thought of arguing with them, but the thought didn't linger long. He grabbed Moises's arm and pulled him away from the armed men. He knew that the powerful drug lords had already taken over sections of these canyons. If Cerro Espinoza were to survive, they would have to find assistance from the other villages.

It was late when Pascual and Moises made it to one of the *ejido* chiefs' huts. There was no electricity in the area, and therefore no lights. They needed to get to the chief's place before it got dark. Only the smell of burned wood reached them first. Pascual pushed Moises behind some bushes. Several men with cowboy hats and firearms had surrounded the *ejido* chief, who was on his knees in front of them, near his charred home.

"Good God," Pascual whispered to Moises. "We have to get out of here."

Moises, however, squatted and began to pray in Rarámuri.

Pascual saw the hatted men move closer to the *ejido* chief. One had a long-barreled gun in his hand that he placed against the chief's temple. Pascual looked to the sky where his baby's face came to him, almost with no mental effort, imprinted in his eye, the last thing he saw before a burst of gunfire broke open the tranquil forest air.

As the evening closed in, Carlos Padilla returned in his car with bags of cement, trowels, and a couple of lounge chairs on the backseat. He left earlier that day with the idea of getting the materials to make a small patio in the backyard where he could situate the chairs—maybe a barbecue grill.

Carlos drove up Meisner Street from City Terrace Drive. As soon as he turned onto De Garmo, he sensed something was wrong. The houses in front looked the same, but surveying in between, he saw that the scenery behind them was radically different. He also noticed the flatbed truck with its door hanging open stashed irregularly next to foliage.

Carlos parked and slowly removed himself from the car. Grace opened her screen door, pulled the blue robe around her, and looked at him. She didn't say anything as the stout, muscular older man stared back. Soon enough, he understood. He walked onto the porch, scrunched his eyebrows in a painful expression, and sat down. Grace put her hand on Carlos's shoulder, and they both watched the sun disappear, raking the sky in red tints, over the tops of flat-roofed houses, across the faintly lit skyline and dry palm trees in the distance.

SOMETIMES YOU DANCE
WITH A WATERMELON

A yyyyy."

A man's voice, the sound of a tumbling body like a sack of potatoes down a flight of stairs.

"Pinche cabrón, hijo de la . . ."

A woman's voice.

"¡Borracho! Get out of my house!"

Next door to the disturbance, Rosalba tossed and turned on a squeaky bed, her fragile mirror of dreams smashed into fragments.

"You dog! Get out of here!" The woman's shrieks continued outside the bedroom window, a raspy stammering over the curses.

"But, *muñeca,*" the man slurred. "Give me a chance, *querida.* Let me in, *por favor.*"

"This house is not for *sin vergüenzas* like you," the woman wailed.

A loud rustling pulsated through the window as the man toppled back onto a row of shrubbery. The whimpers of small children behind a torn screen door followed the man's moans. Rosalba carefully opened her eyes. Early morning sunlight slipped into the darkened room through small holes in the aluminum foil that covered the window. The foil kept the daylight out so that Rosalba's current husband, Pete, could sleep. Rosalba turned away from the heavy figure next to her, curled up in a fetal position.

Rosalba was forty years old, with flawless brown skin and a body that was at times mistaken to be in its twenties. She had rivulets of hair down to the small of her back that she had kept long ever since she was a little girl. Only now, gray strands were intertwined with the profusion of dark ones.

Pete worked the graveyard shift at a meatpacking plant near their apartment on Olympic Boulevard. He slept during the day and labored at night until he wended his way home from the stench and heat. When he got there, Pete climbed onto the mattress, propped up by cinder blocks, to the comfort of Rosalba's warm body.

As the noise outside subsided to an uneasy quiet, Rosalba felt a yearning to go someplace. Any place.

She carefully emerged from under the heavy covers and grabbed a dirty pink bathrobe with loose threads hanging from the hem. She tiptoed through the room, peered backward toward the bed, then slowly opened the bedroom door to a frustrating medley of creaky hinges. Pete, the lump, rolled into another position then lay still.

Rosalba entered the living room and stepped over bodies stretched out on mattresses strewn across the floor. There lay her twenty-four-year-old daughter Sybil; her daughter's four children, including the oldest, nine-year-old Chila; and Sybil's no-good, always-out-of-work boyfriend, Stony.

Rosalba worked her way to the kitchen and opened a cupboard. Cockroaches scurried to darker confines. The nearly empty shelves were indifferent to calls from her nearly empty stomach. The family survived mostly on nonfat powdered milk for breakfast, tortillas and butter for lunch, and cornflakes for dinner—most of which Sybil bought with food stamps.

"This is draining the life out of me," Rosalba whispered, as she stared at the vacant cupboards in front of her.

Rosalba interrupted her futile search for something edible and thought about the twenty years that had past since she first crossed the U.S. border from the inland Mexican state of Nayarit. Her daughter Sybil was five years old then; Rosalba, strong but naïve, was twenty-one.

Rosalba fled her hometown. She fled an abusive husband that her parents had coerced her to marry when she was sixteen. She fled a father who announced he would disown her if she dared to leave. Rosalba finally concluded that the suffocation there would kill her more than being without a father, husband, or even her mother, who sat off by herself, unwilling to challenge the men that eventually overwhelmed Rosalba and her mother to a point of paralysis.

With Sybil, one beaten-up valise held up with tape and rope, and her fortitude, Rosalba managed to stake a ride on a creaky old bus with exhaust fumes that leaked into where the passengers sat, making them groggy. Without arrangements or connections, Rosalba exited the bus in Tijuana, near the U.S. border, crowded with women, children, and single men who also risked everything for another life.

Rosalba cried the first night in the street. In her loneliness, she thought about the *rancho* where she grew up, tending to goats, chickens, and a couple of horses. She thought about their house made of mud and logs, although sturdy, with an open-air dome-covered oven in the patio. She thought about the scorpions and how she had to dust off the bed sheets, how once her mom sliced her skin and sucked the poison from a scorpion bite when Rosalba was a child. She still carried the scar on her back where her mother sewed up the wound with a needle and thread.

Rosalba also remembered how as a little girl she'd take an empty bucket to the village well and fill it with water for cooking or baths. And she recalled walking barefoot along dirt paths with bundles of clothes or baskets of corn that she balanced on her head.

She remembered a time when everything was clear, everything in its place—a time aligned with the rhythms of the universe, it seemed, when she felt her mother's love and her father's protection and a deep internal throbbing to do, learn, and be.

Things changed when she got older. When she became a woman, at the start of her first blood, when she began to hunger for herself. Everything turned toward the men, the chores, and the "duties" of wife and mother. So when she fled her family, she realized, she also fled the fond memories. Rosalba stopped crying and vowed to never let these memories weaken her resolve and force her back to a place where she also felt crushed.

Alone with a small child, Rosalba knew she was in danger if she stayed in Tijuana. She followed other migrants through the permeable line that separated the two countries. Eventually, borrowing rides and the kindness of strangers, she ended up in L.A. She realized then that if she ever harbored any notions about returning to Nayarit to her family, she'd have to let them go from that point on.

Unfortunately, Rosalba endured many scary nights staying in

dingy hotel rooms with other migrants, mostly women, in downtown Los Angeles. She not only didn't have a man to help but no obvious skills except what she learned on the rancho. She had to survive being cast into a peculiar universe of neon and noise. This was a place where winos and the homeless resided on the sidewalk, where women sold themselves for sex to eat or get stoned, and where people on city buses never say anything to you unless they happen to be drunk or crazy.

In the middle of this, she met Elvia, a slightly overweight but vivacious twenty-four-year-old, who also had a five-year-old child, a boy. Rosalba and Elvia became fast friends. She now had someone to share her concerns, her appetites, her hopes. Elvia was also single and fleeing a world similar to Rosalba's, although more urbanized, being from the port city of Ensenada, Baja California.

Rosalba often took care of Elvia's boy while his mother worked in a sewing establishment in the Pico-Union district west of downtown. She loved watching Sybil playing with someone her own age for a change, to know she could finally have a semblance of a child's life. Everything seemed like it would work out fine, where Rosalba could seriously consider a little bit of happiness and stability.

But this part of her life ended with a terrible tragedy—when Elvia's boy accidentally fell three stories to the ground below from an opened window while Rosalba was taking a bath in the middle of the day. Elvia, devastated, left the place and was never heard from again. Remembering these things was difficult for Rosalba, and shaking her head slowly from left to right, Rosalba focused again on the empty cupboard before her.

"*Chingáo*, there was never anything to eat then either," Rosalba grumbled to no one in particular. Even though Pete was now working, his lean check barely took care of the rent, clothing, and bus fares.

She didn't mind the adults not eating, but the children . . . she was prepared to starve so the children could eat.

Rosalba didn't have the same concern for Sybil or Stony. She was certain they were into drugs or other illegal activities.

Why Sybil would end up with an ex-convict like Stony was beyond her. As a child, Sybil was shy and respectful. Someone once commented on the girl's good behavior as she lay in Rosalba's arms while both sat on a sliced-up seat in the smelly bus from Nayarit to Tijuana. Even during their first years in the crumbling downtown hotels, Sybil didn't cause her mother any headaches. She stayed off in a corner, entertaining herself. Sometimes the girl lovingly caressed Rosalba's face to wake her from sleeping on the couch for too long. And despite the tragedy of Elvia's boy's deadly fall, Sybil maintained a good disposition.

That didn't last too long.

By ten, Sybil complained about everything. She spent more time on the sidewalks and alleys, with other children from migrants, next to crazies and drug users and disheveled men. She learned to talk back to her mother and run away when she didn't feel like falling into line. At about that time, Rosalba tried to teach her about helping others by taking her daughter across the U.S.–Mexico border, carefully escorting other migrants through brush and cactus, and assisting them with their entry into city life. But this only made things worse by opening Sybil up to a world fraught with danger and interesting characters—instead of turning away from this, she relished the excitement and uncertainty.

Soon Sybil began to hang out with older guys. One, an undocumented man who already had children back in Sinaloa, got

Sybil pregnant with Chila—she was sixteen, the same age her mother was when she had her. This man was later deported and disappeared from their lives. After that Sybil frequented night-clubs and dance halls. She brought home many a sorry specimen; one of them gave her the other three children she bore—only to leave for Houston with another woman.

Rosalba, who thought her daughter might have learned some-thing from these ordeals, felt further betrayed one day when Sybil brought Stony home. At first glance, Stony seemed nice. But as soon as he smiled, his missing front teeth and beady eyes made him look ominous—like a lizard with fangs. Stony had a look that Rosalba noticed in many Chicanos recently released from the joint. He never worked, but when pushed, somehow coughed up beer money. Rosalba figured Stony sold food stamps to buy booze.

Staring into the vacant cupboard, Rosalba became even hun-grier. She closed the cupboard doors then walked toward the kitchen window that overlooked an alley behind their home; the alley was cluttered with burned mattresses, treadless tires, and weather-beaten furniture.

Rosalba leaned against the streaked glass, fibers of hair spread themselves across her face. She looked over the Los Angeles sky, smudged over with smog, blocking out any semblance of moun-tains or greenery in the distance. In a dirt yard, children played and chattered in broken English and half-Spanish, a language all their own like the pidgin spoken wherever cultures merged and clashed.

What a puzzling place, this Los Angeles, Rosalba thought.

Factory whistles all day long; the deafening pounding of machinery, with cars and trucks in a sick symphony of horns, tires screeching, and engines backfiring. Added to that were the nauseating odors from the meatpacking plants. Rosalba felt the air thick with tension, like a huge rubber band hanging over the streets, ready to snap at any moment.

Two *winitos* staggered by. They sat down on the curb's edge; one of them removed a bottle of Thunderbird out of a brown paper sack. Across the way a young woman pushed a market cart down the street, her three small children crowded inside. In front of newsstands and shops, women in print dresses and aprons, recently arrived from Mexico or El Salvador, sold food and other items from brightly painted stands.

On other days, family quarrels erupted, with children rushing out of houses, intermittent screaming from women and men, and police cars turning sharply around street corners.

Rosalba thought about the Varrio Nuevo Estrada gang: tough, tattooed, *caló*-speaking young men and women with their outrageous clothing and attitudes. They were mostly from the Estrada Courts housing projects, always fighting with somebody—rival barrio gangs, police officers, one another.

Although life in Rosalba's village in Nayarit had been full of want and ill treatment, the world she ended up in was far more threatening. But she mulled that over a while and accepted this fact: She could never return. This was her life now, in East L.A., with Pete. Sharing whatever she owned with Sybil, Stony, Chila, and her other three grandchildren. No, she would never go back.

But still, although she tried not to, she couldn't help but recall the images, voices, and smells of her village in Nayarit. So one day, she promised: *When I die, take me back to Mexico. Bury me deep in Nayarit soil, in my red hills, and along the cactus fields. Bury me in long braids and in a* huipil. *Bury me among the ancients, among the brave and wise ones, and in the wet dirt of my birth. I will take with me these fingers that have kneaded new ground, these eyes that have gazed on new worlds, this heart that has loved, lost, and loved again— remembering that I once lived and suffered in America.*

And often Rosalba thought about Pete. A good man, she almost said out loud. Pete was not like the men her daughter seemed to attract. He was also different from Rosalba's previous two husbands, the one in Nayarit who never saw past his dinner— and an alcoholic in L.A. who lived in the crawl space of her house for a short time until he was shot dead in a barroom brawl.

In Rosalba's eyes, Pete was truly decent. Working nights, gutting steer and hog torsos, pulling out fat-covered organs and yards of intestines, then washing the blood and gore down a large hole with a monstrous water hose—all for Rosalba. And she knew it.

Today, Rosalba needed to get away. The morning beckoned her to come out—to do something, anything.

She sat at the kitchen table—dirty dishes scattered about the tabletop, with bits of hardened tortillas from the night before— and worked on a plan.

Rosalba could take Stony's dented Ford pickup and visit the old furniture stores and used clothing shops along Whittier Boulevard or First Street. Or she could go around the Eastside, gathering newspapers, cardboard boxes, aluminum cans, or whatever she could turn in for extra money. She did this so many times that the men at the county dump site looked forward to

Rosalba's visits, to her bright face and brash approach, and the way she mixed up the words in Spanish and English.

Rosalba dressed quickly, gathering a few loose bills and faded coupons into an old nylon purse. She then worked her way around the bodies on the floor to where Chila was sleeping. Rosalba looked at the child's closed eyes and fingered her small hand.

"'Buelita," Chila moaned as she awoke. "*¿Qué paso?*"

"Come, *m'ija,* I need you to help me."

It took a strenuous moment before Chila made out her grandmother's face in the dimness of the room. The last time she saw her grandmother's face like that, she had convinced Chila to help steal old beaten-up lamps and chairs from broken-into Goodwill bins.

"Oh, 'Buelita, I'm too tired."

"*Mira nomás*—you're tired, eh? You ain't done nothing yet. Now get dressed and come with me."

Rosalba got up and made her way into the kitchen. Chila snarled a weak protest, then tossed a blanket off, unmindful of the younger children next to her, and rolled off the mattress. Chila knew that once 'Buelita put her mind to something, there was no reasoning with her at all.

Chila dragged herself into the bathroom while her grandmother prepared a couple of tacos to eat later from the leftover meat in the refrigerator. A small girl for nine, she had an impish face with large brown eyes.

"What are we going to do, 'Buelita?" Chila asked, as she attempted to brush her hair into some kind of shape. She had grown feisty at her age and, unlike Rosalba, refused to wear braids—just long straight hair, wild like the tails of stallions.

"*Adio—a donde quiera Dios.* Wherever God desires," Rosalba said. "What's it to you?"

"Gee, I was just asking!"

Despite such exchanges, Rosalba and Chila were really best buddies; none of the others in the house were close enough to even talk to each other that way.

Rosalba hurried outside to check the pickup truck. The driveway—overflowing with oily engine parts, boxes of yellowed newspapers, and rain-soaked cartons—was in sharp contrast to the empty kitchen cupboard. She managed to reach the pickup and pull herself inside the cab. She turned on the ignition, and the truck began to gripe and growl. Eventually the engine turned over, smoke spewed like a cloud over the driveway's litter.

"Let's go, *m'ija*," Rosalba yelled over the truck's engine roar. "*¡De volada!*"

By then, other members of the household had awakened. Stony was the first to pop his unshaven face through the window.

"Hey, man, quit gunning that thing—you'll break something!" he managed to holler.

Rosalba pressed the accelerator even more as the exhaust thickened. No sleepy-eyed, ex-con, beer-guzzling boyfriend of her insolent daughter was going to ruin her beautiful day, she thought. It was a day that begged her to do something, anything.

Chila flew out of the house, banging the screen door behind her. Rosalba backed the truck out while Chila screamed for her to slow down as she leaped into the passenger side. The pickup chugged out of the driveway and onto the street.

The truck continued down the block, smoke trailing from behind as Stony bellowed out of the bedroom window, "*¡Méndiga loca!*"

The Ford roared through Eastside streets and avenues, across the concrete river to Alameda Street, where old Mexicanos sold fruit on the roadside while factory hands gathered in front of chain-link fences, waiting for employers in trucks to pick them for day work. Rosalba decided to go to *el centro*—downtown.

They passed the long blocks of Skid Row, with the displaced gathered on street corners or beneath a cardboard-and-blanket-covered "condo" on a sidewalk; they drove past the brick and stone welfare hotels of painful remembrance. Past warehouse buildings and storefront garment sweatshops. Rosalba slowly pulled up to the congestion of cars and humanity along what some people called Spanish Broadway.

In the crawl of downtown traffic, Rosalba had time to look out the window at a gray-haired black preacher, who sermonized from the sidewalk with a dog-eared Bible in his hand. She noticed a newspaper vendor on a corner studying the people who walked by as they scanned the latest news in Mexican publications, including the close-up shots of cut-up and bullet-riddled bodies in crime and disaster magazines. Everywhere, Norteños and Cumbias poured out of record shops.

"How about a shine . . . shoe shine?" exclaimed a half-blind man. *"Para zapatos brillosos."*

The streets bristled with families, indigents, and single mothers shopping. Rosalba spotted a man staggering out of a tejano bar, followed by another man. The second man knocked the first one to the ground and repeatedly punched him in the face. Nobody paused or did anything to stop him.

Another man pushed his little boy out from a group of people gathered at a bus stop and had the child pee in the gutter.

Rosalba and Chila cruised further up Broadway, away from its most crowded intersections. Cholos stood deathly still inside brick alcoves, elderly women strolled along cautiously with heavy bags, winos lay in fresh vomit nearby. More stubble-faced homeless pushed shopping carts filled with squashed cans, plastic bags, and cardboard. The scenery carried the rapid-fire Spanish of the Mexican and Central American shoppers, the foul words of workers unloading merchandise out of six-wheeled trucks covered with gang graffiti, and the seductive tones of pretty women in tight pants enticing potential shoppers to check out the clothing racks.

Rosalba noticed an empty space at a curb and swiftly pulled into it. A sign on the sidewalk warned: NO PARKING, TOW ZONE. But she pulled up the hand brake and turned off the engine anyway.

" 'Buelita, the sign says . . ." Chila began, but she saw that it didn't matter. Rosalba walked off as if by ignoring the sign, it would go away.

"Forget her," Chila muttered, and rushed up behind her swift-moving grandmother.

That day burned and bubbled; Rosalba and Chila felt like chilis on a hot plate being heated before being skinned. Their stroll became torture, especially since Rosalba would stop here and there to browse and barter over items, the majority of which she had no intention of buying. Rosalba was just glad to get out of the house and interact with the world—just to haggle, if need be. Chila, on the other hand, only thought of the mattress and pillow she left behind.

"It's so hot," Rosalba finally conceded. "How about a watermelon, *m'ija?*"

"Sure."

Rosalba and Chila stopped at a Grand Central Market fruit stand. Laid out in front of them, a splash of colors like works of art, were papayas, mangoes, watermelons, apples, bananas, and oranges. Rosalba picked out a sizable speckled dark-green watermelon. She argued over the price with a man, who appeared bored; finally, she assembled her change and paid for it.

"Here Chila, carry this."

Suddenly, to Chila, the watermelon looked like it was at least a quarter her size. She lifted it with her thin down-covered arms, rested it on her belly, helped by a hefty push from her knee. They kept walking, but after a couple of blocks, the weight of the watermelon, the cluster of people, and torrent of smells—all the heat and hubbub—became an unbearable boiling stew.

They stopped to rest at a bus stop bench.

Chila glared at her grandmother.

"I'm tired, 'Buelita. The watermelon is too heavy."

Rosalba stood up, glared back at Chila—sweat beaded on her nose—but then pondered a way to ease the girl's burden. At that moment, Rosalba's thoughts returned to Nayarit, to a time when she was a little girl and strode for miles, carrying loads without assistance of animal or man. Then she turned toward the watermelon, pressed like a boulder on Chila's lap.

Rosalba wrested the watermelon from the girl; Chila let out a long sigh.

Rosalba walked a little, and stopped. With great care, she placed the watermelon on her head, then slowly removed one hand. The watermelon wobbled a little, threatening to fall and splatter into green, red, and black fragments on the sidewalk. Rosalba steadied the wiggly thing, then let it go. She took a few more steps. This time the watermelon stayed upright, as if held by an invisible hand.

Chila stared at her grandmother—stunned.

Even more stunning became Rosalba's efforts to rumba—keeping the watermelon on top of her head while her feet and hips gracefully shimmied along the cement walkway.

A crowd gathered around the woman as she weaved past the dollar stores, the immigration law offices, and through racks of clothes and CDs on display near the street. Merchants stepped out of their shops looking on in disbelief, preachers stopped their exhortations, and bus stop patrons strained their necks to see.

Car horns greeted, hands waved, and some people simply got out of the way.

Rosalba swayed back and forth to a salsa beat thundering out of an appliance store. She laughed and others laughed with her. Chila stepped back into the shadows, stupefied, and shook her head.

"Ahhiiii," Rosalba managed to yell.

Rosalba had not looked that happy in a long time as she danced along the bustling streets of the central city in her loose-fitting skirt and sandals. She danced in the shadow of a multi-storied Victorian—dancing for one contemptuous husband and for another who was dead. She danced for a daughter who didn't love herself enough to truly have the love of another man. She danced for Pete, a butcher of beasts and gentle companion. She danced for her grandchildren, especially that fireball Chila. She danced for her people, wherever they were scattered, and for this country she would never quite comprehend. She danced, her hair matted with sweat, while remembering a simpler life on an even simpler rancho in Nayarit.